THE SECRET STAR

BOOK TWO IN THE BOY FROM MARS TRILOGY

THE SECRET STAR

ROBERT DeLAURENTIS

RARE BIRD
LOS ANGELES, CALIF.

THIS IS A GENUINE RARE BIRD BOOK

Rare Bird Books
6044 North Figueroa Street
Los Angeles, CA 90042
rarebirdbooks.com

FIRST HARDCOVER EDITION

For more information, address:
Rare Bird Books Subsidiary Rights Department
6044 North Figueroa Street
Los Angeles, California 90042

Set in Garamond
Printed in the United States

10 9 8 7 6 5 4 3 2 1

Library of Congress Cataloging-in-Publication Data available upon request

For Francesca and Dani, my lucky stars

It is difficult to say what is impossible,
for the dream of yesterday is the hope of today
and the reality of tomorrow.

—Robert Goddard

PART 1

CHAPTER 1

In the dark of early morning, Thomas was jolted off the ground where he'd fallen asleep the previous night. A strange and sinister vibration unlike anything he'd ever felt ran through his body. A moment later, he felt the enormous heat of the laser and glanced back to see the beam of blue light, thick as a small branch, coming straight at him. Accompanied by a snake-like hiss, it caused everything in its path to explode into fire. His first thought was of Eno, trapped in the cable car a few feet away, disabled by the broken leg he'd suffered in Washington.

Thomas leapt to his feet, climbed onto the platform, and threw open the doors. His wounded navigator was curled in the corner, still in the throes of waking up. But before Thomas could warn him of the Mastership, its laser beam reached the cable car and began to slice its way down the middle of the steel cabin, separating them.

"Can you run?" Thomas said.

"Run?" Eno said. "I can barely walk with this cast on my leg!"

"Okay," Thomas said. "I'll try to divert them!"

Thomas jumped out the back of the cable car as the laser finished cutting it in half. As it did, he caught a glimpse of the cockpit, where High Governor Balthazar was flanked by Bron the Interrogator and Thomas's arch nemesis, Varik. He hit the ground running, ducking into the thickest section of the forest as the ship followed, leaving a trail of smoke and fire. He thought that if he could make it to the bay, the laser would be useless on the water. But the last thing he wanted was to lure the Martian ship to the brink of the sleeping city.

No, he'd somehow need to outrun it.

Thomas dropped into the steepest section of the mountainside, picking up speed, and for a few moments gained ground. He began to zizag back and forth, forcing the big ship into the same maneuver, as it cut a series of Zs behind him. Thomas ran past one of the clusters of boulders that dotted the landscape and noticed that the Mastership took a wider turn than usual. He recalled the escape attempts made by the Returners on Mars, where the ship wouldn't follow them into the Valles canyons due to the risk posed by its granite walls. He knew from Luke that its navigation system would automatically retreat if there was the slightest chance of danger to the high governor.

He spotted the largest cluster of boulders and sprinted toward it. He heard the pitch of the Mastership abruptly change and glanced back to see it hover in place. For a moment, it appeared as if his plan had worked. But then the ship's rear hatch opened and deposited a half dozen *Commandos* on all-terrain bikes. They separated into two flanks and raced through the thick trees. In moments, they surrounded him, leaving nowhere to run.

The Mastership moved into position directly above him, and Bron's distinctive voice boomed from the loudspeaker.

"On your knees, hands in the air, now!"

Thomas had no choice but to obey. As his knees touched the ground, he expected the Commandos to move in, but no one budged.

Finally, the Mastership descended over Thomas, the purr of its engine increasing to an angry roar. It hovered twenty feet over his head and the laser door blinked open like the eye of some mechanical cyclops. Bron looked down at Thomas with his notoriously dark eyes, then gave him a quick wave, as if to say goodbye and good riddance.

With that, a blinding shaft of light seared through his brain.

✦✦

Thomas woke on the cold ground, heart thumping, and looked up to see that the Mastership's laser was merely a shaft of sunlight slashing through the trees. A Steller's Jay, the small blue bird that had been watching him since he first landed on Earth, looked down from an overhead branch as if to assure him there was no danger. That done, it flew into the sky, revealing a sunny day with the only sound being a rhythmic hush of waves on the beach below. So vivid was his dream that he checked the cable car to see if it was intact. Sitting a few feet away, it was still in one piece.

He inhaled a deep breath of morning air and expelled it with relief.

But then the events of the previous night came back to him. Elly at her house, the bus ride from the city, the FBI agents following, the gunshots and knockout gas, and finally, the discovery of the Mastership, here on Earth with the sole purpose of finding him.

He may have escaped the ship in his dream, but for all he knew the real thing was still here, searching for him right now.

Thomas reached for the tiny holograph around his neck, the one given to him by Josef and Lina back at the Returner Compound. It reminded him that his father, along with Ignatius and seventeen orphans, were all depending on him to complete his mission.

He needed to make a decision fast.

A voice startled him. "Are you all right?"

Thomas looked up to see Eno, still wearing the cast on his leg, standing on the platform.

"Did you sleep out there, on the ground?"

Thomas brushed a few leaves from his face and stood up. "Looks that way."

"Any particular reason?"

"Yeah," Thomas said, trying to figure out how to tell Eno what happened without sending him into panic mode. "Got back from Elly's late and didn't want to wake you."

"I heard you a few minutes ago but you were still sleeping. You were making strange sounds, and your feet were moving, as if you were running. Were you having one of your spasms?"

"A dream, yeah."

"It didn't seem like a positive experience."

"No, it was one of the bad ones, what they call nightmares."

"Ah. I had no idea there was more than one variety."

Thomas rubbed the sleep from his face and pushed himself to his knees.

"I suppose we should make some sort of plan to get on with the mission, now that Elly's home safely," Eno said.

"Actually, we have a little problem."

"Do you really mean a *little* problem, or are we talking a huge predicament?"

"That depends," Thomas said, mustering as much calm as possible.

"On what?"

"Whether the Mastership is still where I saw it last night."

Eno's good eye widened in disbelief. "You saw the Mastership here, on Earth?"

"It was hidden in the woods on the other side of the road."

"Are you absolutely positive?"

"Big spaceship, covered in dielectric material, armed with laser cannon? Yeah, I'm pretty sure that was it."

"Did you see any Commandos?"

"No, luckily for me they were distracted by the FBI agents."

"The FBI was there too?"

"They followed my bus, after I dropped Elly off."

"Where are they now?"

"I'm not sure. I was up a tree when I heard gunfire, and then the Commandos shot off a smoke bomb. When I climbed down, the FBI guys were out cold."

"What happened to the Commandos?"

"They went in the other direction, looking for me."

Eno carefully lowered himself into a sitting position on the cable car and tried to slow down his increasingly rapid breathing. Thomas climbed up and sat next to him.

"This is disastrous," Eno said. "The Station doesn't have any time travel technology, so there's only one way they could've gotten it."

"I know," Thomas said. "Ignatius would never have given it to them willingly."

"They must've used neuro-interrogation."

Thomas knew that Ignatius was now in the custody of Bron and the high governor. "That may explain the time travel," he said. "But how did they know where we were?"

"They had to have the Alpha Link, too."

"What's that?"

"A device that tracks our location in space-time. Ignatius showed it to me during one of my training sessions. He was hoping to use it to monitor our progress, but they must've gotten their hands on that as well."

"So, what you're saying is that they can follow us anywhere we go?"

"Basically, yes."

"So, why haven't they found us yet?"

"The link is complicated to use and can only locate the Time Globe at a radius of twenty-two miles. And remember, the Commandos have no knowledge of Earth geography."

"Can you imagine them walking around San Francisco looking for a couple kids from Mars?" Thomas said. "People will think they're lunatics."

Eno almost smiled. "Not only that, but they'll be expecting to find the Time Globe in the shuttle, not a cable car, which they wouldn't know if they fell over it."

"Right," Thomas said. "But we still need to find out if the Mastership's here, and the sooner the better."

"How do you intend to do that?"

"I'll go down to where I saw it last night and use the Tetrascope."

"The Tetrascope?"

"It has a discovery beam that can detect a human heartbeat at ten miles."

Thomas pulled out the Tetrascope and pointed it at Eno. It beeped loudly.

"You're alive," Thomas smiled.

"Tell that to my leg," Eno said, tapping his cast.

"How's it feeling?"

"Dead. Like it's been asleep for days."

"Well, it sort of has been. The alliance doctor in New York said the calcium infusion would cause that. It's the accelerated healing. It should feel better when we take off of the cast."

Thomas unfastened the clips on his cast, then pulled it apart and tossed it to the side.

"Think you can walk?"

"I can try."

Thomas helped Eno into a standing position. He took a step but wobbled. "It'll probably take awhile until you're at full strength. We should get you a cane until then."

Thomas hopped off the platform and located a branch lying on the ground, then measured it against Eno's waist. "Here, this should do. Why don't you take a few practice laps around the cable car while I go check for the Mastership? I'll be back before you know it."

"Don't take any unnecessary chances."

But Thomas had already disappeared into the woods.

After a few minutes, he reached the edge of the tree line and peered out at the fire road that ran up and down the mountainside. He pulled out the Tetrascope, activated its sensor, and aimed it toward the highway. He heard a soft rumble followed by a slight beep.

"Truck driver," Thomas thought to himself.

He moved the Tetrascope in a semi-circular motion.

Not a beep.

Holding the Tetrascope like a flashlight, he continued down the hill until he could hear the buzz of light traffic. He waited for a few trucks to pass, then darted across the road to the bus stop where he'd gotten off the night before. And then he entered the section of woods where he'd found the Mastership.

In less than a minute, he reached the clearing. The two FBI agents that had engaged the Commandos were no longer on the ground. The surrounding trees were stained yellow from the smoke bomb and the only sound was a rustle of branches from the morning breeze. Thomas carefully moved toward the spot where he encountered the Mastership. The discovery beam didn't make a sound, but Thomas knew that the ship's shell, which was strong enough to stop a laser weapon, might prevent it from functioning. And since the Mastership was always camouflaged by its surroundings, he'd probably need to get close enough to touch it.

He continued along, until he reached the spot where he'd nearly impaled himself on the ship's probe. He gently pulled back one of the larger branches to see…nothing.

The Mastership was gone.

Thomas turned off the Tetrascope. But as he did, he heard something moving in the woods behind him. Perhaps it was an animal of some sort. Then he heard it again, more clearly. It was footsteps. Thomas held up the Tetrascope, and it began to pulse.

Using it as a guide, he made his way forward until he noticed a set of fresh footprints in the moist morning ground. It must be one of the FBI agents, he thought, possibly wounded or disoriented. Thomas knew he should run, but he also needed to find out who it was.

The beeping began to accelerate.

The signal was leading him directly toward a large tree about twenty yards away.

He turned off the Tetrascope and slid it into his pocket, knowing he might need to have both hands free if he had to defend himself.

He rubbed his thumbs against the Q-Rings on his fingers, just in case. But after several seconds, whoever was behind the tree didn't move. If it were someone meaning him harm, Thomas reasoned, there was no reason to remain hidden.

"Who's there?" he said.

A moment passed, and a young man stumbled into the clearing. His hair was matted, and his face blackened with dried mud. He collapsed onto the ground.

Thomas hurried to his side and knelt over him. The mud made the stranger unrecognizable, until he saw the tip of a distinctive scar, and couldn't quite believe his eyes.

"Josef?"

CHAPTER 2

JOSEF OPENED HIS EYES through the caked dirt.

"Thomas!" he coughed. "It's you."

"I'm sorry, Josef. I didn't recognize you until I saw your scar."

"I guess my time in the Mirror Factory finally paid off."

Thomas could see that Josef's uniform was damp.

"You're wet."

"I got lost in the dark and fell into some water. Not used to that where we come from, huh?"

Thomas took off his sweatshirt and wrapped it around Josef like a blanket. "You've been out here all night?"

"Since sundown."

Thomas pulled a candy bar Elly had given him last night out of his pocket. He tore off the wrapping and handed it to Josef. "You must be starving. Here, eat this. It'll give you some energy."

Josef took a bite.

"I take it you came here on the Mastership?"

"We landed at dawn yesterday with a group of twenty Redshirts."

"Redshirts?"

"A youth brigade formed by Bron after you escaped. They needed extra men after the fighting broke out, so they recruited a bunch of Varik's friends. But Bron wanted someone besides Varik to make positive identification, and since you helped us escape back on Mars, they took me. Once we got here, Varik led one group while I was assigned to a second, but luckily I—"

Thomas held up a hand to signal to him to stop talking. In the silence they could hear a car slow down and stop. He knew the FBI could return at any moment.

"You can fill me in later. C'mon, we need to get out of here."

Thomas helped Josef up, and they headed toward the road where the FBI car was indeed parked but empty. They darted across the road and started up toward the ridge. Invigorated by the candy, Josef quickly regained his energy and they soon arrived at the cable car.

"Here we are," Thomas said.

Josef looked at the cable car with curiosity.

"Strange, I know. We lost our shuttle and this is our substitute."

He opened the door to find Eno kneeling over the Time Globe, cleaning its outer sphere with one of the towels from the alliance hospital.

"Hey Eno, we've got a visitor."

Eno turned around, completely perplexed.

"Say hello to Josef. I don't think you two ever met."

"No. I saw you on the Magnum Screen during your escape, but haven't had the pleasure."

"Nice to meet you," Josef said.

Eno turned to Thomas for an explanation. "How in the world…?"

"The Mastership brought him along to identify me, but he escaped."

"I came across some large animals," Josef explained. "Five or six, with horns."

"Deer," Thomas said, recalling Eno's run-in with the baby version during the retrieval of the shuttle mirrors in Muir Woods. "You remember them, don't you, Eno?"

"Yes," Eno nodded sheepishly. "I'm familiar with the species."

"They seemed harmless, but the Commandoes were terrified and ran off."

Thomas grabbed a bottle of water and a cellophane-wrapped sandwich he'd brought from New York and handed them to Josef, along with the extra clothes Elly had bought for him.

"Here, these should fit you."

"Thanks."

"Where are the Commandos now?" Eno said.

"Gone. Our orders were to return by daybreak in case things got worse on the Station."

"Worse?" Thomas and Eno said.

"The Redshirts came through the Boys' Quarters and arrested anybody who might know anything about your escape, including your friend Poke. When they put the place on lockdown, riots broke out."

"How did they get you?" Thomas said.

"They invaded the Returner Compound the same night. A lot of the men got away with the women and children, but I stayed to protect Lina and got captured."

"What about Ignatius?" Eno said.

"They took him first."

Eno gave Thomas a look of concern, but before he could speak, Elly's cellphone rang.

Thomas reached into his backpack and pulled it out. "Elly?"

Eno heard Elly's voice in the background but could only make out the word "problem."

"Yeah, we had one here, too. After I left you last night, I was followed by the FBI. I got away but ran into the Station's Mastership. They brought a friend of mine to identify me. He's with us now."

Eno could hear Elly's voice rise with urgency.

"Sure," Thomas said. "Go ahead."

Thomas repeated her instructions. "Take the Chinatown Gate three blocks to the Tin How Temple, turn right to the Sing Fat Building, left down the alley to the Golden Dragon. Got it."

Thomas hung up.

"The Golden Dragon?" Eno said.

"It's the restaurant she told us about, where she and her father have Sunday dinner."

"Who's Elly?" Josef asked, completely baffled. "And what's a restaurant?"

"Long story," Thomas said. "We'll explain on the ferry."

"What's the—"

Eno cut him off. "Trust me, you don't want to know."

✦✦

An hour later, Thomas, Eno, and Josef boarded the ferry for the trip to the city. Josef, who knew even less about Earth than Eno, was awestruck by the vast expanse of water they were about to cross. As they found front-row seats on the upper deck, Josef shifted in his seat nervously.

"Don't worry," Eno said, "It's actually quite safe."

"You must have lots of questions," Thomas said. "Where should we start?"

"At the beginning, if you don't mind."

Over the churn of the boat cutting through the water, Thomas told Josef how his father had built a Biosphere in the mountains to save a group of orphans from the floods that ravaged the Earth. He told him how his father had come up with a plan for him to time travel back in order to transport them to a future when the planet was again habitable, how he and Eno landed here forty-seven years too early, met Elly, and how she helped them get the cable car after their shuttle had been discovered. Finally, he told him how Elly had become their friend and guide on the mission.

When Thomas was finished, Josef could only shake his head at the astonishing story. "It's amazing you've survived," Josef said.

"Eno's been a great Navigator and Protector for me, and Elly's been one for both of us."

A horn sounded as the ferry slowed and approached the dock. Josef looked out at the towering skyline, awestruck. "What is that?"

Thomas smiled. "Welcome to San Francisco."

Just before ten o'clock, a taxi delivered them to the Chinatown Gate, a massive arch that served as the official entrance to the neighborhood. Thomas took a moment to locate the two lion sculptures that framed the entrance. "This must be it. Elly said the lions are there to guard against evil spirits," he said, leading them through the green-tiled arch and into the streets, which were already bustling with people, many with cameras around their necks.

"This is Chinatown," Thomas said.

"So, these people are the Chinese?" Josef said.

"No, they're mainly tourists. Or as Elly would say, another nationality altogether."

Eno nodded. "As you'll soon discover, Elly has a strong opinion about everything."

Thomas led them down the street, weaving in and out of the crowds like an experienced tour guide. After a few blocks, he stopped. "Here's the Tin How Temple." In a few minutes, they arrived at the Sing Fat building and turned down the alley. A neon dragon, not unlike the inflated version on the river outside New York, marked the doorway.

"Elly said we should meet her inside," Thomas said.

He led them into the dark restaurant, the shades still drawn against the morning sun. It was empty, except for someone sitting near the front window. Elly waved and the boys hurried to a circular booth and slid inside. A steaming pot of tea sat in the middle of the table, accompanied by four small cups.

"Josef, this is Elly," Thomas said.

"Welcome to Earth," Elly said, then smiled at Thomas. "I always wanted to say that."

"Why did you want us to meet here of all places?" Eno said.

"First off, it's safe. Second, it's private. They don't open until eleven, but my dad's been best friends with the owner, Mr. Chang, ever since they were kids. He's my godfather. I told him I was hosting some exchange students who might have to go home sooner than expected and he opened early for us. I don't suppose you've ever had tea?"

"I have," Thomas said. "Ignatius let me try some of his."

Elly poured them each a cup. "It helps digestion, calm thinking, and good decision making. I'm assuming we're going to need at least two out of three."

"Why don't you start with your problem," Thomas said. "Then we'll tell you ours."

"I had a visit this morning from our FBI friends. Fortunately, my dad was already at work."

"So, the agents, they weren't wounded?"

"Not unless you consider a Band-Aid on the forehead of the short one a wound. And the tall one was perfectly fine. He wanted to know if I'd been in touch with my friends from Iceland. But I stuck to my story that you went back home. What about your friends from Mars?"

"They went home, too," Thomas said. "From what Josef tells us, they're needed to help quell the rebellion."

"The what?" Elly asked.

Thomas turned to Josef for the explanation.

"As word spread about Thomas's mission, a revolt broke out at the Station. Their plan is to bring him back and try him for treason."

"Treason?" Elly said, stunned. "Isn't that a bit extreme?"

"The high governor believes Thomas is trying to restart a civilization on Earth in direct conflict with the values of Martian society."

"He's obsessed with the notion," Eno nodded.

"Treason's a big deal here on Earth," Elly said. "You can get the death penalty."

"On Mars, you're set adrift," Josef said. "That's what they did to my friend Zev."

"When you say 'adrift' you mean…?"

"Sent into space with no means to stabilize yourself," Eno explained. "To make it even worse, they add a double supply of oxygen to prolong the suffering. If you're fortunate, you get hit by an asteroid before the hypoxia sets in."

"That's horrific," Elly said.

A waiter appeared out of the darkness pushing a cart on wheels. He stopped at their booth and lifted a circular tray of food onto their tabletop. Like the tea, it gave off a cloud of steam.

"I figured you'd all be hungry," Elly said, "so I went ahead and ordered some dim sum. The dumplings are filled with chicken, pork—you name it. I also recommend the steamed buns and Har grow. The good news is you don't have to use chopsticks."

Elly reached out and plucked a dumpling out of one of the steamer baskets, using her thumb and middle finger. "There's something for everyone."

Eno wrinkled his nose in revulsion.

"Well, almost everyone," she said. "Dig in."

Thomas and Josef reached for the dim sum as Eno smelled his tea.

"So," Elly said, "what's the plan?"

"I'm not sure," Thomas said. "But with Ignatius in captivity, I can't see abandoning him."

"I respectfully disagree," Eno said. "As much as we care about Ignatius's fate, our first priority is still the mission. I think Ignatius himself would concur."

"How about you, Josef?" Elly said. "Do you have a point of view on all this?"

Josef seemed surprised that anyone would ask his opinion. "I know how important the mission is," he said, "but if anything happens to Lina, my life wouldn't be worth living. If there's any way you could manage to take me back to the Station, I'd be eternally grateful."

"Lina is Josef's female partner," Thomas said. "They tried to escape together."

"They dragged her out of my arms," Josef said. "I tried to fight them off, but one of the Commandos kicked me in the head and I lost consciousness. That's the last I saw of her."

"I'm sorry," Elly said. "Could she also be…set adrift?"

"She'll be questioned first," Eno said. "which is punishment in itself. They've developed a technique of neuro-interrogation for use on captured Returners."

"Is that like torture?" Elly asked.

"I'm not familiar with that term," Eno said. "They induce unconsciousness and monitor neurological activity until they find what they're looking for."

"Yeah," Elly said. "That definitely qualifies."

"We have to assume they've already done it to Ignatius," Thomas said. "That's the only way they could've gotten the information about time travel in order to follow us."

"What happens to people after they've been interrogated?"

"The timeline is short—a week at most," Eno said. "After that they rarely regain neurological function."

"So, they're zombies," Elly said.

"Not familiar with that term either. Suffice to say they're reduced to a vegetative state."

"Some live in the Returner Compound," Josef said. "They just sit and stare into space."

"So, what you're saying is that if they're not rescued fast, it's pretty much over."

"Yes," Eno said flatly.

"I guess that makes the decision pretty simple then."

"I agree," Eno said. "It's pointless to return."

"That's not what I meant," Elly said. "I think you have to go back into the lion's den."

"Whose den?" Eno said.

"Big terrifying animal," Elly said. "King of the jungle."

"Eno," Thomas said, impatiently. "We've already been gone for five days. We only have forty-eight hours to save them."

"It's the least we can do," Elly said.

"We?" Eno repeated. "Does that mean you'll be coming along?"

"Of course," Elly said, patting the stuffed backpack next to her. "Sooner or later the FBI will want to take me in for questioning, so I need to get out of town for a while. This way I can at least help you guys. I'm sure you could you use another hand."

"Elly, this is not like anything you might run into on Earth," Thomas said. "Our Commandos are ruthless, and Bron is even worse."

"On a scale of one to being eaten alive by megalodons, they can't be worse than that. Besides, we're also talking about the fate of *my planet*. I think I deserve to have a say in it."

Thomas looked to Eno, who shrugged with resignation.

"That settles it then," Thomas said.

"If we're going back to Mars," Eno said, "we'll need hazard suits."

"There's a surplus store on Powell that sells stuff like that. Anything else?"

"Yeah," Thomas said. "Is it possible to take this food to go?"

Elly smiled. "I think we can arrange that."

CHAPTER 3

WITH ONE ARM LOOPED through her backpack, Elly took a cautious step outside the Golden Dragon. Thomas followed with Eno and Josef on his heels. When they got to the mouth of the alley, Elly inserted a thin metal rod, fashioned from an everyday wire hanger, into her backpack. On top of it was a small mirror attached by tape.

"What's that?" Thomas said.

"I rigged a rearview to make sure we're not being followed. Those FBI guys are relentless."

Led by Elly, the four of them started weaving through the dense crowd. In minutes, they passed through the Chinatown Gate and Elly hailed a cab. They rode south, into the same neighborhood as the hardware store where she'd taken Thomas and Eno the day they arrived on Earth. It was hard to believe that had only been a week earlier. The cab dropped them in front of a storefront with the words "Army/Navy" painted on the window.

"Is this a military facility?" Josef said.

"No, just a store that sells military surplus goods. Otherwise I wouldn't shop here. I don't believe in armies. Or navies, for that matter."

They entered the store and approached the man behind the counter. He was bald with a beard that ran down to the top of his chest and wore a black denim shirt with the sleeves cut off at the shoulders. Multi-colored snake tattoos ran around both arms, with their fang-bearing heads on the back of his hands. The name tag pinned to his shirt read: Destroyer.

"How can I help you?" he asked with a politeness that belied his appearance.

"I have a list," Elly said, removing her phone from her pocket.

She handed him the phone to read.

"Hazmat suits?"

"One for each of us," Elly said.

"Level A for radiation," Thomas said, "with full face piece, air respirators, and internal two-way radios. We'll also need steel-toe boots, camouflage clothes, and extreme cold-weather gear."

"Where you going, the moon?" Destroyer said.

"Actually," Eno said, "about two hundred times farther."

"Okay," he said, as if it were a perfectly normal thing to say. "All the camo gear is against the back wall, along with the boots. Dressing room's right next to it. We keep the hazmats in storage downstairs. I'll grab some and be right back."

Elly led the boys to the camouflage section, which included not only shirts and pants, but hats, vests, and even underwear. She picked out a shirt and pants.

"I know my size, but you guys might want to try some stuff on while I keep an eye on the street to make sure our friends from the FBI don't decide to come shopping."

Thomas watched Elly head to the front window while Josef joined him.

"She's amazing, that girl," Josef said. "Reminds me of Lina. I take it you two…"

"We're just friends," Thomas said, blushing.

"Sure." Josef smiled. "That's how it starts."

Thomas grabbed some camo pants and a shirt. "I'm going to try this stuff on," he said, and disappeared into the dressing room, still red-faced from Josef's comment. In truth, it wasn't the first time it occurred to him that his feelings for Elly were unusual. He'd sensed it when they first met, then again in New York. And when he left her off at her house after they returned, he was aware of the emptiness he felt at their separation. He remembered how the prospect of continuing the mission without her had produced a dull ache in his chest—one that didn't lift until she'd announced her intention to rejoin them. Perhaps Josef was right that their friendship was growing into something more. If only he understood what that was.

His ringing phone jarred him out of his reverie.

"Elly?"

Her voice was calm but urgent. "They're here."

Thomas hurried to join her, standing behind a large mannequin of a combat-ready soldier.

She gestured toward the street. "Their car's parked at the corner, in front of that taco place. The tall one's behind the wheel. The shorter one is just coming out of the restaurant."

Thomas looked out to see the smaller FBI agent approaching the car with a bag in one hand, a drink in the other. "How do you think they found us?"

"They must've been working with the plumbers."

"The plumbers?"

"Check out the other end of the block."

Elly pointed to a small blue van. Written across the side in large yellow letters was "Sunset Plumbing." Two dark-skinned men were sitting in front.

"It was the only car on my whole block this morning, parked in front of the Cohens'. I noticed two guys sitting inside, talking. I should've known."

"What do you mean?"

"After last night when they chased you in the woods, they know that you know they're following you. And since they tracked you from my house, they know I'm covering for you. So, they brought in a pair of guys neither of us would recognize."

"I wonder why they don't just arrest us?"

"Because we haven't committed any crime. All they really know is that you've got something to do with the mystery shuttle. I guess they want to see where we're going to help them figure out what we're up to."

"What do you think we should do?" Thomas said.

"I guess we could split up, try to make a run for it. But Eno can't do that on his bad leg, and Josef doesn't know his way around."

"We can't just let them keep following us."

"No," Elly said. "We need to disable their vehicles."

"If I could get close enough, I could try and cut their axel with my laser."

"That's a bit extreme," Elly said. "But since we're in an army/navy store, I have another idea. C'mon."

Thomas and Elly hurried to the back of the store as Destroyer reappeared carrying four silver hazmat suits with outer aluminized shells.

"I've only got small and large, so I brought two of each."

"They should do fine," Elly said.

"Anything else I can get you?"

"Actually, there is one more thing."

"What's that?"

"A forty-caliber ninja blowgun with a package of terminator spikes."

✦✦

Minutes later, Thomas, Eno, Elly, and Josef convened behind the soldier mannequin, their gear now packed in two large duffel bags.

Thomas peered out the window to check on the FBI agents. "Both cars are still there."

Elly checked her watch. "The cab should be here any minute."

Thomas nodded. "Josef, if you can carry the duffel with the hazmat suits and the rest of the clothes, we'll take the other one."

"No problem," Josef said.

"I can carry something," Eno protested.

"The last thing we want is for you to trip and re-break your leg," Thomas said. "Besides, you need to concentrate on the taxi."

"Shall we go over it once more?" Elly asked.

"It's hardly complicated," Eno said, slightly offended. "Josef and I proceed three blocks, to the corner of Castro and Church Streets, where we wait for you."

"Make sure the cab is pointed north," Elly added, "so we can drive straight to the bridge. You remember what to tell the driver, or should I write it down?"

"That won't be necessary," Eno said, as the taxi pulled up in front.

"Here's your ride," Thomas said. "Good luck."

Eno and Josef went out the front door and got into the cab. Thomas and Elly watched as it pulled out. A moment later, the plumbing van followed.

"So far, so good," Elly said.

"Are you sure you're all right with this?" Thomas asked.

"Why wouldn't I be?"

"You said the FBI couldn't arrest us because we haven't committed a crime. I have to think what we're about to do officially qualifies."

"Probably. But I don't see any other way, do you?"

"Let me do it alone. Whatever happens, they can hold me responsible."

"Thomas, you have no experience with this kind of weapon."

"Like you said, all it requires is strong lungs, and I've got those. Besides, isn't blowing darts just another version of throwing darts?"

"You got me there," Elly said.

She unzipped the duffel and pulled out the blowgun, which was the size of a flute. A thin leather shoulder strap dangled from its ends.

He slid the blowgun over his shoulder while Elly pulled out the pack of four-inch terminator spikes. She slid one into the end of the blowgun and handed the rest to Thomas, who slid the other three into the front flap of his camo shirt.

"Ready when you are," Thomas said.

Elly adjusted the rearview mirror on the backpack then slid it over her shoulder. She grabbed the duffel bag and went out the door toward the FBI car on the opposite side of the street.

Thomas watched as she passed the FBI car. Elly glanced over at the two agents and paused for a moment, as if she recognized them.

It was Thomas's signal.

Elly continued down the street with one eye on the rearview mirror mounted on her backpack. The FBI agents were still watching. She adjusted her mirror to see Thomas exit the store and dash across the street, disappearing between two parked cars. Satisfied that he was in position, she turned the corner and was out of sight.

Crouching low, Thomas moved from his hiding spot between the parked cars and onto the sidewalk. Then he crawled toward the FBI car. When he was twenty feet away, he got into a kneeling position and slid the blowgun from his shoulder. Holding it with both hands, he aimed it at the rear tire of the FBI car. After holding his breath for three full seconds, as Elly suggested, he blew with all his strength. The steel spike shot out of the tube and glanced off the side of the tire.

He pulled a second spike from his shirt, loaded it, and aimed again. This time, it landed on the outer edge of the tire. For good measure, he tried a third spike, which hit the other tire smack in the middle.

He slid the blowgun back over his shoulder and stepped into the street.

Walking slowly, he crossed directly in front of the FBI agents. As he did, they started the car and began to pull out. Thomas broke into a run, and the FBI car was forced to turn around on the narrow street. By the time it did, he'd rounded the corner to where Elly was waiting.

"I got both tires," he said.

"Sweet," she said.

They took off, running straight downhill. Within seconds, a car screeched behind them, and they looked back to see the FBI car, flapping loudly, its rear tires almost flat. As they reached the next block, they glanced back to see the two FBI agents pull over, jump out of the car, and proceed on foot. They turned at the next corner onto Castro Street, where a cab was parked. Elly gestured across the street to the Sunset Plumbing van. Thomas dropped into a crouch, loaded a spike into the blowgun. He aimed at the back tire and blew. The spike made a direct hit.

"You're a natural with that thing," Elly said.

Thomas pulled the last spike out of his front pocket. "I should do the other tire."

"No time!" Elly yelled, as the two FBI agents appeared around the corner.

They ran toward the cab, its engine now idling. Thomas threw himself into the back seat with Eno and Josef while Elly took the front seat next to the driver.

"Can you go as fast as possible? We're late for—"

"I know, I know," the driver said. "Your little pal already told me…"

The cab pulled out as the FBI agents jumped into the plumbing van, which started to follow but abruptly stopped in the middle of the block. The van driver jumped out to check the rear tire and was quickly joined by the other three agents. Elly sat back in her seat and took a deep breath.

The taxi driver glanced over at her with a sympathetic smile. "Don't worry kid. They won't start the wedding without the ring bearer."

CHAPTER 4

ELLY GAVE THE TAXI driver an extra ten dollars to take them up the fire road and all the way to the ridge, where they got out.

The driver waved as he made a U-turn and started back down the mountain. "Congratulate the bride and groom for me," he called out.

Thomas led them along the ridge path toward the cable car. Eno's leg, which only hours before was stiff, had already become more flexible, and they made the thirteen-minute walk in almost half the time.

They hurried inside the cabin and shut the platform door, sealing out the sunlight. Josef dropped the big duffel and Elly handed out the hazmat suits. They all fit reasonably well, with the exception of Eno's, which gathered around his ankles like a pair of tiny parachutes.

"I should start programming the globe," Eno said.

"Where exactly do you plan to land?" Josef asked.

"Good question," Eno said, turning to Thomas for an answer.

"We need to get to the Returner Compound and assess the situation first. From there we can figure out the best way to travel to the Station."

"The Ramjets patrol the whole area now," Josef said, "so I'd aim for the Tharsis Rise. It has lots of small craters if we need to stay out of sight."

"I doubt I can put us in a location that exact," Eno said. "The globe is designed for Earth, not Mars."

"Do your best," Thomas said, using his wrist pod to project a grid map of Mars against the darkened cabin wall. "Josef, you said the Returner Compound is deserted?"

"It was when I was captured," Josef said. "There's a lot of rubble, so it may be hard to get around, but we should be able to get to the munitions cave."

"Munitions?" Elly said.

"The Protectors hid some emergency weapons in one of the terra farms."

"Wow," Elly said. "We're going to use real weapons?"

"I don't think we have much choice," Thomas said. "Let's get going."

But as they started stowing the duffels, the low growl of an engine sounded outside. Thomas grabbed the binoculars and scrambled onto the roof, where he could see a small section of the highway. It was enough to reveal a car, with a light flashing on its roof.

"See anything?" Elly asked, leaning out of the cable car.

"A car, with a flashing light." Thomas said. "Make that two…I mean, three."

"The FBI," Elly said. "They must've gotten a look at the taxi's license and called for back-up. Can you see where they're going?"

"Yeah, they're coming up the road."

Thomas jumped off the roof and ducked inside as Eno made one last adjustment on the Time Globe. He started to close the platform door when he spotted several men in suits, running toward them on the ridge path. "Eno, time to go!"

Eno nodded. "Counting down!"

As the four of them got into position, Elly glanced at Thomas and smiled.

"What?" Thomas said.

"It's hard to believe…I'm actually going to Mars."

The cable car began to spin, creating a ring of leafy debris across the bluff, obscuring the ocean below and the sky above. Thomas couldn't help feeling slightly disheartened. He thought he'd left the red planet forever, and now here was, only a week later, going back.

Elly held on tight and closed her eyes, and Thomas noticed that they entered the wormhole more slowly than previous time jumps. It was thick and sludgy, like galactic mud, as if the Time Globe were equally relunctant to return to Mars.

Thomas opened his eyes to see that Eno and Josef had slid to the opposite corners of the cable car, unconscious. Elly was leaning against his shoulder, no longer smiling. The time flies, unlike before, were a dark reddish hue, as if they reflected the surface of Mars itself.

Thomas listened for Ignatius's voice but heard only a high-pitched moan, as if someone were in pain. It was soon drowned out by a loud crackling sound.

Elly opened her eyes. "What's that?"

"It's something hitting the mirrors," Thomas said.

Thomas peered through one of the small openings between the mirrors but couldn't see a thing. As his eyes adjusted, he could make out a brown vortex swirling around them. "We're in the middle of a dust devil."

"What's that?" Elly asked.

"Like one of your tornadoes. Only with sand."

Eno sat up. "Remember, Mars is basically one massive desert."

Josef opened his eyes and sat up. "Are we here?"

"Yeah," Thomas said. "Though I can't exactly say where *here* is." He opened one of the side panels, revealing the mass of dust. A hint of light appeared at the center, as if the sun were trying to force its way through.

"Will it pass?" Elly asked.

"Eventually," Thomas said. "But unlike the storms on Earth, these can last months."

"Months?" Elly repeated.

"Maybe less," Thomas shrugged. "The problem is, there's no way to know."

"So, I guess it doesn't make any sense to wait it out." Elly said.

"Not unless we're willing to starve to death," Thomas said. "How's your leg, Eno?"

"Much better. I'd say it's about eighty-nine percent. But I hope you're not thinking about walking. The bigger devils can be five or six miles wide."

"He's right," Josef said. "There was a smaller one when we escaped. Lina and I were in the truck for most of it but had to go the last mile on foot. You can only see a few feet in front of you, so you're walking blind. And the wind is incredibly strong, so it's really slow going."

"Our wrist pods should show us where we are," Thomas said.

Eno pulled off his glove and checked. Several coordinates sprang to life. "According to this we're at the northern end of Tharsis."

"Is that good?" Elly asked.

"Yes and no," Eno said. "It puts us just a few hundred miles from the Returner Compound, but we can only expect to cover a few miles per day. With the food and water we have, we can't last more than a day or so."

Thomas turned back to the viewing panel. "I have an idea."

Eno turned to Josef. "This happens with regularity. We encounter trouble and Thomas comes up with a plan, usually involving the risk of life and limb."

"But it always seems to work," Elly said.

"I grant you we've been fortunate to this point," Eno said.

"What are you thinking Thomas?" Elly said.

"There's a shelter between here and the compound called the Graveyard."

"Really?" Eno said. "That's news to me."

"I saw it from the rocket car when we flew out to Olympus Mons the first time," Thomas said. "You had your eyes closed, as I remember."

"Ah, yes." Eno said, shrugging sheepishly.

"It was the first staging ground for the Mars project, when the original group of workers arrived to build the Station. It's been deserted for forty years, but the shelter should still be intact. It's filled with old supply ships, so there's a chance we could find a transport of some kind to take us the rest of the way."

"Maybe we could even find food and water," Elly said.

Eno glanced back at his wrist pod. "I don't see it on the Station map."

"It wouldn't be there," Thomas said. "They have no reason to think anybody would use it. Switch over to topography. The satellite should read all that metal in a different color."

Eno made an adjustment on his wrist pod and the Olympus Mons came into view, a huge black mound towering over the flat red landscape.

Slowly, a smaller black mound came appeared.

Thomas pointed. "Look, right there…"

"How far is it?" Josef said.

"Seventeen miles," Eno said.

"We could walk there in two days," Thomas said.

"It's still too risky," Eno said. "We're better off trying another jump to get closer."

"You said yourself the globe wasn't programed for Mars," Thomas said. "How do you know we won't wind up farther away? Every minute we lose could be fatal for Ignatius—and Lina. I say we give ourselves two hours. If we can't get through the storm, we can come back and time jump then."

Eno thought about it for a moment, then nodded.

✦✦

It was agreed that they would travel as lightly as possible, leaving most of their supplies behind, though Thomas insisted on taking the Sonic Inducer in his backpack. Without an actual weapon to protect themselves, it was better than nothing. And after what happened the last time, Elly could hardly object. For her part, she brought the Chinese takeout, in the event that they got stranded overnight. Eno, in charge of mapping their trek, removed his wrist pod and had Josef tape it around the outside of his glove for easy visibility. Thomas grabbed the marine rope he'd taken from the Star of the Sea after his mother's rescue and tied it around his waist.

"This is to make sure we don't get separated," Thomas said, handing the rope to Eno, who tied off his waist and passed the rope on to the others. "Elly, you go next, then Josef can anchor the rear. All right, everybody ready?"

They all nodded. Thomas opened the cable car door and was hit with a powerful blast of wind. He lowered his head and pushed his way onto the platform. The others slowly followed.

Outside, Eno checked his wrist pod to determine their location. A tiny digital map sprung to life as a reflection in Eno's face shield. Thomas started walking, with Eno, Elly, and Josef trudging behind, leaving a fresh set of footprints on the Martian surface.

Footsteps that quickly vanished into the mouth of the storm.

CHAPTER 5

THEY WALKED FOR A little over an hour. Other than the crackle of sand against their suits, the only other sound was the steady rhythm of their own breathing. With the wind pushing against them, their pace was agonizingly slow. Thomas turned around and walked backward for a few steps so he could check on everybody. Eno had his head down, and Josef was at the rear, barely visible. Elly gave Thomas a little wave, thinking about the time he walked backward on Stinson beach, and how she could never have imagined repeating the same moment on the sand of a far-off planet.

"How we doing?" Thomas panted through the internal communication system.

"It feels like walking in a giant vacuum cleaner," Elly said.

"Why don't we take a little break," Thomas said, "to rest our legs."

"Legs?" Eno said. "You mean those two numb appendages connected to our waists?"

"Let's form a circle," Thomas said. "So we can see each other." He looped around to find Josef, and the four of them sat on the sandy ground. "You think you guys can make another hour?"

"Sure," Elly said.

"But can you do another two hours back to the cable car?" Eno asked.

"Ye of little faith." Elly said.

"Faith has nothing to do with it," Eno said, bringing his wrist pod to his face shield. "We've gone a little over a mile. At this rate it will take a Martian year to get to the Mons. That's 669 sols, or days, as you would call them."

"Look," Thomas said, "all we have to do is get through this storm, and then we'll be able to make much better time."

A strong gust of wind kicked up around them, whipping the sand against their face shields with a hard rattle.

"Unfortunately, it's getting worse," Eno said.

"Maybe that's good news," Josef said.

"What do you mean?" Elly asked.

"We could be at the outer rim of the storm, which is the most intense. It was like that when we escaped from the Station. Maybe we're almost though it."

"How would we know?" Eno said.

"We should start seeing some light," Josef said.

The wind continued to pick up speed, nearly blowing them over.

"Link arms!" Thomas yelled. But within seconds, the sand piled up in drifts that nearly covered their ankles.

"If we stay here much longer, we'll be buried alive!" Eno shouted.

Suddenly the wind seemed to weaken slightly.

Thomas raised his head. "It's slowing."

"And there's a little light coming through," Elly said. "Look, there's something over there behind you."

Thomas and Josef craned their heads to see the hazy outline of a rectangular object, about ten feet long and almost as wide, some thirty yards away.

"Let's see what it is," said Thomas, struggling to his feet.

"Proceed with caution," Eno said. "This area's filled with abandoned drill sites from the water mines. We don't want to fall into an empty shaft."

With Thomas in the lead, they headed toward the mysterious object. As they got closer, they could make out a thick column of metal protruding upward.

"It looks like a machine of some kind," Thomas said.

"Probably a drill rig," Eno added.

"Drill rigs are much taller," Josef said. "I worked on one until I got transferred to the mirror factory."

Elly let out a shriek. "I think I know what it is!"

"What?" Thomas asked.

"Curiosity."

"What are you talking about?" Eno asked.

"A Mars Rover sent from Earth. We launched it eleven years ago, in 2012."

"Are you certain?" Eno asked.

"Of course," she said. "It was a big deal at the time. My father and I watched the coverage on TV. I even did a report on it."

"When you were four years old?" Eno said, dubiously.

"Okay, it was mainly a drawing for my preschool class. Look, that thing on top of its robotic neck, it's the panoramic navigation camera. And the platform is its heat shield."

In a few more steps the unmanned vehicle came into full view. It had three wheels on each side, all half buried in sand.

"It's stuck," Elly said.

"I wonder if we could we use it to ride to the Graveyard?" Thomas said.

"It should hold us," Elly said. "It weighs a couple thousand pounds."

Thomas turned to Eno. "You think you can get it going?"

"I don't see why not." Eno said, moving in for a closer inspection. "It looks like it has an old-fashioned radioisotope thermoelectric generator with lithium ion batteries. The batteries are dead, but I should have something in my Time Globe kit to regenerate them."

"Good," Thomas said. "While you do that, we'll dig out the wheels."

Thomas gave Eno his Tetrascope and—with Josef's help—lifted him up onto the rover's heat shield, which acted like a kind of platform. While Eno went to work on the batteries, Thomas, Elly, and Josef used their gloved hands to clear the sand that had gathered around the wheels like a snowdrift. Several minutes later, the rover suddenly came to life, its navigation neck craning around as if looking for the best way out of the storm.

"Incredible," Josef said. "That was really impressive, Eno."

"Repairing exotic vehicles is his specialty," Elly said.

With the wheels free of sand, the three of them climbed onto the Rover's heat shield next to Thomas and sat with their legs dangling over the side.

"Ready when you are," Thomas said.

Eno fiddled with the steering mechanism, and they could feel the cleats of the rover's tires gain traction. Slowly, they began to move. In another ten minutes, they drove through the outer rim of the dust devil, revealing an otherwise normal day on Mars. There was virtually no wind, and on the horizon, they could even make out a pale, pinkish sun.

Elly sat up and looked around. This was her first real look at the planet.

"Wow," she said. "It really is red. I guess you can pinch me now."

"What?" Thomas said.

"An expression that means I'm not dreaming. I really am on Mars."

"Actually, you just made history," Thomas said.

"How's that?" Elly said.

"You came from Earth in the year 2023. That makes you the first person to step foot on the planet."

"That's merely a technicality of time travel," Eno said.

"Did anyone ever tell you you're a buzzkill?" Elly said.

"Unfamiliar with the term," Eno said.

"I'm adding it to my list," Thomas smiled. "I think it might come in handy."

✦✦

THEY ARRIVED IN LESS than an hour at the outskirts of the Graveyard, where a pair of massive twenty-wheel supply trucks acted as a sort of entrance. The encampment was much larger than Thomas had thought from the air. A hundred or so vehicles were scattered around the perimeter, all in various stages of decay, with a thick coat of red Martian dust.

Thomas pointed toward the interior, where a large plastic bubble ballooned over the vehicles. "Let's head over there. It looks like some sort of habitat."

Eno steered the rover in that direction, but after a few minutes the big trucks were parked too closely together to drive between. "I'm afraid we'll have to go the rest of the way on foot."

Eno shut down the rover, and Thomas undid the rope around his waist and climbed down. The others followed suit. They walked single file through the mass of vehicles, each bearing the Science Alliance insignia along with identification from their country of origin. As they passed some Canadian and Japanese trucks, they arrived at a series of smaller bubbles joined to form a warehouse-sized compound. Taken together, they reminded Elly of the model of an atom from her science class. Written in faded block letters was "ALLIANCE HABITAT #1."

"Hopefully it still has pressurized oxygen," Eno said.

Thomas pointed to a set of doors, and they entered a large open space that contained a variety of inflatable furniture, most of which was now deflated. On one side was a doorway leading to living and sleeping quarters, including a mess hall. The other side was filled with containers of various sizes and shapes. The two areas were simply marked with the letters "A" and "B." Both were deserted, and by all appearances had been so for years.

Eno checked his wrist pod. "There's over 1,025 millibars of oxygen in here."

"Great," Thomas said. "Then we can breathe easy."

They unzipped their helmets and pulled them back.

"Aaaah," Elly said. "Nice to be out of this thing."

"We have some time to rest," Josef said. "The Station fleet does daily patrols, so we can't travel to the Returner Compound before dark anyway."

"It's almost two hours until sunset," Eno said. "We should see if we can locate an equipment log for the vehicles."

Thomas nodded. "Elly and I will check for food and water."

The foursome separated. Eno and Josef went toward the "B" wing of the compound, while Thomas and Elly headed into the "A" wing, which was filled with supplies. The walls were filled with oxygen tanks, hazmat suits, electric drills, handheld spotlights, sledgehammers, shovels, sections of pipe, and spare vehicle parts.

Elly pointed to some containers. "Water?"

Thomas tore one open and pulled out four large metallic bottles, one for each of them.

They continued into the mess hall, where they came upon several containers of dehydrated food and removed a few packages of indistinguishable items.

"What do you think this is?" Elly asked, ripping open one of the packages.

"Not sure," Thomas said. "But it'll have to do for now."

A voice echoed from the entrance area. "Thomas!"

They turned to see Josef holding up a handheld monitor.

"We found the vehicle log."

"Good work," Thomas said. "Where's Eno?"

"He was right behind me…" Josef said.

A whirring noise came from the "B" wing and they turned to see Eno walking out with a small remote device. "I found something else that might come in handy," he said, as two small robots, no more than three-feet tall lumbered into view. "They're Drill-Bots. They must have been used for digging in locations the big rigs couldn't access."

"Do they have names?" Elly asked.

"Of course not," Eno said. "Why would you name a robot?"

Elly kneeled down in front of the little robots. She ran a gloved hand over their dust covered torsos, revealing two nameplates. "This one's Frank. And his buddy is...Stein. Ha. Someone had a real sense of humor."

The three boys looked at each other, puzzled.

"Frank and Stein?" Elly repeated. "Doesn't ring a bell?"

"Are they famous Americans?" Thomas asked.

"No, they're fictional characters—and British, at that. Actually, it's actually only one character, made from combining two different names to make Frankenstein." Elly could see that the boys were becoming even more confused. "Never mind. Who wants some water?"

They sat on the floor. Elly passed around the water bottles.

Eno pulled out a strip of dehydrated food and held it up for examination. "What is this?"

Elly took a piece and chewed off a bite. "Turkey jerky. It's a little stale, but not bad for a fifty-year-old old snack slathered in preservatives. Fortunately, we still have our Chinese food, which gives new meaning to the term *takeout*."

She passed around the dim sum. After the long trek, they were all starving, and even Eno gobbled the food down. "Don't forget to leave room for dessert," she said.

"Dessert?" Josef asked, confused.

"The thing you eat after dinner, usually on the sweet side?"

Eno shrugged. "Never encountered it."

"You're in for a special treat then." Elly pulled out several small packages individually wrapped in cellophane.

"What are those?" Thomas asked.

"Fortune cookies. Your first dessert comes with a bonus life lesson."

"How does that work?" Josef asked.

"First, you determine the order of fortunes, like this." Elly emptied the cookies onto the floor between them. "Steps one and two. Take the cookie that's pointed at you and open it."

The boys each picked one up and tore apart the wrapping.

"Step three, break the cookie in half and gently remove your fortune." Elly demonstrated by removing the small piece of white paper in the middle of hers. "Step four, read your fortune. I'll go first. 'Expect a life-changing surprise.' I guess this was last week's cookie. Who wants to go next?"

Josef opened his. "The object of your desire comes closer."

He looked up, stunned. "How would it know about Lina?"

"The cookie knows all," Elly said. "Eno, your turn."

"Life does not get better by chance. It gets better by change."

"Some real wisdom there. You should tape it to your wrist pod," Elly said. "All right, Thomas, you're up."

Thomas read silently, then aloud, clearly trying to understand it. "Do not follow where the path may lead. Go where there's no path and leave a trail."

"Interesting advice," Eno said, "given where we just came from."

"Or where we're going," Elly added.

Thomas carefully folded the fortune and tucked it into his pocket for safekeeping.

"What happens now?" Eno asked.

"Step five," Elly said. "Dessert."

They each took a bite and chewed in silence for a moment.

"This is the best thing I've ever tasted," Josef said.

"Not as good as spaghetti." Eno shrugged, and added, "But not bad at all."

"There's a couple more in here if anybody wants a snack," Elly said.

As Eno and Josef split the rest of the cookies, Thomas checked his wrist pod. "It's getting late. We should start looking for a transport."

Josef handed the monitor with the vehicle log to Thomas. "Check out the Australian F-600. It has a top speed of sixty miles an hour. According to the log, there should be four of them here, so hopefully we can find one in decent condition. Or one that Eno can fix."

Thomas pulled up the image of a cumbersome looking rectangular vehicle. "It looks solid enough, but is there anything faster?"

"Most of the trucks were designed for moving equipment and supplies," Josef said, "so they're not really build for speed."

"What about an ambulance?" Thomas said. "They're fast, and they must've had one for injuries in the field."

"Good thought," Eno said. "We'll need one for Ignatius. If he's been through neuro-interrogation, it's more than likely he'll be unconscious."

Thomas scrolled through the inventory. "There's only one listed, a Swedish model. It's small but has a top speed of a hundred miles an hour."

"Might take a while to find it," Josef said. "According to the log, there's ninety-three vehicles here, scattered around a two-mile radius."

"Maybe Frank and Stein can help," Elly said. "What do you think, Eno?"

"They're easy enough to program," Eno said.

Within minutes, the foursome were back in their hazmat suits and walking toward the habitat entrance. Frank and Stein whirred along behind Eno.

"Elly and I will search everything to the left," Thomas said, "while Eno and Josef you take the right. We'll send Frank and Stein down the middle, and meet up at the other side."

With that, they separated. As Thomas and Elly started out, a brilliant orange glare began to reflect off the windows of several vehicles. They turned to see the sun setting in the distance.

It took Thomas and Elly almost twenty minutes to reach the end of the perimeter, moments before Eno and Josef approached from the other direction.

"Nothing on our side," Thomas said.

"Nothing on ours either," Josef said.

Suddenly the remote in Eno's hand began to flash.

"Hold on," he said. "It's Drill-Bot 2. He seems to have a vehicle match."

"Do we know where he is?" Thomas said.

"The coordinates are coming in now. Follow me."

The four of them worked their way through the labyrinth of vehicles to find Frank and Stein standing at the rear of a massive thirty-wheel cargo truck.

"So much for getting help from a pair of bots," Eno said.

"Hold on," Thomas said.

He jumped up on the rear bumper of the truck and threw open the doors. Inside was the Swedish ambulance. "They must've put it in here to protect it from the elements."

Elly patted Frank and Stein on their heads. "Way to go, guys."

"How do we get it out?" Eno asked.

"There must be a ramp," Thomas said, "or they couldn't have gotten it in there in the first place. Check the cab."

Josef hurried around the side of the big truck and jumped into the cab. Within seconds, a ramp emerged from a panel at the bottom, and angled down to the ground.

Thomas got into the driver's seat of the ambulance and backed it out. "Let's go," he said.

"Uh, aren't we forgetting something?" Elly said, gesturing toward Frank and Stein, who stood behind the truck looking like abandoned children.

"You're not suggesting we take the bots?" Eno asked.

"They came in pretty handy already. They might be useful in the Station."

"Can't argue with that," Thomas said.

Together, they lifted Frank and Stein into the back of the ambulance.

And as the sun set on the Martian landscape, they drove toward the darkness.

CHAPTER 6

JOSEF, AS THE PERSON most experienced with the Martian landscape, took the driver's seat for the three-hour drive to the Mons. Thomas rode next to him, monitoring the sky for station aircraft. Eno tracked their drive on his wrist pod while Elly gazed at the two moons sitting above the volcano, a pair of suspicious eyes set over an unusually large nose.

"You don't know how strange it is to see two moons," Elly said.

"Almost as strange as seeing only one," Eno countered.

A soft alarm emitted from his wrist pod. "We've only got another five minutes before we reach the compound."

Elly leaned forward. "Thomas, once we rescue Ignatius, what then?"

"I figured we'd get him back to the Returner Compound and go from there," Thomas said.

Josef glanced at Thomas. "The compound may not be safe for him."

"The same is true for the entire planet," Eno said. "Bron won't rest until he's found him."

"Then we'll just have to take him back to Earth," Thomas said.

"With the FBI breathing down our necks in San Francisco it won't be much safer there." Elly said. "He might be better off in a different country. Or even a different time."

"Maybe both," Thomas nodded.

"But where?" Eno said.

"I think Elly would be the best judge of that," Thomas said. "Any ideas?"

"Let me think about it, okay?" Elly said.

Josef slowed down as he reached the tunnel that led to the entrance of the Returner Compound, coming to a stop in front of the massive doors.

"If it's deserted, who's going to let us in?" Elly said.

"We can't force our way through those doors," Josef said. "They were built to withstand a missile attack. Our best chance is to trip the locking apparatus."

"How do we do that?" Elly asked.

Eno glanced back at Frank and Stein, standing in the rear. "I might be able to use the Drill-Bots to triangulate the signal. But I'll need them outside."

Thomas and Josef unloaded Frank and Stein from the back of the ambulance and positioned them at opposite sides of the doors. Eno stood in the middle and worked the remote. A light went on in Frank's forehead, followed by a similar light in Stein's.

"Look," Elly said. "They're thinking."

"Hardly," Eno said. "Just computing."

A moment later, they heard a loud pop, and slowly, the doors began to open.

"Quick!" Thomas said.

Josef jumped back into the ambulance and drove it through the opening, while the others, including Frank and Stein, followed.

Elly got out and looked up at the waterfall in astonishment. "We're under a volcano?"

"It's not active," Eno said, "in case you were wondering."

"We should check out the caves right away," Thomas said, retrieving the flashlight. "Frank and Stein can stay here with the ambulance."

They quickly made their way past the amoeba-shaped pool and under the small waterfall. The living quarters appeared to be deserted, and Thomas led the group forward.

Elly looked around in amazement. "How many people lived down here?"

"About a hundred, though it grew a lot during the last year," Thomas said.

"Remind me again," Elly said. "When was that?"

"2086."

They hurried past the terra farms and the recreation area, but as they entered the tunnel, which led to the training center, the lights went out, plunging them into darkness. Thomas turned on the flashlight but could see nothing. As he did, the sound of footsteps echoed from the tunnel. He moved the flashlight back and forth until he could make out several men, armed with laser rifles, approaching. A surge of bright light lit up the tunnel, forcing them to cover their eyes.

A disembodied voice followed. "Thomas?"

Thomas dropped his hand, but it took a moment for his eyes to adjust. "Luke?"

The men lowered their rifles, revealing four Protectors. A short distance behind them stood a handful of women carrying small children.

"I thought the compound was deserted," Thomas said.

"It was," Luke said. "After the attack, we evacuated the women with children to a secure bunker on the other side of the Mons. But now that the battle's moved to the Station, we felt it was safe to bring them back. We were just returning when we heard the doors open and thought it was the Commandos. You were the last person I expected to see. What are you doing here?"

"We came back for Ignatius. He's still alive, isn't he?"

"So we hear. He's being held captive in the Station."

Luke turned to the Protectors. "Get everyone settled and meet us back in Cavern 10."

As the women and children were ushered toward the living quarters, Luke turned to Thomas. "Come along. I'll take you to headquarters and our leader can fill you in."

Luke drove them into the deepest recess of the compound, passing the cave where Thomas had his Q-Ring training. Finally, they reached a small doorway and Luke led them down a narrow flight of stairs to a small room with an open archway. Inside, a man was sitting in the dark at a table, his back to them. He faced a three-dimensional holograph of the Station interior.

"We have some visitors," Luke said. "I think you might know one of them."

The leader swiveled around. His arm was wrapped in a sling and he had a patch over one eye.

Thomas was stunned. "William? I thought…"

"Bron went to great pains to spare me, so I could be interrogated. But Luke came to my rescue before he had the chance."

Thomas gestured behind him. "You remember Eno and Josef?"

William nodded, though his attention was focused on Elly.

"I see you've brought a guest?"

"This is our friend Elly, from Earth."

"It might not've been the best time to bring a visitor."

"I insisted on coming," Elly said. "Thomas's mission has as much to do with the future of my planet as it does yours."

"The Mastership almost found us," Thomas said, "but we got away. Josef told us about what happened, and we decided to come back for Ignatius."

"You needn't have. I've just been going over plans to free him. With any luck, we'll have him out of the Station by tonight."

"But where will you take him?"

"We'll figure that out once we get him. Mars is a big planet."

"Not as big as Earth," Elly said.

"Elly's right," Thomas said. "We're thinking he'd have a better chance to recuperate there, where no one's looking for him. And we can hide him in a different year."

William glanced at Luke.

"They've got a point," Luke said.

"Maybe," William said. "But Ignatius is only the architect of the revolution. Balthazar knows that you're its chief executor and holds you responsible for the escalation in fighting."

"Escalation?" Thomas asked.

"Last night, a group of your classmates got their hands on some small arms and barricaded themselves in the planetarium. More join them by the hour. Balthazar will stop at nothing to get his hands on you, and Bron will make sure you don't survive the experience."

"I know," Thomas said. "But we're here now, and can take Ignatius back to Earth, where he'll be safe. It's his only chance."

William glanced at Luke, who nodded agreement.

"Can I ask what your plan is to free him?" Thomas said.

The two men turned to the holograph of the Station's interior.

"The Returners captured in the initial attack are being held in the prison, so it's become the focal point of the rebellion, but Ignatius and a few others were moved to the government center for interrogation. It's fortified with Redshirts."

"What about Commandos?"

"There's only a small group. Most of the others are scattered between the prison and the rest of the Station."

"How do you plan to get inside?"

William pointed toward the holograph of the Station. "The Commandos destroyed the tunnel we used to use to bring you in and out, but they still don't know about the one that leads to Ignatius's quarters. We plan to attack the government center and lure the Commandos into the Station. While we engage them, the Q-Ring team will go in and get Ignatius."

Thomas stepped forward to view the holograph up close. "How will you get the Commandos out, if you don't mind my asking?"

Luke stepped forward and pointed to an area Thomas and Josef knew well. "We're going to plant a pair of explosive devices in the Propellant Depot. The damage will be significant, so they'll have to send Commandos in to repair the radiation leaks. When they do, we'll be waiting."

"How many Protectors do you have?"

"The four you saw in the tunnel," William said, "plus Luke and I."

"Only a half-dozen men, altogether?"

"We have to make do with what we have."

"If I understand your plan, you need to hold off the Commandos long enough to allow the Q-Ring Instructors to find Ignatius, so you'll need all the Protectors at the government center. I happen to know it's seven hundred steps away. It'll take four minutes for the others to rejoin you."

"It's not ideal," William said, "but there isn't a better choice."

"Maybe there is," Thomas said. "The explosives could be planted by bots."

Luke gave out a laugh. "Bots?"

"We brought along a pair of drillers who are more than capable," Thomas said. "They helped us break into the compound."

"If they plant the explosives," Eno said, "you can use all your men to engage the Commandos. Then the four of us can go in for Ignatius."

"No," William said. "It's far too dangerous."

"I've spent the last week with Thomas," Elly said. "We've escaped giant sharks, the FBI, even your Mastership. I've seen firsthand what he can do."

"Me, too," Eno said. "Besides, Ignatius had enough confidence in Thomas to choose him to lead our mission. The least you can do is honor his conviction."

Elly smiled at Eno, proud of the way he spoke up for Thomas.

William nodded. "All right then. We stole some uniforms used by the cleaning crew in the government center. They have special clearance, so you can avoid undue scrutiny. But you'll still need weapons."

✦✦

An hour later, Thomas, Eno, Elly, and Josef, armed with small laser guns, convened back at the ambulance for the trip to the Station. Elly was initially reluctant to carry a weapon, but William assured her that they were designed to temporarily disable, rather than permanently injure, a potential attacker. When their gear had been stored, they put on the uniforms provided by Luke.

Elly gave Frank and Stein a pat on the head. "Good luck, boys. And thanks for your help."

Eno rolled his eye. "They can't actually process gratitude, you know."

"Maybe so, but my father says that it's always important to acknowledge it."

"Very well," Eno said. "Thank you both for your assistance."

With that, they got into the ambulance and drove out of the compound. During the trip to the Station, both Eno and Josef drifted off, leaving Elly to keep Thomas company.

She glanced in the rear view to see Josef sleeping. "What's going to happen to him?"

"Josef? I guess he'll stay here and join the fight."

"Won't the authorities come down exra hard on him for escaping?"

"You can count on it," Thomas said.

"It's a shame he can't come back to Earth with us."

"Yeah. But he'd never leave Lina behind. I know I wouldn't leave without…"

Thomas suddenly became tongue-tied.

"Without what?" Elly said,.

"My girlfriend," Thomas said. "If I had one."

He turned away, relieved to see that they were approaching their destination at an outcropping of rocks a few miles from the Station.

He pulled over and turned off the ignition. "We're here."

Eno and Josef sat up, and they all silently zipped up their hazmat helmets. They stepped outside, and Elly peered around the largest rock. The Station glowed in the distance.

"Wow. It looks like a giant metallic lizard."

Thomas smiled to himself. Despite the fact that he and Elly came from planets fifty million miles apart, they seemed to share a way of seeing things.

"This is it, huh?" Elly asked. "No turning back now."

Thomas felt a pang of regret. Elly was right. Once they entered the Station, there'd be no way to prevent her from being harmed, or even imprisoned. Part of him wanted to turn around and take her home, but he knew she'd never hear of it. Elly was a force of nature, and by letting her accompany them, he'd unleashed it.

Thomas opened the hatch. Josef and Eno disappeared inside.

Elly stepped up next. "Here goes everything."

As Thomas watched anxiously, Elly disappeared before his eyes.

CHAPTER 7

Thomas closed the hatch and climbed down the ladder into the dark tunnel. He noticed that the wall was still scarred with laser fire from the battle that wounded William. Hopefully they wouldn't have to fight their way out this time. At the bottom of the ladder, the tunnel car was parked and waiting. Eno, Elly, and Josef got in and Thomas drove them toward the government center.

After a short ride, they arrived at the entrance to Ignatius's library. Worried there might be Commandos lurking nearby, Thomas pointed his Tetrascope upward. The discovery beam emitted no pulse, confirming no human presence.

"All clear," Thomas said.

He climbed up through the hatch, then pulled the others into the library. Thomas turned on the lights and surveyed the room. The shelves were bare, the floor covered with Ignatius's books. The last of his precious tea had been tossed onto the heap, scattered like ashes.

Elly had never seen Eno look actually angry.

"What idiots," Eno said. "They were probably under the delusion they could find the secrets to time travel by simply going through his books."

Thomas activated the wall monitor he'd used to see Balthazar and Bron for the first time. Ignatius's living quarters, including the hallway outside, were dark and deserted. "It's almost midnight," Thomas said, "so we have a few minutes before they blow the Propellant Depot."

Eno plopped into a chair while Josef pulled out his laser gun, checking it over in case he needed to use it. Elly knelt down to examine some of the books on the floor when something caught her attention. She picked a slim blue volume out of the pile.

"Find something to read?" Thomas said.

"Actually, I've already read it," she said, holding up a dog-eared volume. "It was written by my father."

"Really?" Thomas said. "I thought your father was a professor."

"He is, but he's also written several books, mostly about plant species in New Zealand. Wonder why it's here?"

"Ignatius didn't just collect books on time travel," Thomas said. "He was interested in anything that had to do with the survival of life on Earth."

"How amazing to find this on another planet in the future. I'll have to remember to…"

"Tell him you saw it on Mars?" Eno said.

Before Elly could respond, a muffled bang reverberated from the Station. A second quickly followed.

Elly put down her father's book. "Frank and Stein."

Thomas nodded. "That's our signal."

On the monitor, several Commandos began to run through the hallway shouting orders. A few moments later, they were gone.

"Let's go," Thomas said.

They hurried through the living quarters to the door that led into the government center.

Halfway down the corridor, the floor shook with another explosion. Moments later, they could hear footsteps running toward them. Thomas gestured to follow him into the nearest connector. They flattened themselves against the wall as more Commandos passed, and Thomas was surprised to see a group of boys wearing bright red armbands. Even in the dim light, he recognized Varik and the Moons leading the way. The moment they passed, Thomas led his small group to the infirmary that catered to those who worked in the government center.

Thomas peered through a small glass panel in the door to see that it was occupied by twenty or so patients, all sedated. A male nurse went from bed to bed, checking the medical monitors.

Eno whispered. "What now?"

Josef held up his laser gun in response.

"No," Thomas said. "We might hit one of the patients. Wait here."

Thomas burst through the door. The nurse looked up, alarmed. Thomas shouted, "Hurry, there's been an explosion at the Propellant Depot, and they're calling for all medical personnel!"

The nurse looked flustered. "But I'm not supposed to—"

"It's an order from the high governor himself!"

The nurse hesitated, looking Thomas over. "Aren't you a little young to be a maintenance worker?"

"All the available adults were pressed into service because of the prison riots. Me and some of my classmates volunteered to help."

Still, the nurse didn't move.

"Do what you want," Thomas shrugged. "But don't say you weren't told."

The nurse considered this for a moment, then hurried out the door on the other side of the room. Thomas waved for Eno, Elly, and Josef to enter.

"Do you see Ignatius?" Eno said.

"No. We'll have to check the beds, one by one."

They moved to the four corners of the room, and systematically began to inspect each patient. Thomas paused at the bedside of a young woman. "Josef, over here!"

Josef hurried over to find Thomas standing over Lina. He put his free hand on her forehead and his mouth to her ear. "Lina?"

"She can't hear until you remove the sedation patch," Eno said. "It's at the base of her neck."

Josef reached down and gently removed the patch.

"It'll take a few minutes for her to come around," Eno said.

Footsteps approached from the other direction, and the door opened to reveal a large man.

Josef aimed his laser gun.

Thomas put his arm out. "No, he's a friend."

Eno popped up from behind one of the beds. "Dr. Jax!"

"Good to see you, boys."

"We came to find Ignatius," Thomas said.

"I know. William got word to me about the plan, but I was with Balthazar at the time and couldn't get away."

"Where's Ignatius?" Thomas asked.

"In the Council Meeting Room. They've converted it to an interrogation facility."

"He's all right then?"

"I'm afraid not. Once they got everything they needed out of him, he lapsed into a coma. You have to get him out of here right away. Come on."

"What about the others?" Thomas asked, glancing at Lina.

"They're on the waiting list for interrogation, so they're still sedated."

As they hurried to the door, Thomas turned back to Josef. "Stay with Lina. We'll pick you up on the way out."

Josef nodded.

Dr. Jax led them down the hallway toward another area of the complex. "You're lucky you came when you did. Everybody's either fighting or sleeping."

"Is Ignatius alone?" Thomas said.

"There's another doctor on duty, with a pair of guards. But I think I can distract them. Wait here."

Thomas, Eno, and Elly stayed inside the room while Dr. Jax crossed the hall and went through another door. In a few moments, a doctor hurried out followed by two guards. As they disappeared down the hallway, Dr. Jax peeked out and gestured for them to enter.

"I sent the doctor on break, then told the guards I suspected him of being a Returner spy, so they're following him. But they could be back any time, so we need to hurry."

Ignatius was lying on a gurney with several micro-wires protruding from his head and ears. They were connected to a monitor above the bed, which displayed a video of a blue sky.

"What's that?" Elly asked.

"The interrogation protocol allows them to download his unconscious activity. He's still hooked up and having a dream."

The image changed to a rugged forest, and Thomas instantly recognized the mountain in Colorado where his parents lived before the final evacuation.

"I'll need to remove all the filaments before you can take him anywhere."

Dr. Jax put on a pair of high-powered magnifiers and, using a small metal instrument, detached the wires. When the last one was disconnected, the video screen went blank. He wrapped Ignatius's head in a protective bandage so that his silver hair disappeared in a white skullcap.

"How long will it be until he wakes up?" Thomas asked.

"The deep sedation will wear off in several hours, but the effects of the neuro-interrogation could last days. The process doesn't simply extract information. It sucks out the soul."

They each took a corner of the gurney and pushed it to the door.

"If anyone stops us, I'll stay I'm moving him for a medical emergency."

Dr. Jax opened the door and they began to wheel the gurney down the hallway. As they approached the infirmary, Elly glanced over at Thomas.

"I'll get Josef," she said.

Thomas nodded, and Elly ducked into the infirmary.

"Where will you take Ignatius?" Dr. Jax asked.

"We're not sure," Thomas said. "Somewhere on Earth."

"Then you should also take this." Dr. Jax dug into his pocket and pulled out a small disc that fit into the hollow of his palm.

"What is it?"

"His original photo-disc, the kind we were all issued for travel to Mars. I found it hidden in his desk when he was first brought in. I assume it contains important photos, but it might also store a type of written communication, what we used to call 'letters.' I was worried it might include incriminating material, so I took it before it could fall into Bron's hands."

Thomas took the photo-disc from Dr. Jax, slid it into his pocket, and zipped it shut.

Eno looked back toward Lina's room. "What's taking so long?"

The infirmary door suddenly opened and Elly stepped outside. She paused and held the door. A moment later, Josef pushed the groggy Lina out in a wheelchair. They hurried to the end of the hallway and paused before entering the connector. Dr. Jax pointed up to a mirror positioned at the ceiling, where they saw the reflection of two men who'd been guarding Ignatius.

The guards were moving toward them.

"I'll try to hold them off," Dr. Jax said, "while you make a run for it."

He approached the guards as Thomas and the others hurried in the other direction, but the guards saw what was happening and shoved Dr. Jax aside.

"Stop!"

Josef pulled out his laser gun and spun into a shooting position. He got off two quick shots and the guards fell to the floor. He caught up to the others as they turned the corner that led to Ignatius's quarters. A handful of Redshirts suddenly appeared from the other direction, blocking the entrance. Leading the group, armed with a laser gun, was Varik.

Thomas pulled up at the other end of the hallway as Varik stepped forward, smiling. "You weren't actually going to leave without saying goodbye, were you, Thomas?"

Josef raised his laser gun, but again Thomas put his arm out to stop him. "All right, Varik, I know when I'm beaten."

"I'm happy to see you've come to your senses. But I'll be even happier to escort you to Bron, where he can give you a proper welcome!"

As Varik and the Redshirts started toward them, Thomas whispered to Eno, directly behind him. "Unzip my backpack."

"And if you're still in command of your senses" Varik continued, "you'll get to witness Balthazar present me with the Station's patriot award for your capture."

"Sorry I won't be able to hear his speech," Thomas said. "Then again, neither will you."

"What are you talking about?"

Thomas slid his arm around his waist and into his backpack, whispering to the others. "Cover your ears."

He pulled out the Sonic Inducer he'd gotten from Matthew and fired it into the ceiling above Varik's head. The cartridge exploded with an ear-splitting noise, raining down a shower of debris. Varik and the Moons dropped to the floor with their fellow Redshirts, holding their heads and writhing in pain.

Thomas, Eno, and Elly ran the gurney down the hall with Josef right behind with the wheelchair. They reached Ignatius's library, and Thomas pulled up the tunnel hatch.

"The sedation's wearing off," Lina said. "I can help."

"Good," Thomas said. "Elly, come with me. Josef and Eno can lower Ignatius down to us."

Thomas and Elly dropped into the tunnel. A moment later, Ignatius was lowered, legs first, into their arms. They laid him in the back seat of the tunnel car, then did the same with Lina. Elly and Josef sat opposite her, while Eno held onto the unconscious Ignatius for the bumpy ride ahead. Thomas jumped into the driver's seat and they drove off into the tunnel.

A few minutes later, Thomas pulled up in front of the wall ladder and popped the outside hatch. The sound of battle boomed from the Station. Lina, now fully conscious, helped carry Ignatius to the ladder, where Thomas pulled the marine rope out of his backpack and made a harness under his arms. Thomas and Elly scrambled up the ladder, and with the others pushing from below, managed to get Ignatius out of the hatch. Eno, Josef, and Lina followed, and together they got him onto the gurney and into the ambulance.

"All right, let's go," Thomas said.

"Not yet!" Elly said.

"What now?" Eno said.

Elly pointed toward the Station, where two small figures were moving toward them in the darkness. It was Frank and Stein, blackened by the explosions.

"How did they find us?" Thomas asked.

"Robot instinct," Elly said.

"Hardly," Eno said, holding up his wrist pod. "I programmed myself as a homing terminal back in the graveyard and forgot to delete the coordinates."

"Well, they're here now and we can't just abandon them," Elly said.

"Why not?" Eno asked. "They're just machines."

"We wouldn't have gotten this far without them," Elly said. "You have to admit, they've been pretty valuable so far."

Thomas nodded. "And we can always use the help."

Eno shook his head with exasperation as they loaded the bots in next to Ignatius. Finally, they got into the ambulance themselves. Thomas slid into the driver's seat as an explosion thundered from the Station. The power grid, situated in the Station's left foot, went dark. A second explosion darkened the right foot. It looked like the big lizard had stopped moving.

Thomas turned to Elly. "I don't suppose you thought about where we could take Ignatius?"

"I had an idea, but maybe we should talk about it first."

In the background, Thomas could hear the muffled but unmistakable sound of the Defense Dome retracting and knew that within seconds the Mastership would be airborne. He started the ambulance. "It's too late for that. Besides, I trust you."

And with that, he pulled out, leaving the crippled lizard in a cloud of Martian dust.

CHAPTER 8

THOMAS WOKE IN A flurry of time-flies, but unlike the small clouds that usually gathered around his head, they now meandered around the entire car, as if they couldn't quite make up their mind where to go. He could hear Ignatius's voice somewhere in the distance, despite the fact that the man himself was sleeping right next to him. He half expected Ignatius to scold him for returning to Mars, but his words were jumbled, as if Ignatius were mumbling to himself from the deepest recesses of his mind. The darkened interior of the cabin was a tangle of arms and legs. Elly was on the other side of Ignatius, while Josef and Lina were draped across each other. Eno had managed to find a private space, tucked between Frank and Stein like a third bot.

"Eno?" Thomas whispered, hoping to let the others come around gradually.

Eno opened his eyes.

"You all right?" Thomas asked.

"Yes, surprisingly good in fact," Eno said.

"Maybe you're getting used to time travel."

"Actually, I think it's due to the fact that I didn't shoulder any responsibility for choosing our destination. Once Elly picked the spacetime, I simply locked in the coordinates."

"Where did she decide we should go?"

"A small town in the country of England called Shrewsbury."

"I don't think I've ever heard of it."

"A mysterious choice, I agree," Eno said. "Though the year is even more exotic."

"What do you mean?"

"1824. She said it would be extremely tranquil, ideal for Ignatius's recovery. And with no chance of encountering the FBI."

Elly yawned. "Did somebody say FBI?"

"I was just telling Thomas that we shouldn't expect to see any."

"That's because they haven't been created yet. England barely has a police force, and hopefully they're in some sweatshop cracking down on child labor."

Elly unzipped her helmet. "How's Ignatius?"

"The same," Thomas said. "Dr. Jax said it could take a long time for him to come around."

Josef and Lina began to stir.

"How are you guys doing?" Thomas asked. "Time travel can leave you a little woozy."

"I'm just so happy to be away from the Station," Lina said.

"You'll feel even better once you get some fresh air," Elly said.

"Fresh air." Lina smiled. "What an incredible concept. I can't wait."

Thomas and Elly got to their feet, and Josef helped Lina up.

Eno stretched out to take advantage of the extra room.

"You coming?" Thomas asked.

"No, I'll stay with Ignatius. I can't imagine there's much to see anyway."

Thomas, Elly, Josef, and Lina climbed out of their hazmat suits. With the exception of Lina, in her gray station uniform, they were still wearing the red maintenance uniforms William had supplied.

"Should we change clothes?" Thomas asked Elly.

"I wouldn't bother," Elly said. "We've gone back in time a couple centuries, so any way you cut it we're gonna look like aliens. Actually, with the exception of yours truly, most of us are."

Thomas opened the panel that led to the front platform of the cable car, revealing a gentle hill framed by several large magnolia trees.

Elly sniffed the air. "Smells like June to me. I asked Eno to aim for the summer, since England is fairly damp the rest of the year, and I think he stuck the landing."

Thomas inhaled deeply. "It smells great, whatever time it is."

Lina took a few deep breaths. "I actually feel a bit lightheaded, in a good way."

Elly put her finger to her ear. "Hear that?"

A soft gurgling echoed in the distance.

"It sounds like the pool in the Returner Compound," Lina said.

"We must be close to the Severn River," Elly said, as they climbed down from the platform. They were in a thinly wooded area, broken by large sections of grass. A line of silver light flashed through the trees about a hundred yards ahead. "That must be it over there. Come on."

They followed Elly down to the river, which wasn't much wider than the length of the cable car.

Lina was mesmerized. "It's so unbelievably beautiful. I couldn't have conceived such a place in my wildest imagination."

Elly nodded. "It's one of the prettiest places on Earth."

"Have you been here before?" Lina asked.

"No, but I've seen plenty of photos. My father promised he'd take me on my sixteenth birthday, though it would've changed a lot by then. Two centuries worth. By the way, we're looking for a large brick mansion. It's called the Mount because it sits at the top of a hill."

Thomas pointed in the distance off to the right. "There's a building over there."

Sure enough, a massive brick house sat perched on a hill across the river.

"That's the place," Elly said.

"Who lives there?" Josef said.

"It's the boyhood home of Charles Darwin, one of our most famous scientists, though that's still a ways in his future. If it's 1825, he should be about your age, Josef."

"Really?" Josef said.

"I thought it might help to ease the transition. And since his father's the local doctor, I figured he could oversee Ignatius's recovery. But first we have to cross the river."

"It doesn't look all that wide," Thomas said. "We could probably swim it."

"Yeah, but we don't want to show up soaking wet. There must be a footbridge somewhere. We'll just walk along the riverbank until we find one."

"I'm not sure I can keep up," Lina said, leaning on Josef. "They wouldn't let us have solid food prior to the neuro-interrogation, so I haven't eaten in a few days."

"I'm surprised you're still standing after what you went through," Elly said. "Maybe Josef should take you back to the cable car so you can rest until we're able to suss out the situation."

Thomas nodded. "It's probably better that Elly and I approach the house anyway. The four of us might be a little overwhelming. We'll try to bring back some food."

"Thanks," Josef said. "Good luck."

Thomas and Elly headed downriver. In about fifty yards, it narrowed to reveal a small wooden bridge.

They crossed the bridge onto the large estate where a few sheep were grazing, then trudged up the hill to the mansion door. Elly knocked firmly.

"Anything I should know?" Thomas asked

"Don't mention San Francisco. It hasn't been founded yet."

The door opened, revealing a plump, middle-aged woman. "Yes?"

"Excuse our appearance ma'am, but my friend and I are part of a group of foreign students engaged in a scientific exploration in your lovely country. Our professor has had an accident, and I was wondering if there might be a doctor in the neighborhood?"

"A doctor?" the woman asked.

"Teasely?" a voice boomed from somewhere inside the house. "Who is it?"

"A pair of foreign students, looking for a doctor!"

"Hold on, I'll be right there."

Elly winked at Thomas as a man appeared on the stairs.

"Hello, there. I'm Dr. Robert Darwin. How may I be of service?"

"We're part of a group of students from Iceland on a field trip with our professor. He took a fall nearby and someone in the village told us you were the local doctor. We were wondering if you would be kind enough to see him?"

"Is he ambulatory?"

"Unfortunately not," Thomas said. "We bandaged his head, but he's still unconscious."

"Best bring him here then. I'll have Charles take you in the ambulance."

"Charles?" Elly said. "Your son?"

"Yes, how did you know?"

"Oh," Elly said, "I think someone in the village mentioned it."

"Despite his youth, he's an apprentice doctor, so he knows how to transfer patients with head injuries. I'm just finishing with another patient, but I'll be done by the time you return."

The doctor disappeared toward the back of the house.

Elly turned to Thomas, almost giddy. "I know this probably doesn't mean much to you, but meeting Charles Darwin could be the highlight of my life."

A few moments later, a gangly sixteen-year-old appeared in the doorway.

"Good day. My father says you require the ambulance?"

"Yes," Thomas said.

"Follow me."

Charles waved them into the house and out the back door toward the barn.

"I'm Thomas, by the way. And this is Elly."

"It's a pleasure," Charles said. "We don't get many visitors up here, particularly foreigners. Not enough to see or do."

"The countryside is beautiful," Elly said.

"I suppose," Charles shrugged. "Personally, I'd rather be collecting specimens in the Firth of Forth, but my father insists I stay here as his apprentice."

"You don't want to be a doctor?" Thomas asked.

"I'm not very comfortable with human beings. I'd far rather spend my time with marine invertebrates."

"Well, you never know," Elly said. "Maybe you'll get the chance later on."

"I highly doubt it," Charles replied. "My father has other plans for me."

"I know the feeling," Thomas said.

"Like it or not, I'm being sent to the University of Edinburgh medical school in September," Charles said, as they reached the barn. "You can wait here while I get the horse."

As Charles entered the barn, Thomas glanced at Elly.

"The horse?" Thomas said, unable to hide his excitement.

"To pull the ambulance," Elly whispered. "No spontaneous combustion for another half century or so. That's why it's so quiet around here. Awesome, isn't it?"

Charles led the horse out of its stall. "This is Erasmus."

As he harnessed him to a wagon a few feet away, Thomas whispered to Elly. "I know this probably doesn't mean much to you, but meeting Erasmus could be the highlight of my life."

Elly scrunched her face into a fake smile. "Ha."

Finished with the harness, Charles rejoined Thomas and Elly. "Will anything else be required for transferring your professor?"

"No," Elly said. "But perhaps we could impose upon you for some food. We were on our way into the village for provisions when the accident happened, and one of our fellow students became light-headed."

"I'll pop into the kitchen on the way out and get some biscuits," Charles said. "Mrs. Teasely makes the best in all of Shrewsbury, a fact that she'll quickly share when you meet."

✦✦

THERE WAS ONLY ROOM for two in the driver's seat of the carriage, so Elly sat up front with Charles while Thomas sat in the back under a small canopy. They went in the opposite direction from where they'd come, crossing a wider bridge to reach the area where the cable car was located. Elly and Charles talked non-stop for the entire ride, though with the noise of the heavy wheels against the unpaved ground, Thomas couldn't hear a word.

"Over there," Thomas said, pointing to the pair of towering magnolias.

Josef and Lina were sitting in the grass, while Eno sat on the cable car platform.

Elly made the introductions. "These are our fellow students: Eno, Josef, and Lina. This is Charles, everyone. He's an apprentice doctor. His father kindly agreed to see Ignatius."

Thomas jumped out of the wagon and Elly handed Lina the basket of biscuits Charles had gotten from the kitchen.

"Here you go, Lina—courtesy of the Darwins' housekeeper."

"Thank you so much."

She took one of the biscuits and began to eat as Charles eyed the cable car.

"What an extraordinary wagon," he said. "But where are your horses?"

Thomas glanced at Elly, hoping she had an answer.

"After our professor was injured, we took them into town to be fed and stabled," Elly said.

As Eno glanced nervously at the horse, Thomas helped Charles onto the platform. "Our professor's in here," Thomas said, leading him into the cabin as Elly followed.

Ignatius was lying on the floor, still unconscious, but as Charles entered, his attention was drawn to Frank and Stein.

"What on Earth are those?"

"Drill-Bots," Elly said. "They're mechanical specialists that help with collecting samples."

"Amazing," Charles said. "I'd love to see how they work."

"Perhaps we can concentrate on Ignatius for the moment?" Eno said.

"Sorry," Charles said. "I'm afraid I'm not much of a doctor, even as an apprentice. As you can see, my focus is naturally drawn elsewhere." Charles knelt down and took Ignatius's pulse, then put a hand on his forehead. "I won't hazard a diagnosis, as it's beyond my expertise. We should get him back to the Mount and see what father thinks."

"Would it be all right if we brought along our fellow students?" Thomas said.

"Of course," Charles said. "You can even bring your Drill-Bots if you like. I don't suppose they have names?"

"They do," Elly said. "Frank and Stein."

For the first time, Charles cracked a smile. "That's quite the funniest thing I've ever heard!"

Thomas turned to Elly. "Let's get Ignatius back to the Mount, and then maybe you can give Charles a demonstration."

"Good idea," Elly said.

With that, Thomas and Josef carefully lifted Ignatius out of the cabin and into the back of the wagon, which was padded with what looked like a blanket-sized pillow.

When the horse-drawn ambulance pulled up outside the Mount, Dr. Darwin was there to greet them. He was standing next to a tall muscular man in his forties.

"This is Jeremiah, my loblolly-boy," Dr. Darwin said.

Elly turned to Thomas and translated. "The doctor's assistant."

"The finest in all of Shrewsbury," Dr. Darwin added. "He'll carry your professor upstairs to the examining room."

Thomas jumped off the wagon and opened the back panel as Jeremiah lifted Ignatius into his arms and carried him into the house.

"Charles, escort our guests into the kitchen. I had Mrs. Teasely prepare them breakfast."

Thomas turned to Elly. "You go ahead. I want to check on Ignatius first."

As the others followed Charles, Thomas accompanied Dr. Darwin up the stairs and into the consulting room, where Ignatius was now lying on a padded examining table.

Dr. Darwin looked closely at his skull. "Who bandaged his head?"

"I did."

"I daresay you have a knack for medicine, Thomas. Certainly more than my Charles. He's done his share of binding, and not nearly as well."

Using a small scissors, Dr. Darwin cut the bandage and carefully unraveled it. He then used a magnifying glass to examine Ignatius's head. "Do you know how he suffered the injury?"

"No, we found him on the ground. How bad is it?"

"There's no sign of blunt trauma, though there are minor contusions at regular intervals along his cranium. Very peculiar."

Thomas could see that Dr. Darwin was referring to the places where the interrogation wires had been removed. "Is there anything that can be done for him?"

"I'm afraid our knowledge of the brain is still quite primitive, so we haven't much choice but to let him rest and bide our time. The first twenty-four hours are critical. I have to go into the town hospital and make my rounds, but I'll be back shortly and look in on him regularly."

"I can't thank you enough," Thomas said.

"Your concern for your professor is evident. I sense that you have a relationship with him that transcends that of your fellow students."

"I didn't have parents growing up, so Ignatius has been my mentor."

"A father figure, I see. Do you or your fellow students have lodging?"

"The wagon we've been using for travel is big enough for us to sleep in."

"Nonsense. You'll all stay at the Mount. We have fourteen bedrooms, most of them unused. That way you'll be close to your professor and can look in on him whenever you want."

"I wish there was something we could do to repay your generosity."

"Your presence is payment enough. In truth, my son has been in quite a state this summer. He's having a difficult time reconciling his future, so it will do him good to have the distraction of other people his age. Mrs. Teasely will get you settled and make sure you're well fed." Dr. Darwin started for the door, then paused. "I know it's a difficult thing to consider right now, but you should give some thought to the possibility that the outcome here might not be positive."

"You mean that he won't completely recover?"

"That, or worse."

CHAPTER 9

THOMAS SAT BY IGNATIUS's side for the next two hours. He tried to think about what Dr. Darwin had said, but couldn't hold the thought for more than a fleeting moment. The possibility of Ignatius's death was too jarring to consider. Without him, Thomas would've spent his entire existence in a state of complete ignorance about his past and family, not to mention his future. He'd never have spent a single day on Earth, or ever met Elly. For those two things alone, he owed him everything.

A soft tap at the door jarred him.

Eno poked his head into the room. "How is he?"

"The same, I'm afraid."

Eno quietly entered. "Mrs. Teasely has served lunch, if you're interested."

"I'm not hungry," Thomas said.

"You'll be pleased to hear that Lina seems completely recovered."

"Good," Thomas said. "That gives us hope for Ignatius."

"I'm not so sure. Lina was never actually interrogated. We got her out just in time."

"It's a shame we couldn't get there earlier, for Ignatius's sake."

"The truth is, the damage was done long before we even knew about his plight."

Thomas nodded, though the knowledge didn't give him any consolation.

"The question now is what to do going forward," Eno said.

"Dr. Darwin has offered us lodging."

"Be that as it may, we can't stay here forever. And we can't drag Ignatius along with us. Not in his condition."

"No," Thomas agreed.

"I don't expect you to make a decision right away. I say we give it until tomorrow."

"Right." Thomas stood up. "If we're spending the night, I better head back to the cable car and get the rest of our things."

"Don't forget the Time Globe. Given our exposure to the dust devil on Mars, I need to check it for contamination. I'll keep an eye on Ignatius while you're gone."

Thomas nodded, though he was distracted by the sound of laughter that echoed from somewhere outside.

He left the room, but stopped at the landing and looked out through a back window. He saw Frank and Stein digging small holes in the ground near the barn, much to Charles's delight. Elly stood next to him, using the remote. She caught sight of Thomas and handed Charles the remote, then headed toward the house. She was waiting for Thomas when he came down the stairs.

"How's Ignatius?" Elly said.

"The same. Eno's keeping an eye on him while I go back to the cable car for our things."

"Are we spending the night here?"

"Yes."

"Good. I think we can all use a little rest, especially you."

"How are you feeling?"

"A little wobbly, to be honest. It must be the time travel. But I don't know how much time I'll get with Charles, so I should make the most of it. He has the most fascinating mind. You can tell he's bound for greatness."

Thomas glanced out the back door to see the gangly Charles with the Drill-Bots. "I guess I'll take your word for it. I should go."

He went out the front door and sprinted down the hill. At the bottom, he slowed to a brisk walk. The one thing he'd never counted on was being responsible for Ignatius's well-being. And if his condition didn't radically improve, he'd have to decide what to do about it.

Before he knew it, Thomas found himself back at the cable car, barely recalling how he'd gotten there. He went inside, gathered all the backpacks, and put them at the platform door. He then tucked the Tetrascope and Sonic Inducer into his rolled-up sleeping bag and slid it into a compartment under one of the seats. Lastly, he changed out of the maintenance uniform into his "San Francisco" clothes, being careful to transfer the photo-disk Dr. Jax had given him into his back pocket for safe-keeping. When he finished, he was gripped by an overwhelming wave of fatigue. The escape from the FBI in San Francisco, followed by the trip to Mars and Ignatius's rescue, had finally caught up with him.

Elly was right, he needed a rest.

Thomas went back outside, where the sun was high in the sky, and a gentle breeze nudged him toward the river's edge. He sat on the grass next to the water, which seemed to be moving in slow motion. He lay back and looked up through the trees as the clouds crossed above him, alternately covering the sun and letting it burst through. As he tried to make himself comfortable on the ground, he felt something sharp in his back pocket.

He rolled onto his side and pulled out Ignatius's photo-disk. The very contact with his thumb and forefinger brought it to life. It contained several beautiful pictures of Colorado, and he couldn't resist scrolling through them. As expected, some were of Ignatius with Thomas's parents, but most were with a young woman he assumed was his wife. Toward the very end, he came to a photo of them holding an infant, somewhere in the Returner Compound. Thomas was surprised, as Ignatius had never mentioned having a child. For a moment, he thought the child might be him, but its complexion was much darker than his own. He tried to scroll forward, hoping to find other photos that might clarify the identity of the child, but it was the last on the disc. As he stared at the photo, a strange feeling came over him, as if he suddenly found himself in a place he'd never been before and at the same time recognized. But the sensation was interrupted by the din of voices from beyond the trees. He sat up to see Elly—along with Charles, Josef, and Lina—heading down the embankment on the other side of the river.

"Thomas!" Elly shouted. "We've decided to take a swim. Come join us!"

Thomas got to his feet and put the disc back into his pocket.

Elly shed her jumpsuit, revealing the shorts and T-shirt she was wearing the day they left San Francisco. She kicked off her sneakers and untied the binding that held back her hair, which sprang around her face, framing her eyes in a way that made them appear more vibrant than ever. While the others were still stripping down, she slid into the water and disappeared under the surface. A few seconds later, her head popped up, directly in front of Thomas.

"Come on in, the water's spectacular. It's like liquid velvet."

Thomas, still in the throes of the photo on Ignatius disc, was momentarily speechless.

"Is everything okay?" Elly said. "You look like you've just seen a ghost."

Thomas didn't know the expression, and used his ignorance as cover. "Uh…"

"Like you've just had a shock or something," Elly said.

A shock, Thomas thought, was the perfect word for what he'd just experienced. But he couldn't explain to Elly what he was thinking, and didn't want to alert her to his suspicion.

He reached for the easiest excuse.

"I should go back and check on Ignatius."

"Nothing's changed. I just checked in with Eno and offered to take a shift so he could bathe, but he wanted no part of the river. Shocking, huh?"

Thomas forced a smile, as the others tentatively waded into the river. Charles groaned as he tested the water with his foot, while Josef held Lina's hand as she screamed with delight.

"So, you're really going to pass up the chance to swim?" Elly said.

"Under the circumstances, I think so."

"Look, I understand how worried you are about Ignatius, but he's in good hands. I spoke to Dr. Darwin before I left, and he said that Ignatius could stay as long as was necessary."

"Just the same, I don't feel right being out here while he's unconscious. I should get back to the house in case he comes to. I'll see you there."

Thomas walked briskly down the riverbank. After a few moments, he glanced back to see that Elly had rejoined Charles, still trying to coax him into the water. But any jealousy he'd felt now appeared petty in light of Ignatius's photos, and the secret he'd potentially uncovered. He was desperate to know the truth, but only Ignatius could provide that, if and when he regained consciousness. He crossed the footbridge and looked down the river a final time. He could hear the sound of happy voices, but Elly was nowhere to be seen.

✦✦

THOMAS SPENT THE REST of the day with Ignatius. Dr. Darwin looked in on him several times, encouraging Thomas to take a break. But he insisted on staying. In the event that Ignatius came around, he had to be the first to talk to him.

It was almost seven o'clock when Dr. Darwin, dressed in a fresh jacket and trousers, entered. "It's dinner time, Thomas."

"I'm not really hungry."

"Nonsense. You're a growing boy, under enormous stress. As long as you're under my roof, I'm your doctor. And your doctor says you must eat."

Thomas tried an excuse. "I don't really have any clothes other than what I've got on."

"We're a household of freethinkers. We don't adhere to the rules of formal dining that constrain the rest of the English populace. Your working clothes, while admittedly unusual, are quite acceptable here. If, however, you'd prefer more regional attire, I'm sure we could get you something from Charles's wardrobe."

"No," Thomas said, "that's all right."

Dr. Darwin smiled, having called his bluff. "Come along then."

Mrs. Teasely was putting out the serving dishes when Thomas and Dr. Darwin arrived in the dining room. Elly was already at the table, along with Josef, Lina, and Charles.

Eno sidled up to Thomas and spoke in a low whisper. "Where did you put the Time Globe? I can't find it anywhere."

Thomas suddenly remembered that he'd left it behind in the cable car, along with the rest of their things. "Sorry. I didn't bring it back."

"I thought you went there for the sole purpose getting it."

"I did, but I got distracted and forgot. I'll go back right after dinner and pick it up."

The dinner bell rang, and everyone assembled around the table.

"We don't stand on ceremony here at the Mount, so the seating is pell-mell," said Dr. Darwin, who sat at the head of the table. The others took the chair where they were standing, with the exception of Charles, who hurried to Elly's side. Thomas and Eno sat across from them as Dr. Darwin raised his glass for a toast. "I'd like to officially welcome all of you to the Mount, and encourage you to take full advantage of the property during your stay. We have seven lovely acres, as well as a marvelous 'thinking path.' I also encourage you to visit our town of Shrewsbury, which has a glorious castle and abbey, as well as a splendid station."

"A train station?" Thomas asked, perking up. "With actual trains?"

"Which, if you're lucky," Charles added, "will take you far from Shrewsbury."

"Thomas is obsessed with trains," Eno said.

"Though I've never actually seen one," Thomas admitted.

"Don't they have them in Iceland?" Charles asked innocently.

"Not where we're from," Elly said. "It's a small rural town in…"

Elly glanced at Thomas for help.

"Hofn," Thomas said.

"I'm not acquainted with your diet in Iceland," Dr. Darwin said, "but hopefully you'll find something in our native cuisine to your liking. We have rabbit soup, mashed turnips, roast shoulder of mutton, fish pie, oxford dumplings, calf's foot jelly, and stewed pigeons. I highly recommend the potted eels and the cranberry tart—both specialties of Mrs. Teasely's."

As the plates of food began to circulate, Thomas glanced at Eno, who looked as if he were going to be sick. For the first time since coming to Earth, Thomas found that his own appetite was missing, and he took only enough food to be polite.

Elly turned to Josef and Lina, who were already devouring their meal with relish as Mrs. Teasely looked on with obvious satisfaction.

"Mrs. Teasely," Lina said. "This is the most amazing food I've ever tasted. The flavors are remarkable. I can't imagine how you created them!"

"The secret's in the ingredients, dear. Fresh eels from our river, meat from our piggery, and fruit from our very own orchard, tended by Dr. Darwin himself."

Dr. Darwin smiled. "Mrs. Teasely is too modest. While every good meal begins with fine ingredients, it's ultimately in the hands of the chef. If you're interested, I'm sure she'd be happy to demonstrate her culinary artistry."

"Would you really?" Lina asked. "I'd give anything to learn."

"Consider it done," Mrs. Teasely beamed.

"So, Thomas," Dr. Darwin said, "perhaps you can regale us with an account of your adventures so far in our fair country."

"I'll defer to Elly. She's a much better spokesperson."

Elly sat up in her chair, warming to the task. "We've only been in England a short time and came down from the north only a few days ago. We stayed off the beaten path to pursue our primary objective, collecting native species."

"Charles is an avid collector himself, aren't you boy?"

Charles beamed with pride. "Mainly bird eggs, rocks, fossils."

"We've concentrated mostly on small grubs and insects," Elly said.

"Charles tells me you're accompanied by a pair of robotic creatures?"

"Frank and Stein," Elly said.

"Fantastic fellows," Charles added. "Named after my favorite book to boot."

"They're brilliant at searching and digging," Elly said. "I've charged them with finding me a rare six-spotted green beetle."

"Then their search will lead directly to my rooms," Charles said. "I have not one but two!"

"No!" Elly said. "You can't be serious?"

"Yes, they're the prize of my collection! Would you like to see them now?"

Dr. Darwin shook his head. "There'll be plenty of time for that after dinner, Charles." He turned to Elly. "As you can see, my son is far more excited about collecting insects than medical school."

"I'm a naturalist by temperament," Charles said. "There's not much I can do about it."

"Perhaps," Dr. Darwin said. "But one can't allow one's life to be determined by youthful passion. If you're still keen on it after medical school, then we'll see."

Charles slumped in his chair, a portrait of frustration.

"What would you like to do after medical school?" Elly asked.

Charles was about to respond but glanced at his father warily.

"Don't be modest on my account, boy."

"Well," Charles said. "My lifelong dream is to visit an archipelago off the coast of Ecuador. You've probably never heard of it but…"

"The Galapagos Islands?" Elly said.

"How did you know?" Charles asked, visibly impressed.

"I saw the books on the subject in your room," Elly said, which was true.

Dr. Darwin looked up with his own frustration. "My dear Charles, you might as well wish to go to the Moon. What on Earth would you do in…the Galapagos Islands?"

"Pursue my theory of evolution."

Dr. Darwin put down his fork, fully exasperated. "Charles is consumed by the notion that man is another form of animal, and that we've evolved from the lower forms, perhaps even apes!"

"What a fascinating theory," Elly said.

"One that will make him the laughingstock of the civilized world," Dr. Darwin said. "But I'd love to hear more from our guests. What line of study do you intend to pursue, Elly?"

"I'd like to spend my life doing everything I can to insure the survival of the planet."

"Oh?" Dr. Darwin smiled. "I wasn't aware the planet was in jeopardy."

"Maybe not at this moment. But if we don't make the right choices in the future, particularly in our use of fossil fuels, that could easily change."

Thomas could see that Dr. Darwin was baffled. "It's one of Professor Ignatius's favorite themes. The preservation of all species is his greatest concern, including the Earth itself."

Dr. Darwin listened patiently to Thomas and even seemed to consider the validity of the idea. "Your professor must be a bit of a futurist then."

"You have no idea," Elly said. "Hopefully you'll get the chance to talk to him…"

A strange look suddenly came over Elly's face and she stood up abruptly. "Excuse me, I think that I'm about to..."

Thomas jumped up and raced to her side just in time to catch her fall.

"My dear," Dr. Darwin said as Thomas lowered her to the ground.

"She gets these spells from time to time," Thomas said.

"I'll get my medical bag," Dr. Darwin said.

As he hurried away, Thomas helped Elly into a sitting position while Charles knelt on her opposite side.

"I'm sorry," she said. "I've never had one like this before."

"What do you mean?" Thomas said.

"I had an aura just before it hit."

"What's that?" Thomas said.

"It's like a warning that something's about to happen," Charles said. "I've observed the phenomenon before with one of my father's patients."

"The doctors always used to ask me if I had one before a spell," Elly said. "But I never did until now. It felt as if I was falling off the planet."

"Are you sure you're all right?" Charles asked.

"Positive. Let's finish dinner."

Thomas and Charles helped Elly up and got her back into her seat.

"Now," Elly said, "where were we?"

But before Charles could answer, a voice rang out from upstairs.

"Thomas! Hurry!"

He sprinted to the bottom of the stairs to find Dr. Darwin on the second-floor landing.

"Your professor! He's just opened his eyes!"

CHAPTER 10

Thomas raced up the stairs and into the consulting room, only to find Ignatius still unconscious. Moments later, Dr. Darwin entered behind him.

"His eyes were open for several seconds, long enough for me to see that they were clear. His heart is strong, and both signs bode well for recovery."

"Did he say anything?" Thomas asked.

"No. He's still very weak, but I assured him that he was in a safe place and there would be plenty of time to talk."

Eno and Elly entered the room behind them.

"I better stay in here tonight," Thomas said, "in case he comes around."

"Very well, but you have to promise to notify me if he wakes again, regardless of the hour."

"I promise."

Dr. Darwin turned to the others. "Come now. Let's finish dinner. There will be plenty of time for visitation in the days to come."

Everyone but Eno followed Dr. Darwin out of the room.

"I can take a shift for you during the night," Eno said.

"Thanks, but that won't be necessary."

Thomas had no intention of leaving Ignatius. If he did regain consciousness, Thomas would need to talk to him privately. He was still holding out the slim hope that he'd somehow misinterpreted the photo-disc, but until Ignatius could confirm or deny his suspicion, there was no point in sharing it with Eno. If Thomas was right, it would mean the mission was compromised. Even worse, perhaps it never even existed in the first place.

"I'll be in the room at the end of the hall," Eno said. "Call if you need me."

Eno left, and Thomas turned off the gas lamp. He pulled up a chair next to Ignatius. The moon was framed in the window and left a small pool of light next to Ignatius, though his face was still hidden in darkness.

The room suddenly felt warm. Thomas went to the window and threw it open. The wide swatch of green that surrounded the property was interrupted only by the silver strand of river that seemed to go on forever. If not for the mission, Thomas could imagine himself traveling downstream, fishing for food, cooking over an open fire, sleeping under the stars. If it turned out that the mission couldn't continue, he'd happily settle for a normal life on Earth.

His fantasy was interrupted by the sound of voices from behind the house, and he saw two shadowy figures, led by a single lantern, enter the conservatory. He recognized the silhouette of Elly, who was standing close enough to Charles that their heads were almost touching. Charles lifted something into the palm of his hand, and Thomas realized that the young Darwin must be showing off his prize beetle. He leaned out the window to hear what they were saying. But he could only detect a pleasant patter, as a light rain began to fall and the water ran down the glass panels, obscuring their faces. Charles removed his jacket and draped it around Elly's shoulders, then ushered her outside. With one arm around her waist and the other holding an umbrella, he guided her across the lawn toward the house. As they disappeared inside, Thomas hoped that Elly might be headed upstairs to visit him. But he heard their footsteps go in the opposite direction.

A voice whispered from the darkness. "Thomas?"

Startled, he turned to see Ignatius staring at him.

"Ignatius!"

Thomas was so happy to see him alive that any discontent he'd been feeling immediately disappeared. "How are you feeling?"

Ignatius's voice was so faint that Thomas had to lean closer to hear him. "I have a strange headache. I take it I've been through some interrogation?"

"Yes. We came back to the Station last night and brought you to Earth."

Ignatius looked around the room with curiosity. "I dreamt that a man was looking after me. He said he was a doctor."

"It wasn't a dream. It was Dr. Darwin. We're at his home in England."

"Dr. Darwin? Charles Darwin?"

"His father actually. Charles is my age."

Ignatius suddenly realized what Thomas was saying. "So, we're in the nineteenth century?"

"We thought it would be the safest place to hide you."

A smile came over Ignatius's face. "What an inspired idea."

"I can't take any credit. It was Elly's."

Thomas searched Ignatius's face for a reaction, but in the darkness couldn't make out even a hint of recognition. "Elly?"

"A friend we made when we landed in San Francisco. She's been a great help to us."

Again, Thomas waited for a reaction, but Ignatius had none. Thomas was desperate to ask him about the photo-disc. If his suspicions were true, it would be a difficult conversation, and in Ignatius's fragile state, possibly harmful. He said nothing, but Ignatius seemed to sense his mood.

"Thomas…is there something on your mind?"

"We don't need to talk about it until you feel better."

"That day may be a long way off. What is it?"

Thomas hesitated, but knew that the question had to be asked. "When we went back to rescue you, Dr. Jax gave me your photo-disc. He didn't want it to fall into the hands of the high governor."

"That was wise of him."

"Yes. And well…I looked at the photos." Thomas waited for Ignatius to react, but his face was still unresponsive, so Thomas had no choice but to continue. "In the last photograph, you were holding an infant. At first, I thought it might be me, but…the baby had a darker complexion."

"And?"

"And…I was wondering who it was?"

Ignatius held out his hand. "Help me up. I could use some oxygen. I haven't breathed fresh air for years."

Thomas got him to his feet and over to the window.

Ignatius took a few deep breaths. He seemed to gather strength with each one. Finally, he spoke. "The child in the photograph is my daughter." Ignatius seemed to be composing his thoughts carefully, as if each word was accurate. "She was born the year after we arrived at the Station. The photo was taken shortly before my wife died."

Ignatius stopped in a way that made Thomas think he might not be able to continue.

"Why didn't you tell me you had a daughter?"

"Like so much that took place in the aftermath of leaving Earth, it was connected to painful memories."

"What happened to her, your daughter?"

Ignatius hesitated, and Thomas wondered if that's as far as Ignatius would go.

"It sounds as if there's a question behind your question, as they say."

Thomas was reluctant to say what he thought, but there was no going back now. "You told me you time-traveled twice, the first in a failed attempt to find my father. I think that's when you were timeblown."

"Correct."

"And the second time?"

"That's the question, isn't it? The one behind the question?"

"Yes."

"It sounds like you already have a theory, Thomas. What is it?"

"I think...you went in search of a place where you could hide your daughter, where she might have a happy childhood—on Earth. I know it sounds crazy but I think your daughter is Elly."

Ignatius let out a sigh that seemed to fill the entire room.

For a moment, Thomas thought he'd made a terrible mistake, and insulted the man he admired more than anyone in the world. He was about to apologize when Ignatius spoke.

"You're right, Thomas."

Thomas felt the hair on his neck stand up. Hearing Ignatius verify the truth was even more overwhelming than his suspicion.

"How did you figure it out?" Ignatius asked.

"I didn't—until I first saw the photo. And then all the pieces fell into place."

"Pieces?"

"On our last night in San Francisco, after I took Elly home, I had a strange conversation with Mr. McAllister. He said he was sorry he didn't have children of his own, but that fate had another plan for him, something more amazing than anything he could've ever imagined. And then he told me that I was the future, which was the same thing you said to me when I left Mars. I still didn't make the connection, but then I remembered that Elly found one of her father's books in your library, which was an amazing coincidence, to say the least. And then I saw the picture."

"You recognized her, even as an infant?"

"She has your smile."

"That's what my wife used to say."

Now that the truth was out, Thomas felt a wave of relief. But in moments it darkened to something that bordered on resentment, even betrayal. "Why you didn't tell me?"

"I never intended to deceive you, Thomas. I hope you understand that. I had every intention of telling you the story in due time, back on Mars. But as you know, we ran out of that."

"So, my mission to save the Earth was really just a pretext to save your daughter?"

"Is that what you think?"

"I don't think the Time Globe took us to Muir Woods on its own. Eno thought he damaged it when he dropped it, but I think it was your doing."

Ignatius nodded, as if he was admitting something to himself as well as to Thomas.

"I'll admit, I programmed it for Muir Woods in the year when she would be just about your age. Dr. McCallister told me he went there almost every day when mourning his wife's death. He found great joy and solace in the place. But there was no guarantee you'd meet Elly there."

"Then how did it happen?" Thomas said, his voice ringing with skepticism. "Are you going to tell me it was the tide of time?"

"I know it's hard for you to believe, especially now. But for some reason, Muir Woods seems to have a special magnetism in your time field. It does for Elly's as well."

"So, you knew she'd be there?"

"I've been able to follow her over the years with my Alpha Link, so I knew she spent summers there, though I'll admit the timing of your encounter does seem like cosmic serendipity. But I couldn't know for certain. That's the truth, Thomas, I swear."

"Why didn't you just tell me to begin with, when we first met?"

"I didn't want anything to distract you from your mission, which remains the most important reason for your return to Earth. I naively thought you'd never find out."

"And what am I supposed to do about Elly now that I have?"

"Why do you need to do anything at all? You said yourself, she's been a great help. I believe there's a reason she's with you. The mission is part of her destiny, just as it is yours."

Thomas had to admit the truth of what Ignatius was saying. But at the same time he couldn't help feeling that he'd been used and continuing on with Elly would only be an extension of that.

"I'm sorry, but now that I know who she is, I can't risk her life. When we leave here, I'm taking her back home, to be with her father."

"Thomas…"

But before Ignatius could continue, he was out the door.

CHAPTER 11

THOMAS RAN FROM THE house and into the night, quickly losing track of time. A handful of black clouds rumbled overhead. Rain began to fall but he kept running anyway, oblivious to the elements. At some point, he found himself back at the cable car, exhausted and wet, seeking shelter.

He woke at sunrise to the gentle ripple of the river, removed the Time Globe from its chamber, and put it in Eno's backpack. The morning sky signaled another beautiful summer day. He went down to the river's edge, overcome by a deep sense of regret about his conversation with Ignatius. Thomas had been selfish, he thought, thinking only about himself. After all, how could he blame Ignatius for wanting to save his own daughter? Particularly when that daughter was Elly?

He sat down and dangled his feet over a small stretch of mud. It reminded him of the wet sand at the beach outside San Francisco. He picked up a large stone and began to carve out the four letters of Elly's name. His printing was still primitive, but the act demanded so much concentration that his mind was freed from the distress that had consumed him over the past day. As he drew the last letter, there was a flash of movement near his hand, and he spotted a sleek brown fish, no more than a foot away. It turned toward the opposite bank and swam away. As the water settled, he could make out a reflection in the water. It was a pair of black tennis shoes. He recognized them immediately, and looked up to see Elly, standing on the opposite bank.

"Glad to see you're practicing."

Thomas glanced down at Elly's name, shimmering below the water. "I'm afraid I'm not getting much better."

"Some things just take time," Elly smiled.

Thomas stood up, and slid his foot over the mud, erasing Elly's name.

"Where have you been?" Elly said. "I woke up in the middle of the night and went to Ignatius's room to find you, but you weren't there. I got worried."

"Sorry. I forgot the Time Globe and had to come back to pick up it up last night. While I was waiting for the rain to stop, I fell asleep."

Elly nodded, but in a way that made Thomas think she didn't completely believe his story. "I wish you would've told me you were leaving."

"I saw you in the conservatory with Charles, and I didn't want to interrupt."

"Why not?"

"You seemed to be having a great time."

"Yeah, if you can call looking at somebody's insect collection a great time."

"You were laughing so hard, I couldn't really tell."

"Thomas, I think we need to talk, but not on opposite sides of the river."

"I'll meet you at the footbridge," Thomas said.

"Beat you there."

Elly sprinted toward the bridge, while Thomas jogged along a parallel path, which at one point detoured into the trees. By the time he got to the bridge, Elly was already there waiting.

"Are you getting slower or am I getting faster?" she said with a coy smile.

"Both, I think."

Thomas walked onto the footbridge and stood next to her.

"Are you all right?" Elly asked.

"What do you mean?"

"You don't seem like yourself. You were so distracted last night at dinner. I've never seen you like that. Are you upset about something?"

"No."

"This isn't about Charles is it?"

"Charles?"

"I know you didn't have much experience with girls on Mars, but I want you to know that as much as I admire Charles, the father of evolution, the teenage version leaves a lot to be desired."

"What do you mean?"

"Let's just say that I don't find his kind of Beatle-mania very appealing."

"Beetle mania?"

"Bad joke, not worth explaining. But getting back to you, I can tell something's wrong. If it's not Charles, what is it?"

For a moment, Thomas felt the urge to tell Elly everything that had transpired with Ignatius. He didn't feel comfortable keeping anything from her, let alone such a huge secret. But there was no way he could do it without upsetting her.

"I'm just worried about Ignatius," Thomas said.

"He's doing much better," Elly said.

"How do you know?"

"I ran into Dr. Darwin in the kitchen getting him some tea. He told me."

"But you haven't actually seen Ignatius, have you?"

"No, I didn't exactly know how to explain who I was. I was hoping you'd introduce us."

"Introduce you?"

"He's obviously one of the most important people in your life, if not the most important. I can't wait to meet him. I have so many questions."

Thomas nodded. Perhaps it was only fitting that Elly meet her real father. Maybe the best thing he could do now was to make sure she had that chance. For her and Ignatius as well.

"C'mon," he said. "Let's go back to the house and we can see him together."

✦✦

IT WAS ALMOST NINE o'clock when Thomas and Elly passed the glass conservatory. They entered the house as Dr. Darwin was coming down the stairs.

"How is he?" Thomas asked.

"Conscious, but still quite unsteady. He almost took another fall. We should take pains not to overtax him."

Thomas turned to Elly. "I should probably make sure he's ready for visitors."

Elly nodded, trying to conceal her disappointment. Thomas ran up the stairs and opened the door to the consulting room. Ignatius was sitting at the window. In the harsh morning light, he looked as if he'd aged several years. Thomas realized that his ordeal had taken more of a toll than he thought. He closed the door to announce his presence and Ignatius turned to see him.

"Thomas..."

"Dr. Darwin said you almost took a fall."

Ignatius shrugged. "I no longer have my cane."

Thomas had completely forgotten that Ignatius needed it to walk.

"I'm afraid we left it back at the Station. I should've thought of it."

"Yes, you should have," Ignatius said. "In the course of rescuing me, and getting back to Earth to save civilization, it should've been foremost on your mind."

It took a moment for Thomas to realize that Ignatius was joking. He smiled.

"Dr. Darwin kindly offered to get me a walking stick when I'm ready, though right now he wants me to do as little as possible.

Perhaps you can open the window. I'm desperate for some life-affirming atmosphere."

Thomas threw open the window, letting the summer breeze rush into the room, as if it had been waiting all along for the chance. Ignatius closed his eyes as the air washed over his face.

"How are you feeling?" Thomas asked.

"Like someone's taken my brain apart then reassembled it, with the neurons not quite reconnected. I should be grateful it's functioning at all."

"Ignatius, I just want to say…"

Ignatius raised his hand. "I'll be deeply offended if you even attempt to apologize, Thomas. It's I who should apologize, and I do. I'd feel even better if you let me explain."

Thomas didn't object.

"Do you remember how you used to dream about Earth?"

"Yes."

"Did you ever ask Eno about his dreams?"

"He's never had any."

"That's right. None of the Station children did. The Birth Design Group was quite proud of that. They called it part of the 'Martian Evolution.' They thought dreaming was the cerebral equivalent of burning fossil fuels, polluting the brain and diverting energy better served for scientific research. What they didn't understand is that dreams are part of the fabric of our souls."

Soul. Thomas remembered the word from his list of "S" words he found in the Information Archives. While he didn't really understand what it was, it seemed to be an important part of every person. Maybe even the most important part.

"I had no choice but to keep you on the Station because it was your father's wish to prepare you for your mission. That was your fate, which was also mine. But there was no reason to make it my daughter's. I simply couldn't bring myself to raise her in a world where children didn't dream. So, I decided to hide her the same way you've chosen to hide me, in another time and place."

Thomas couldn't help admiring the boldness of Ignatius's plan. "How did you find Mr. McAllister?"

"I was already familiar with him, through his books. I was moved by his compassion and wisdom, so I did some research and discovered that like me, his wife had died prematurely. Unlike me, however, he was left childless. So, I showed up at his workplace one night, out of the blueshift, so to speak, with an infant and a mind-boggling story."

"And he believed you?"

"As a scientist, he understood that what I was saying about time travel was theoretically valid. In truth, Elly did the rest."

"Elly?"

"She was an irresistible child. It was love at first sight, as they say, and he agreed to raise her as his own. For my part, I promised never to intrude on their lives. In fact, McAllister's only condition was that he be allowed to shorten her birth name, Elpis, to Elly."

"And that was the last time you saw her?" Thomas asked.

"In the flesh, yes. I thanked him from the bottom of my broken heart and kissed her goodbye. It was the most difficult thing I've ever done in my life. But only fitting."

"What do you mean, fitting?"

"Your father made the same sacrifice with you, and it was only fair that I do the same."

Thomas pictured Ignatius as a young father, handing over his daughter to Mr. McAllister.

"I've been thinking," Thomas said. "I could leave Elly here with you while Eno and I continue with the mission."

"A kind thought. But it wouldn't be advisable, or even safe for that matter."

"Why not?"

A serious look came over Ignatius. "Dr. Darwin said she had a fainting spell last night."

"Yes. She gets them from time to time. She says they're nothing serious."

"I'm not so sure. Living in the past is the one potential negative side effect of time travel that always concerned me. But since no one's ever actually lived in the past, other than Elly, I had no way to study it, let alone prove it. Elly's been living in the early twenty-first century for fifteen years, and now she's landed another two centuries back. There's a strong likelihood her condition might get much worse if she were to stay here."

Thomas suddenly recalled what Elly said the last night they were in San Francisco. "She once told me that she thought she belonged in the future."

"I believe she's right. And in the future, the best place for her is with you, Thomas. I trust that won't be too much a burden."

"A burden? Just the opposite. We wouldn't be here without her."

"Actually, that's not the burden I was referring to."

"What do you mean?"

"I'm afraid Elly can't know her true identity, or my relationship to her. It must remain our secret, at least while Mr. McAllister is alive."

"But why?"

"If she was told the truth, it wouldn't be fair to her. I'm part of her past, but no longer her present. I gave up that right the day I handed her over."

Thomas was about to object, when there was a knock on the door.

"Come in," Ignatius said.

The door opened, revealing Elly. "Sorry to interrupt, but Dr. Darwin wanted me to bring this up," she said, holding out a carved walking stick.

Ignatius slowly got to his feet. He reached out for the cane, but his hand was shaking. Thomas could see his eyes glistened.

"Ignatius…this is Elly, the girl I told you about."

Elly put out her hand, and Ignatius enveloped it in both of his.

From the look on his face, Thomas wondered if he'd ever let it go.

CHAPTER 12

Ignatius's face glowed with a mixture of excitement and pride. All the outward signs of his ordeal on Mars suddenly seemed to vanish.

"Are you sure I'm not interrupting?" Elly asked.

"No," said Thomas. "You came at the perfect time. Ignatius was just telling me how anxious he was to meet you."

"Thomas has told me how helpful you've been to him and Eno."

"Well," Elly said, "I've had the time of my life."

"I told Ignatius that it was your idea to bring him here," Thomas said.

"Inspired, I must say," Ignatius said.

"I really can't take all the credit."

"How's that?"

"My father and I have been playing a game ever since I was little where we talk about the place we'd most want to visit if we could time travel. His was always the Mount. He's a big Darwin fan. I started reading up on him, and it got me hooked."

"Your father was a visionary man."

"That's kind of you to say. When we were back on Mars, I saw that you had one of his books in your library."

"*Everlasting Earth*. It's one of my prize possessions. I had to smuggle it to Mars."

"Thanks for that," Elly said. "It's nice to know his work survives into the future."

"Not only was he a brilliant man, but he had an enormous generosity of spirit. A rare combination."

"It almost sounds like you knew him."

Thomas and Ignatius made quick eye contact.

"I certainly feel as if I did," Ignatius said. "It comes through in his work."

Thomas suddenly got the feeling that he'd become what Elly called a "third wheel." He pretended to check his wrist pod for the time. "Hey, I better check in with Eno. Is there something I can get you downstairs?"

"I'd do anything for a cup of tea," Ignatius said.

"I think that can be arranged." Thomas said, smiling at Elly.

As Thomas left the room, he could already hear the buzz of conversation coming from inside. He hurried down the stairs, where Eno was waiting.

"Well, how is he?"

"Good. Make that great. He's talking to Elly."

"Well if he has enough energy to do that, he must be…what's the expression…out of the woods? Did you get the Time Globe?"

"Yeah," Thomas said, handing over Eno's backpack.

"Thanks. I'll take it to the conservatory and do a thorough inspection."

"Good. We need to leave as soon as you're done."

"You've got no argument on that."

Thomas went down to the kitchen and ordered Ignatius's tea from Mrs. Teasely, who offered to bring it upstairs as soon as it was ready.

He thanked her and went out to look for Dr. Darwin, who Mrs. Teasely said would be in the orchard. He found him in a tree, or at least his lower half, his torso hidden by the upper branches.

"Dr. Darwin?"

"Thomas," Dr. Darwin said, his head still hidden. "How's your professor?"

"Much better," Thomas said. "Mrs. Teasely's making him some tea right now. She told me I'd find you down here."

Dr. Darwin climbed down, revealing his head. "The orchard's a hobby for me. I was just looking after one of my prized fruit trees."

"Ignatius loves fruit. In fact, he used to have a few small trees on…"

Thomas suddenly realized what he was about to say and stopped.

"I'll bring him some pears for lunch," Dr. Darwin said. "Nothing like the pyrus communis to lift the soul. Will you be joining us?"

"No. In fact, I came to tell you that we're leaving."

"Leaving?"

"Eno, Elly, and I need to get back home and let everyone know what happened. But I was hoping Ignatius could stay here and recover, along with Josef and Lina, who can help out."

"Of course. They're welcome as long as they like. We can use the companionship."

"Oh, and if it's all right, we'll be leaving the Drill-Bots for Charles."

"That will certainly make him happy. He's been having a difficult time lately, as I'm sure you noticed."

"He's been very kind to us. As you have. We owe you both a lot."

Thomas pulled out one of the small gold bars that Ignatius had given him back on Mars from his backpack. "This should cover any additional expenses while we're gone."

Dr. Darwin raised his eyebrows at the sight of the gold.

"Thomas, I can't possibly accept this. Thanks to my forebears, we're quite well off. Besides, any cost we might incur will be offset by the pleasure of having such a learned man as your professor in the house, particularly with Charles off to university in a few weeks. I can't tell you how much I'm looking forward to having something other than insects to discuss over dinner."

"If you won't take it for expenses, then I'd like to make a donation to your hospital in town. I'm sure there are some needy villagers who could use it."

Dr. Darwin nodded. "In that case, I graciously accept your gift, thank you."

In less than an hour, Thomas and Eno appeared on the front lawn, packed and ready to leave. Josef and Lina stood between the stone columns outside the front door while Charles and Erasmus brought the ambulance around.

Josef helped Thomas load the backpacks into the wagon, as Eno waited impatiently. Elly emerged from the house walking slower than usual, as if the time spent with Ignatius had left her in a daze.

Josef put his arm around Lina and turned to Thomas. "Thanks for saving my life Thomas—both of our lives, both times."

Lina nodded. "Thanks to you as well, Elly. I hope these boys appreciate what a remarkable girl you are."

Elly gave her a big hug. "Enjoy your time here."

"I'm sure we will," Josef said. "Charles promised to take me angling later today. He says the river's overflowing with salmon, which it turns out are actual fish."

"And Mrs. Teasely's agreed to let me help her in the kitchen," Lina said. "I'm excited to master the art of cooking."

Mrs. Teasely appeared from the house with two large baskets of provisions and handed them to Elly. "I packed the remainder of last nights' supper with a few surprises for good measure. The eels are lovely cold."

Eno glanced at Thomas with horror as Dr. Darwin appeared at the door.

"Thomas, your professor asked if you could stop by his room for a minute. He said there was something he forgot to tell you."

"I'll be right back," Thomas said to the others.

He ran into the house and up the stairs, where the door to Ignatius's room was wide open. "Dr. Darwin said you had something to tell me?"

"I just wanted to thank you for the chance to meet Elly. It was a dream fulfilled. She's an amazing girl and I know you'll take good care of her. But make sure you do the same for yourself."

Thomas nodded "I'll try. Hope I'll see you again, soon."

"As do I, Thomas. But we shouldn't count on it. It's been my privilege to know you. Your father would be very proud."

Thomas started for the door, then paused.

"Oh, I almost forgot, there's something I meant to ask you about."

"What's that?"

"After every time jump, there's a cloud of small particles in the cable car…"

"Ah yes, my messages. I figured out a way to record them in molecular fashion so they'd quickly disappear and be undetectable. I hoped they might serve as notes of encouragement."

"They did. Though the last time I thought I heard you…in pain."

"Hmnn. That I can't explain. I suppose we'll just have to chalk it up to one of the mysteries of time travel. Perhaps you'll figure it out for me."

"I'll do my best."

Ignatius took his hand and they shook. "Good luck, Thomas."

As Thomas came out the front door, Dr. Darwin was standing at the ambulance, waiting. Elly was sitting on the driver's bench with Charles.

"Thanks again for your hospitality, Dr. Darwin. And your kind help with Ignatius."

"It was my pleasure, Thomas. Travel safe."

Thomas jumped into the back of the ambulance with Eno. He noticed Elly looking up at Ignatius's room. He was at the open window, waving. She waved back as they pulled away.

On the ride from the property, Elly wasn't her usual talkative self, and Thomas wondered if she had any inkling of her true relationship to Ignatius. But it was now his job to make sure he never said anything that might even hint in that direction.

They quickly reached the cable car, and Charles brought Erasmus to a halt. Thomas and Eno got out of the wagon and began transferring their backpacks.

"Where are your horses?" Charles asked.

"They're not supposed to be delivered for another hour," Elly said, jumping down from the bench seat. "No need to wait around, Charles, you've done more than enough. Thanks again for everything. And don't forget to take good care of Frank and Stein."

"I'll have them polished to perfection by the time you return."

"If we don't get back soon, good luck on your trip to the Galapagos."

"The truth is, I doubt I'll ever make it."

"Why do you say that?"

"I get terribly seasick. I can't even ride our little river skiff without retching."

"Hold on," Elly said.

She disappeared into the cable car and came back with a bottle of pills. "Take one of these an hour before you get on the Beagle and you'll be fine."

"The Beagle?"

"I had a dream last night, that you were leaving on your journey. It was so vivid I could even see the name of the boat."

"The Beagle," Charles smiled. "I'll keep an eye out for it."

And with that, Erasmus pulled him away.

As Elly entered the cable car, Eno pushed the Time Globe into position.

"Have you already programmed it?" she said.

"Last night," Eno said. "I cleaned it thoroughly, so hopefully its exposure to the dust devil on Mars won't have an adverse effect. But there's only one way to find out."

Thomas and Elly took their positions and began to strap themselves in. Elly did so distractedly, her mind clearly elsewhere.

"I'm sorry you didn't get to spend more time with Charles," Thomas said.

"I had my fill." Elly smiled. "But I do wish I could've spent more time with Ignatius."

"You two seemed to really hit it off."

"The moment I met him I had the strangest feeling, like I knew him in another life."

"Another life?" Eno said, joining them on the floor.

"Just an expression," Elly said. "Not to be taken literally."

"The timer is set. Colorado, 2071…here we come."

PART 2

CHAPTER 13

When Thomas opened his eyes, Elly was already awake, watching a small cloud of perfectly white time-flies that floated near her head, accompanied by a distant voice.

"Do you hear that?" she said. "It sounds like Ignatius."

"Hmmm," Thomas said.

Elly listened closely, but the words were already fading into oblivion, along with the time-flies themselves. "I can't hear what he's saying, can you?"

Thomas shook his head, though he could make out a phrase that sounded very much like "our secret." He jumped to his feet. "Let's see where we are."

Elly leaned over an unconscious Eno to retrieve her backpack as Thomas opened the front door. A blast of cold air assaulted the car. She turned on the flashlight and joined Thomas. Together, they stepped under a canopy of stars even brighter than those they'd seen on their boat ride to Washington. But unlike that trip, there were no trees and no signs of civilization.

Elly moved the flashlight in a horizontal arc, illuminating a barren landscape covered by sand dunes, most of them waist high but some as tall as the cable car itself.

"Any idea where we are?" Thomas asked.

"No," Elly said. "But it's a pretty safe bet we're not in Shrewsbury anymore. From the dunes, I'd say we're in some sort of desert."

"I don't suppose there's any desert in Colorado?' Thomas asked.

"Not that I know of."

Elly looked up at the moon, which was dark, except for the sliver of orange on its lower half, as if someone had underlined it with neon. It was enough to reveal the outline of the mountain range in the distance. "But maybe we're not as far away," she added, aiming the flashlight to reveal a flat stretch of black asphalt that cut through the dunes. "That looks like a road over there."

They climbed over the dunes, passing the remnants of broken trees, many of them smashed into twigs by some unknown force. After five minutes or so, they reached the asphalt. A broken white line revealed a two-lane highway that vanished into the darkness in both directions.

The road was deserted. "It's probably too late in the night for any traffic."

Thomas pointed to the side of the road. "Isn't that a sign?"

They walked toward it, but as they got closer, saw that it was riddled with bullet holes.

"Looks like someone's been using it for target practice," Elly said.

There were two words, and Thomas tried to spell out the first. "E. A. T. And I think there's an H at the end, so maybe it spells Earth.?"

Elly traced her fingers along the holes. "I actually think the first letter is D, which would make it *death*."

Elly went around to the back of the sign and held up the flashlight. The light shot through the bullet-sized shafts, freckling Thomas's face.

"The second word definitely has a pair of L's in the middle," Elly said. "And there's a Y at the end. "Maybe an A at the other end?"

"Death Alley?" Thomas asked.

"I think the missing letter must be V. My guess is we're in Death Valley."

"Is that as bad as it sounds?" Thomas said.

"Yes and no. It's basically a massive desert on the eastern border of California. It brushes up against the state of Nevada, which is not all that far from Colorado."

"Can we walk there?"

"I'm afraid it's too far," Elly said. "A long day's drive even by car. Also, it can get up to a hundred and twenty degrees during the day, so you'd need more water than you could carry."

A chill ran through Elly's body and she rubbed her arms for warmth.

"You're freezing," Thomas said. "Let's go back to the cable car and light a fire. By morning we'll have a better chance to see where we are."

As they started walking, Thomas gathered some large pieces of wood while Elly picked up some twigs for kindling. When they reached the cable car, Elly cleared a circle in the sand and dug a shallow hole. Thomas dropped the wood into the depression, and Elly arranged it into a pyramid, leaving room for air between the pieces. She then lit it with her hand lighter. Within seconds, the fire was sending up a small cloud of sparks.

Eno appeared on the car platform, holding a pair of binoculars. "Where are we?

"Death Valley," Thomas said. "About a day's drive from Colorado."

"So, the Time Globe worked?"

"Sort of," Thomas said. "We still don't know what year it is. And since it's too far to walk, we decided to wait until morning to figure it out."

"The desert gets really cold at night, so we built a fire," Elly said. "But we're missing something critical."

Elly dashed into the cabin. A few moments later, she reappeared with a small plastic bag.

"What's that?" Thomas asked.

"Marshmallows. I completely forgot about them, but on the off chance we might be doing some camping, I threw some in my backpack. They're the key to a great campfire experience."

Elly held the bag open for Thomas and he pulled one out and squeezed it lightly.

"How do they work?" Thomas said.

"I'll show you," Elly said.

She snatched the marshmallow out of Thomas's hand, impaled it on the sharp end of a long stick, then handed it back. "You just hold it over the fire. When it gets toasty brown and gooey inside, it's ready to eat. Shame we don't have some chocolate or we could make s'mores."

Elly put another on a stick and held it out for Eno.

"I'll pass," he said, scanning the sky with the binoculars. In the pitch black of the desert, it was filled with more stars than they'd ever seen on Earth.

"See any of your favorite planets?" Elly asked.

"No, but there's a shooting star low on the horizon. It's moving toward us."

"Let me see," Thomas said. He took the binoculars to see a shimmering white light moving toward them. "It seems to be breaking up."

"What do you mean?" Elly said.

"It's more like three smaller stars now," Thomas said.

Elly took the binoculars to see three bright lights, illuminating some sort of giant truck. It was leaping over the dunes like a giant toad, producing a loud growl in the quiet night. As it got closer, Elly could see that the three stars were powerful lights mounted on struts above eye-level, dwarfing the headlights below. The tires were at least ten feet in diameter, and its cab twice as high. Instead of a normal grill, it had a rounded nose, like the front of an airplane, with a pair of tubes shaped like massive torpedoes running the length of each side.

"I think it's a truck of some sort," Elly said, "though not like any I've ever seen. It looks like a cross between a moving van and a fighter jet. And that's not even the strangest thing."

"Which is what?" Eno said.

"It doesn't look like anybody's driving."

Eno glanced at her anxiously. "Do you think it intends to slow down?"

"Doesn't seem that way," Elly said.

"Maybe we should take evasive action," Eno said.

"Get behind the fire," Thomas said, as he ran into the cable car.

A moment later he reappeared with the Sonic Inducer and stood in front of Elly and Eno. The brakes on the phantom truck suddenly let out a squeal as it rolled to a stop about fifty feet away. Just as Elly said, there was no sign of a driver. Both doors popped open, and two small figures spilled out, one from each side, presumably a driver and passenger. Thomas holstered the Sonic Inducer as they crossed in front of the truck's lights. The driver was taller than Eno but shorter than Thomas, while the passenger barely came up to the driver's shoulders. Both were dark-skinned, the driver at least two shades darker than Elly, his passenger's face a light bronze.

As they approached the fire, the two kids stopped. The driver seemed to be only a couple years younger than Thomas and wore a leather bomber jacket with a white captain's hat over a head of hair that popped out several inches on each side. His passenger, no older than twelve, was outfitted in a camouflage suede vest with matching headband. It ran around his forehead, meeting in the back of his head with a large feather that stood up like an antenna. His hair, a color of black so dark it seemed covered in oil, was pulled into a single braid that ran down his neck.

The driver held up his hand. By the light of the fire, they could see it was a girl.

"Hey, there. The name's Angel, though I don't quite look the part, so everybody calls me Ajax. And this is Duck, also know by his Shoshone name Eagle-eye. He's my Native American blood brother," she said, throwing her arm around the small boy.

"I'm Thomas. That's Elly and Eno."

"Pleasure to meet y'all," Ajax said with a slight drawl.

Thomas and Elly came around the fire to meet them, while Eno stayed in place.

"Where's your plane?" Duck asked.

"Our plane?" Thomas asked.

"We saw the blue light," Ajax said, "then the fire. We figured you crashed."

"Actually," Elly said, "we made the fire, and we didn't come by plane."

"So, how'd you get here then?" Ajax asked.

Thomas glanced at Elly, wondering how much of the truth he should share. "It's complicated," he said, "but we travel in that transport sitting behind us."

Ajax and Duck glanced at the cable car, confused. The truck's lights bounced off the mirrors, making it look even stranger than their truck.

"What the heck is that?" Ajax asked.

"It's a cable car," Elly said. "They were used to travel around the city of San Francisco in the early part of the twenty-first century."

"San Francisco," Ajax nodded. "I was there once. Saw the big bridge just a few months before it went under."

Duck stepped up to get a better look. "What kind of engine does it have?"

"It doesn't have one," Eno said, still standing on the platform. "The mirrored panels draw negative energy from the atmosphere, which in turn enables it to…travel."

Duck nodded casually, as if he didn't find the explanation in the least bit strange.

"Whaddya know," Ajax said. "Where you headed?"

"Colorado," Thomas said. "How far is it, anyway?"

"About twelve hours away, give or take. Close enough to drive."

"That's not exactly an option for us," Elly said.

"Your truck's got wheels," Duck said, observing the obvious.

"Technically accurate," Eno said. "But it's been repurposed, rendering them obsolete."

Duck nodded thoughtfully. "So, the mirrors are your wheels?"

"Precisely," Eno said, surprised at the speed of the boy's deduction.

"So, why not use them to get to Colorado?" Ajax asked.

"It's complicated," Thomas said. "The cable car has a device for programming our destination, but it isn't always completely accurate. So, if we leave again, we have no guarantee of getting any closer to where we want to go."

"I hear you," Ajax said. "Transportation's a real challenge these days. The open road is full of surprises, and there's always water on the way."

"You mean floods?" Thomas asked.

"Yeah," Ajax said. "We're settled in Las Vegas, or Last Vegas as we like to call it, and when we first got here, we were livin' on the ninth floor. We're up on twenty-six now, and the next one promises to be the mother of all gushers."

"You're in a hotel?" Elly said.

"It's abandoned, like the rest of the city, but it's got a first-class emergency generator, so it still works fine. We can give you a lift there, after we finish in the boat yard."

"The boat yard?" Thomas asked.

"It's the end of the valley where everybody used to keep their boats," she said. "When the flood before last hit, most of them got trashed."

"So, you're looking for a boat?" Thomas said.

"No, we're buildin' one. Actually, it's more like a raft, and we're scavengin' for parts."

Duck looked up to sky; the sun was threatening to make an entrance.

"We better get a move on," Ajax said. "You interested in a lift or what?"

"Thanks," Thomas said. "But we wouldn't want to slow you down. And we can't abandon our transport."

Duck leaned over and whispered into Ajax's ear. They stepped away to talk for a minute, then came back.

"Duck just reminded me we're kinda on a deadline, and we could use help with our salvage operation. If you're willin' to help, we'll give you our truck, and you can be on your way."

"You won't need it anymore?"

"Nope. We expect to use our raft to ride the next flood out—right, Duck?"

Duck nodded.

"We could put your transport in the back of the truck if you like."

"It would fit?" Eno said, suspect at the possibility.

"It's a custom-built German Liebherr, made for drivin' through deep water and suckin' it up so it's got a thousand cubic foot belly. Right now it's empty, so we could fit a couple of your transports in there."

Thomas glanced at Eno, who didn't seem enthusiastic at the prospect.

"As you can see, it's also got a pair of external tubes filled with liquid, which also make it amphibious. If you hit a flash flood on your trip, you couldn't find a better ride."

"What does it run on, if you don't mind my asking?" Elly said.

"Electricity, like everything else," Ajax said, as if it were obvious.

"Ah," Elly said, glancing at Thomas. "So, it must've have been built…recently?"

"It's a sixty-nine, barely a year old."

"That would make it 2070 now, right?"

"Yep," Ajax said. "Not that anybody's countin' anymore."

Eno's body sagged with disappointment. Thomas knew what he was thinking. If they went to Colorado now, the Biosphere might not even be built yet.

"Ajax, you mind if I talk with my friends for a minute?" Thomas asked.

"Go ahead."

Thomas huddled Eno and Elly together. "I think we should take her up on the offer."

Eno looked baffled. "Thomas, you heard what she said, it's only 2070. We're here too early. We have no choice but to time jump again."

"If we jump again, there's no guarantee we'll get any closer. Right now, we're in striking distance. Even if the orphans aren't there yet, maybe we could find the Biosphere."

"I take your point. But we've already had one detour to save your mother."

"Thanks, if I haven't already said it. But maybe there was a reason for that we don't understand. Ignatius did say that with time travel we're on a different kind of journey."

"The tide of time," Eno said dismissively.

"You may not believe it," Thomas said, "but I do."

"I'll tell you what I believe: if we're in Colorado at the wrong time, you'll be timeblown to who knows where and when."

"Say what?" Elly said. "Timeblown?"

"It's one of the rules of time travel," Eno explained. "Thomas can't encounter another version of himself without dire consequences. There's a window of six months, from the time he's born on January 1, 2071, until he leaves on the Shuttle on July 4, that we have to avoid."

"True," Thomas said. "But we should be able to do that easily."

Eno threw up his hands. "It's your decision, as always."

Thomas turned back to Ajax and Duck. "Is there someplace where we could get an accurate view of the current time?"

"Sure thing," Ajax said. "There's a big clock tower on the hotel across from ours that keeps the time down to the second."

"How long before we get there?" Thomas asked.

"We're an hour from the boat yard now. We'll need a few hours for salvage, then a couple hours back to the Odessa. We should be there before dinner, unless we run into cowboys."

"Cowboys?" Thomas asked.

"Renegades from the Old South who hooked up with bandits from the New West."

"They hunt long pig for food," Duck said, as if they'd know what he meant.

"That's why we travel mostly under cover of dark," Ajax said. "We aim to be at the boat yard by daybreak, work fast, then hightail it back to the hotel soon as we're done."

"We should get going then," Thomas said. "I'll grab our stuff."

As Thomas disappeared back into the cable car, Eno turned to Ajax. "Just out of curiosity, what exactly is long pig anyway?"

"You're lookin' at it."

CHAPTER 14

As Ajax and Duck walked back to the truck, Eno turned to Elly.

"What did he mean by us being 'long pig'?"

"I don't have a clue," Elly said.

"Ah," Eno said with satisfaction. "So there is something you don't know."

"But I do," Thomas said, appearing with their backpacks. "I just looked it up."

"Enlighten us then," Eno said.

"It's what the Polynesian natives used to call humans."

"Makes sense," Elly said. "After all, the pig is the closest animal to us, anatomically speaking."

"Wait a minute," Eno said. "Are you saying there are people who eat other people?"

"Yes. It's called cannibalism," Elly said.

"I read about that in the Information Archives," Thomas said. "It happened on one of the frontier crossings."

"The Donner party," Elly nodded. "It was a long time ago, in the middle of the last century. But we rarely see it anymore. The only people who do it are either dying of starvation or flat out crazy. Sounds like these cowboys might be both."

✦✦

The Liebherr backed up toward them. Ajax jumped out and, using a small remote on the truck keys, guided it into position.

"Okay, Jack, just a little more."

"Who's Jack?" Eno asked.

"That's what we named the truck. He just seemed like a Jack to us—didn't he, Duck?

Duck nodded, motioning for Ajax to move the truck slightly to the left.

"You can communicate with it?" Elly asked.

"Yeah," Ajax said. "Comes in handy sometimes. Bring out the lift, Jack."

As a pair of long streel prongs emerged from the truck and lowered to the ground, Eno turned to Elly. "What is it with Earth people naming their machines?"

"If you'd like to hear my theory, we can discuss it on the way."

"That's quite all right, thank you," Eno said.

The prongs reached the ground and Ajax gave it one last request. "Now pick up the transport and bring it on board."

The prongs slid under the cable car then raised it to the level of the truck bed and pulled it inside. When the cable car was safely tucked inside, Thomas, Eno, and Elly followed Ajax and Duck to the cab. They slid into the spacious back seat, which was wide enough for five adults. Ajax sat up as straight as possible, and though she could still barely see over the instrument panel, put her hands on the steering wheel.

"Hit the road, Jack."

The Liebherr surged forward, and in seconds they were on the highway, pushing ninety miles per hour. While Ajax drove, Duck kept watch in the wraparound rearview mirror that ran along the top of the windshield and provided a hundred-and-eighty-degree view of everything behind them. Other than the stars, there was still nothing but darkness.

Ajax kept up a constant stream of dialogue. "Don't get me wrong. I don't condone cannibalism, but we were all carnivores in the years before the floods, so when there was no more meat in the world, some people just couldn't deal."

"Just out of curiosity," Elly said, "what *do* you guys eat?"

"Most of the hotels were abandoned five floods ago, but the kitchens were still well stocked, so we've been workin' our way through the freezers. We're savin' the canned goods for the voyage, but everything else is fair game, so to speak. I'm partial to Mexican myself, never met a taco I didn't like, but my sidekick here likes to eat a few steps down the food chain, insects mostly, and plants. Duck's a master forager, aren't you?"

Duck shrugged modestly.

"He whips up some beetle larvae most nights that tastes just like popcorn."

"What's popcorn?" Eno said.

Ajax glanced in the rearview at Eno, surprised by the question.

"The boys are from Iceland," Elly said, by way of explanation.

"Livin' in the desert, it's either vulture or sand rats. Duck won't eat vulture on principal, and trust me, there's just no way to dress up a sand rat."

"I can imagine," Elly said. "By the way, I've done some foraging myself, and have nothing against eating insects. They have a much higher protein conversion rate than cows."

Ajax burst out laughing. "Cows? That's a good one."

Duck turned around, suddenly curious. "You seen one?"

"A cow?" Elly said. "Sure, I've seen lots."

Ajax raised her eyebrows in disbelief. "No fooling?"

Elly realized that cows must've become extinct. "When I was a little kid, that is."

For the first time, Duck seemed impressed. "Seen any megalodons?"

"More than we'd like," Thomas said.

"Wow," Ajax said. "Maybe you can give us some tips on how to handle 'em if we encounter any on our voyage."

"For sure," Thomas said. "When are you leaving?"

"Any day now," Ajax said. "When the next flood hits, we plan to be on it, right, Duck?"

But Duck had his head out the window, distracted by the roar of a jet somewhere above. They looked up to see a large plane heading west toward the mountains.

"Isn't that a passenger jet?" Elly asked.

"Sure is," Ajax said. "Fly-to-Die."

"What?" Elly asked.

"Random groups of survivors. They load up on booze and gourmet edibles, then head off into the sunset. When they run out of fuel, the Fly becomes Die."

"Seriously?" Elly said in disbelief.

"Yeah, we used to see 'em all the time, but they're pretty rare these days. Good thing for us though. Keeps the cowboys occupied. Right, Duck?"

Duck nodded. "Plenty of long pig, already cooked."

They watched as the plane cleared the mountains and slowly began to descend. A minute later they heard a muffled explosion.

Ajax shook his head in sympathy. "Bad way to go. Rather take our chances on the high seas, right, Duck?"

Duck nodded, then pointed to an upcoming road sign in the distance.

"Dante's View, that's our next-to-last turnoff," Ajax said.

She pulled off the main road at a sign that was broken and unreadable. The first light of morning began to reveal the desert, and several abandoned fire pits, littered with skulls and bones.

"The cowboys used to use this as their ambush spot," Ajax said. "Soon as somebody went off road, they were cooked, if you know what I mean."

They drove in silence for a short while, and arrived at a second road sign.

"This is it," Ajax said, making the turn.

Elly looked up at the sign. "Badwater Road?"

"Somebody's idea of a joke." Ajax said. "But the folks anchored here didn't think it was so funny."

The sun was now sitting on the desert floor, announcing the official start of another day.

"Here we are," Ajax said.

Thomas leaned forward, and Eno, who'd fallen asleep, slid onto the back window with a thump. Hundreds of boats, between thirty and fifty-feet long, were scattered across the desert. Many had their anchors still stuck in the sand.

"What happened to them?" Thomas asked.

"Flood hit in the middle of the night. Most of the boat people were in dreamland."

Ajax pulled off the road. They all got out and surveyed the bizarre landscape. The boats were in various states of decay, with most lying on their sides or upside down, as if they'd fallen from the clouds. Ajax led them toward a large sailboat that was broken neatly in half. A skeleton sat crumpled near the stern, its skull leaning on the steering wheel.

"Between the vultures and the sun, flesh doesn't last long out here," Ajax said, slipping off her heavy leather jacket to reveal a black tank top over a pair of well-toned arms. "We've made a bunch of trips out here already and got most of what we need, so we're now down to essentials."

Ajax pulled a list out of her pocket. "Three toilets, eight portable bilge pumps, four hundred feet of canvas tarp, a pair of fifteen-foot inflatable lifeboats, three 250 horsepower outboard motors, and most important of all, as many first-aid kits as possible."

"How should we divide it up?" Thomas asked.

Ajax tore the list in half and gave the top part to Thomas.

"You take the top while Duck and I take the bottom. If you find something too big to carry, just holler and we'll bring Jack around to pick it up."

Ajax and Duck waded into the sea of lifeless boats, while Thomas, Eno, and Elly went in the opposite direction. Thomas concentrated on the toilets while Eno collected bilge pumps and

Elly did the meticulous work of finding first aid-kits. Some she had to pry from the skeleton bones of clenched fingers.

It was four hours later when they regrouped in front of a long thin cigarette boat named Hellmaker and stood under its shadow to escape the sun. They were layered in sweat and covered in a thin coat of sand.

"I think that's it," Elly said, plopping down on the ground.

"I certainly hope so," Eno said, collapsing next to her.

Thomas wiped his brow and surveyed the boat desert, then sat upright. "I'll be right back. I thought I saw something on my way back I want to check out."

"How will you ever be able to find it in all this wreckage," Elly said.

"Blue Eagle," Thomas said.

"What?" Eno muttered.

"The name of the boat," Thomas said.

Thomas went off alone, trying to remember his route in the confusing landscape. After a few false turns, he found the fifty-foot boat with a small blue eagle painted on the side.

"Ajax!" he shouted.

Ajax shouted back from the deck of a boat nearby.

"Yeah?"

"There's something over here you might want to check out."

"Hold on, we're comin'."

Ajax and Duck appeared a few seconds later.

"Nice find," Ajax said. "Coast Guard rescue boat."

"How do you know?" Thomas said.

"Right after one of the first floods, my mom got me a sticker book with all kinds of boats, just to show me the many ways a person can conquer the water. I remember the Coast Guard one from the eagle insignia. The Latin underneath is their motto, 'Semper Paratus.' It means 'Always ready.' Guess they weren't quite ready for what hit 'em here. You see anything worth keeping?"

"On the back," Thomas said, leading them toward the stern, where a huge outboard motor was mounted. "You said you were looking for outboards? Is this one too big?"

Ajax looked up at the huge outboard, which had an eagle of its own on the back. "Holy mama. This is the queen of all outboards, the legendary triple eight—as in eight hundred and eighty-eight *horsepower.*"

"That's big, I take it?"

"None bigger, or more valuable. Only eight in existence, all government owned."

"So you can use it?" Thomas said.

"Use it? With this baby we can go around the world forever."

✦✦

They spent the most of the next hour loading all the equipment into the back of the Liebherr, saving the huge outboard motor for last. It took all of them to move it just a few feet to the hydraulic lift. When that was done and the truck closed, Ajax removed her captain's hat, wiped her brow, and used her fingertips to pull up her hair, which had matted down to half its size.

"If you're in a hurry, we can hit the road now, or grab a quick lunch."

"I wouldn't mind eating," Elly said.

"I'm with Elly," Ajax said. "We can all shower first, clothes and all. The sun out here dries you off in five minutes."

Elly looked puzzled. "You have a shower on the truck?"

"Four of 'em," Ajax said, nodding toward a pair of giant tubes that ran along each side. "Just stand underneath and I'll man the water valve."

While Ajax headed back to the cab, Duck removed his camo vest and the headband that held his feather in place and positioned himself under the front tube.

"Here comes!" Ajax shouted, as a torrent of water gushed out.

Thomas and Elly each stepped under a tube while Eno stood back. Ajax jumped down from the cab and joined them.

"This is fantastic," Elly said, as the water rushed over her.

"Eno," Thomas shouted. "At least put your hands in."

Eno cautiously held out his hands to catch some water. He then used them to wipe his face.

After a few minutes, Ajax shut off the water, and called, "All right, let's eat!"

They piled into the massive rear section of the truck, where Ajax pulled out a large cooler and laid it between them on the truck bed. Duck retrieved some fruit juice and plastic cups, while Ajax opened the cooler to reveal a layer of crushed ice. She slid one of the cups into the ice, filled it halfway, then handed it to Duck, who passed it along. When everyone had a cup, Duck filled it with juice. As they all gulped down the cold liquid, Ajax located an oversized white shopping bag with the distinctive "O" logo of the Odessa hotel. Then, plunging both hands into the ice, she pulled out two massive jars of peanut butter and jelly. Each was about half full.

"This is certainly a sight for sore eyes," Elly said.

"We found a couple cases a few months ago," Ajax said. "Far as I know, this is the last on the planet."

"It's nice of you to share it," Thomas said.

"Consider it payment for a hard day's work."

Ajax passed over the jars along with some soup spoons, then reached down to the bottom of the cooler and pulled out a package of hot dog rolls. She held them in the air triumphantly.

"Here we go, final dozen. Duck and I had one for breakfast, so there's ten left, two for each."

They quickly spooned out the precious peanut butter and jelly and spread it on the inside of the rolls. Famished, they ate without speaking.

As they finished, Ajax got to her feet. "Dessert?"

"I've never been known to pass it up," Elly said. "What do you have?"

Ajax reached back into the cooler and pulled out a black and white package.

"Eskimo pies?" Elly said. "You have to be kidding."

"We found a whole freezer full last week. Have as many as you want."

She started passing them out, when Duck suddenly shot to his feet.

Ajax stopped in mid-motion when Duck put a finger to his nose and sniffed the air.

"What is it kid?"

"Gas engines."

"I thought you said everything was electric," Elly said.

"Cowboys still favor the old combustion jobs. Duck can smell 'em a mile away."

Duck popped open one of the rectangular ventilation windows and scanned the horizon.

"See anything?" Ajax said.

"Four buggies, coming fast."

"Afraid we have to postpone dessert," Ajax said, tossing the Eskimo pies into the cooler.

She turned to Thomas, Eno, and Elly. "Stay here and hang on, it's gonna be a rough ride."

She and Duck scrambled through the back of the truck, into the front seat.

Thomas glanced over at Eno and Elly. "I'm gonna see if I can help."

He climbed into the backseat of the cab as Ajax started the truck and pulled off the main road. In seconds, they were bouncing over the rough terrain.

"Why not stay on the highway?" Thomas asked.

"Easy target. We'd be sittin' ducks. Right, Duck?"

Duck pointed to the wraparound rearview mirrors and Thomas could see several strange looking vehicles racing in a parallel line about fifty yards away. They looked like black metal boxes sitting on tires half their size. As they begin to move toward the truck, Duck reached down and pulled up a bow with a quiver full of arrows. Looping his arm through the quiver, he climbed up through the moonroof of the truck, his feet still on the seat.

Thomas looked into the rearview to see four buggies catch up to them. One stayed on their rear while two more pulled up on opposite sides. The fourth raced ahead then veered back in front of the truck in an attempt to slow them down. But when Thomas sped up, it dropped back to join the others.

A panel flapped open on the roof of the lead buggy. A man, naked to the waist and wearing a black cowboy hat, stood up. His chest was covered with a red, white, and blue tattoo of the Confederate flag. He lifted a high-powered rifle, looked through its sight, and pointed it at the cab.

"Duck!" Ajax yelled.

Thomas, not sure whether Ajax was talking to him or his sidekick, lowered his head, as a bullet richoted off the side of the truck. Ajax looked at Thomas and winked.

"Did I mention Jack was bullet proof?"

"No, but thanks."

As a second cowboy prepared to fire, Duck's arrow tore into his shoulder, sending the rifle flying into the sand. The buggy fell in behind the truck.

"Anything I can do?" Thomas asked.

"Kerosene balls," Ajax shouted. "They're in a blue metal box in the back."

Thomas climbed into the rear of the truck, where Eno and Elly were doing their best to hold on as the truck careened wildly over the dunes.

A pair of gunshots bounced off the side, as Thomas grabbed the metal box and climbed back up to the cab.

"Open it up," Ajax said. "And pass one up to Duck."

Thomas tore the box open to find a dozen palm-sized balls of rags, soaked in a liquid he didn't recognize. He grabbed one and climbed up through the roof, where Duck was pulling another arrow from his quiver. Thomas held out the rag ball, and Duck pushed it onto the end of the arrow. Using a small lighter, he put a flame to it, and it quickly caught fire. As he did, the buggy to the right turned toward the cab. The cowboy took aim at the truck. But before he could get off a shot, Duck shot his arrow, which hit the buggy in the front grill, covering it in cloud of fire and smoke. With no visibility, the buggy swerved behind the truck and slammed into a second buggy, sending them both end over end in a tangle of black metal.

That left two buggies, both now in the rear.

Thomas dropped back down to the seat next to Ajax. "What now?"

"See that big dune up ahead?"

Thomas looked toward a dune that was almost as high as the truck.

"We're going through it. The buggies can't handle the sand like we can. Hold on!"

Ajax plowed the Liebherr though the dune, sending a shower of sand in every direction. The closest buggy hit the dune sideways and flipped, but the second one managed to fishtail its way over it.

Now there was only one buggy left.

Thomas stood back up through the moonroof, next to Duck, who was retrieving another arrow. He impaled the rag ball on Duck's arrow and lit it. Duck squared off against the cowboy, who aimed his rifle in a faceoff. A shot rang out, and the arrow went skyward. The bow clattered to the floor as Duck slumped against Thomas, holding his arm.

"Duck!" Ajax yelled from below, her voice filled with panic.

"He's hit," Thomas said, grabbing the boy by the waist and lowering him down. They were both covered in blood.

"Elly!" Thomas shouted.

She crawled toward them and examined Duck's wound.

"How bad is it?" Thomas asked.

"Worse than my shark bite, for sure. I can use the laser on your Tetrascope, but not while we're being chased."

"It's in my side pocket."

Elly reached into Thomas's pocket and pulled out the Tetrascope.

Thomas could see Ajax watching anxiously in the rearview.

"Ajax, if you help Elly get Duck into the back of the truck. I'll drive."

Ajax nodded, and Thomas slid next to her, gripping the steering wheel with both hands. Ajax released the wheel and slid under Thomas as they exchanged positions. The truck slowed for a moment as Thomas got his foot on the acceleration pedal, but in seconds were back up to speed.

"See these two buttons?" Ajax said. "They release water from the tubes, one for each side. If they get close, soak 'em."

Thomas nodded as Ajax and Elly moved Duck into the back of the truck.

Alone now, Thomas looked out the window to see the last buggy pull alongside, with a cowboy aiming a rifle at his head. Thomas hit the first button and water gushed from the tubes on the passenger side of the truck. The cowboy tried to back away, but the water soaked the sand, turning it to mud, which grabbed the buggy's wheels on one side and nearly turned it over.

Thomas pushed the accelerator to the floor, putting some distance between them. But in seconds the buggy was next to them again, though it now kept its distance from the water tubes. Out of the corner of his eye, he saw a cowboy put his rifle out the window and get into firing position. Thomas swerved toward the buggy, forcing it to make a fast turn to avoid a collision. It cut behind the truck as Thomas glanced in the rearview to make sure it was directly behind him.

In seconds it was only about ten feet away. But every time it tried to make a move to the left or right, Thomas steered in that direction, cutting it off. While it kept the driver at bay, he knew he could only do that so many times. He needed to lose the buggy once and for all.

Thomas tightened his hands around the steering wheel and yelled to the back. "Hold on, everybody!"

With that, he sped up. It took the buggy about five seconds to catch up, and the moment it did, Thomas slammed his foot on the brakes as hard as he could.

The Liebherr strained against the soft sand but held its ground as it skidded to a stop. A moment later, Thomas heard a crash from behind and glanced back to see that the buggy had slammed into the rear of the truck.

As it burst on fire, Thomas hit the accelerator, and Jack pulled away.

Moments later, an explosion rocked the desert floor.

Shards of black metal flew into the sky like startled crows.

CHAPTER 15

As the burning buggy blended into the background, Jack chewed the desert floor into a wake of sand. The gunshot to Duck's hand landed in the web of skin between his thumb and index finger, tearing away a chunk of flesh. Elly put his hand on ice, and when it was numb, used the Tetrascope laser to cauterize it. In the aftermath of the battle, Duck's main concern was the well-being of his bow, which was a gift from his grandfather and the only thing left from his family. He worried that it had fallen out of the truck, but Ajax found it under the back seat, and put his mind at rest.

Thomas continued to drive as Ajax stayed by Duck's side. Neither of them said a word during the two-hour trip. It was almost five o'clock when Thomas saw the golden glare of a glass city in the distance. The sun, dropping toward the horizon, shimmered like a fire ball. The skyline of Las Vegas sat directly underneath, as if propping it up.

"How's the patient?" Thomas said.

"Not bad," Ajax said. "Your girlfriend did a great job."

Thomas glanced at Elly in the rearview, but she didn't correct her.

"Is that Las Vegas?" Elly said.

"Yup," Ajax said. "Home sweet temporary home."

"Is there a road somewhere?" Thomas asked, looking for any sign of black asphalt in the sea of cream-colored sand.

"We're on it, or at least where it used to be. The floods buried it years ago. Good for us, though. Keeps out unwelcome visitors."

"What about the cowboys?" Elly asked.

"They live up in the mountains, above the water flow. Only come down to hunt. And they never come near the city. Afraid they might run into the I-Men."

"I-Men?"

"International security guards. They left a long time ago, but the cowboys don't know that, and we don't advertise it."

As they got within a hundred yards of the city, Thomas could see that it was surrounded by a fifty-foot wall. In front of that was a twenty-foot moat of stagnant green floodwater.

"The wall was built for the floods?" Elly asked.

"Yeah. It worked for a few years, but when the bigger ones hit, the water came right over the top. The tourists left after that. Some of the hotel workers stayed on for the free rooms, but when the fourth flood took out the first twelve floors they packed up and hit the road."

"When did you get here?" Elly asked.

"A couple years ago. My dad came for a medical conference, but then he got assigned to one of the Mars programs and was told he had to go. No children allowed."

"So, he just left you?"

"He tried to sneak us out in the middle of the night, but a group of I-Men grabbed most of the kids for ransom money to buy onto a shuttle."

"How did you manage to avoid them?" Elly asked.

"I hid out in a potato cellar and survived on spuds until they were gone. Then I joined up with a bunch of older kids for a year or so, but they were all guys and didn't really want a young girl taggin' along. Anyway, they left town a few months later and I was on my own. One day I took my bike out to check the area, but it broke down a few miles west, and I ran out of water. On the walk back, I got dehydrated and lost. Duck appeared like a mirage and saved my butt."

"A mirage?" Thomas said.

"Somethin' that looks real but isn't. Lucky for me, Duck was real as rain. He had just come from the mountains after saying farewell to his family."

"Why did he leave them?" Elly asked.

"It was kind of the other way around. They were killed in an ambush by a band of cowboys. Duck was the last man standin' and and when it was all over gave his family a sky burial."

"What's that?" Thomas said.

"A funeral in the Duckwater Shoshone tribe. They lay the bodies on top on a wooden pyre, light a fire. Their spirits go up to the great beyond in the smoke."

Eno looked to Thomas, stunned at what he was hearing.

"He's pretty courageous," Thomas said, "your friend Duck."

"You bet. He's been my little blood brother ever since we met."

"He came back with you?" Elly asked.

"Yeah, and good thing, too. He realized my hotel was filled with ghosts, so we moved over to the Odessa, which was ghost free. Ivan, the kid who runs the place, took us in."

"So, it's just the three of you?" Elly said.

"Oh no, there's another nine of us, an even dozen altogether. Some were leftovers, like Ivan and me, some were hidin' out in other hotels. We found Thor livin' in the boat yard and Momoko crashed right out front in a stolen glider a few weeks later. Zeffi escaped from some cult out in the desert. They all have a story. You'll meet 'em at dinner. Most are at work now."

"Work?" Eno repeated.

"The raft is a full-time job for everybody. All hands on deck, that's our motto."

"Where you headed, if you don't mind my asking?" Elly said.

"Headed?" Ajax laughed. "We just plan to go with the flow, wherever the water takes us. From what we know, the whole world will be under it in another year or so. The raft will be our forever home."

Ajax looked up as they approached the city. "Here we go. Welcome to Vegas."

Thomas drove through the entrance and onto the sandy streets. An ambulance appeared at the first intersection. Behind it was a limousine with the name Odessa painted on the doors.

"You can pull over," Ajax said. "We stop out here for security reasons, just so nobody could follow us to our hotel."

Thomas turned off the ignition. A girl about Ajax's age jumped out of the ambulance and came to greet them. Her skin color was somewhere between Ajax and Elly's, set off by a turquoise turban. Thomas and Ajax got out of the truck, then helped Duck. Eno and Elly joined them.

"Thomas, Eno, Elly, this is Pooja," Ajax said.

Pooja gave them a quick bow, holding her turban with one hand so it wouldn't fall off.

"Poo's from Mumbai. Her mom was a doctor, and she grew up in a hospital, so she's our chief medical officer."

"Nice to meet you," Thomas said.

"Truly," Elly added.

Pooja turned to Duck. "What happened to our boy here?"

"We met up with some cowboys," Ajax said. "Duck took one to the hand."

"Oh dear," Pooja said. "Is it bad?"

Duck shook his head and held up his bandaged hand.

"Elly here fixed it right up," Ajax said.

"Then we owe you a great debt of thanks," Pooja said. "While Ajax is our captain and the heart of our little group, Duck is its soul. Will you all be staying for long?"

"They're our guests for the night," Ajax said, "then taking the truck on to Colorado to make their stand in the Rockies."

"That's ambitious," Pooja said. "Take it from someone who spent six months stranded in Kaṣhmir. Perhaps you'll change your mind when you see the amazing raft that the captain's built with her own bare hands."

"She's jokin', of course," Ajax said. "It's been a total team effort."

"The captain's too modest," Pooja said, "It was *her* vision. We're merely the executors."

"I couldn't build a toy boat if my life depended on it," Ajax said. "All I did is paste one together from the stickers in my boat book. It's a floating Frankenstein if you know what I'm sayin'."

"We do," Thomas and Eno said.

"Anyway, we better get our guests settled. Been a long day."

"I'll take Duck to the infirmary and put a fresh bandage on his hand," Pooja said.

As Pooja led Duck toward the ambulance, the waiting limousine pulled forward. Ajax opened the rear door and gestured for everyone to get in. She then slid into the passenger seat.

Eno glanced at the empty driver's seat. "Who's driving?"

"I am," came a disembodied voice.

Ajax pushed a button on the navigation screen. The chiseled face of a boy, roughly their age, appeared. With a prominent nose and oversized jaw, his face looked like it was about to push through the screen. He was dressed in a black suit and bow tie with an old-fashioned top hat that looked like it had seen better days.

"Thomas, Eno, Elly, meet Ivan. He's Ukranian."

Ivan spoke a bit formally, with only the slightest hint of an accent. "Glad you and Duck managed a safe return. I heard you had an escort."

"We sent them back up the mountain, where they belong."

"Your guests will find refreshments in the door: bottled nuts and boxed water for your transfer to the hotel. Now, sit back and leave the driving to me."

Ivan held up a small remote control and pushed a few buttons. And with that, the limousine turned and headed into the city. Thomas and Eno looked out the window in amazement as they entered an area of deserted hotels, exotic structures with wild flourishes of glass and steel. In short order, they passed the Bora Bora, the Canary, the Fiji, and the Madagascar, each with its own external projection system displaying notable features of their once-thriving destinations.

"You'll notice that most of the hotels in the superflood era are named after different vacation lands, each a living monument to a bygone paradise. Our hotel was the last to be built."

They pulled in to the circular driveway of the most magnificent hotel of them all, the Odessa. While most of the other hotels had suffered flood damage to their projection systems, causing them to go dark, the Odessa maintained a display of famous beaches flanked by the Carpathian mountains.

"Odessa was my father's favorite place as a child, though it was under water before I ever had a chance to visit. But hopefully you can at least get a taste of it's unique beauty."

The moment the limousine stopped, the doors opened, revealing Ivan himself.

"I take it your transfer was satisfactory?"

Ajax nodded. "Have to admit, Ivan, you're getting pretty good with that remote."

Ivan acknowledged the compliment with a tip of his top hat. "If Ajax hasn't already informed you, I'll be your official host for your stay in our fair city. My father was the original manager of the hotel, and I was born here, up in suite 1452. Do you have a room preference?"

"Ajax was telling us there's a big clock tower," Thomas said.

"That would be the Palm Beach. Not my favorite hotel personally, but a testament to Florida, which as you know was the first state in the country to entirely vanish."

"It would be helpful if we could see the clock from our room," Thomas said.

"I can put you face-to-face with it," Ivan said. "If you open the window in your suite and reach out, you can almost wind the second hand."

"If your arm was a few hundred feet long," Ajax said. "As you'll soon find out, Ivan exaggerates a little."

"Though it's not an exaggeration to say that the P suite is not only the largest room in Last Vegas but the world, at least since the Dubai went dark. How about you, Miss Elly?"

"I can do without the clock. But if it's got a bed and a bathtub, I'll be in heaven."

"Then heaven you shall have. The suite has five of both, in mint condition and never used, a tragic waste. The president of Bolivia was headed here, along with the Group of Five. But as you probably recall, their chopper was blown up en route."

"I'm sorry," Elly said. "I actually don't know about the Group of Five."

"The presidents of all the countries who voted against the Mars Project. Probably before your time. I was only three myself, but my father never got over it. It was his last chance to show off the suite. He'd be ecstatic to know it's finally getting used. Now, where are your things?"

"In the back of Ajax's truck," Elly said.

"I'd send someone out to fetch them, but as you might imagine, we're a little short on staff. All available personnel are at work."

"We can carry our own things, no problem," Thomas said.

"I have to get over to the fish tank for a raft test," Ajax said. "If you want, come over and visit. It's at the other end of the hotel."

"You've got plenty of time," Ivan added. "Dinner's being served in the main dining room at seven sharp. Cap, you'll be happy to hear it's in Louie's."

"Good news after a hard day," Ajax said. "I'll leave you in Ivan's hands."

"Thanks for the hospitality," Elly said.

"And for not being a mirage," Thomas said.

"Hey," Ajax said. "Without you guys, we'd all be cowboy barbecue."

✦✦

After Thomas, Eno, and Elly gathered their things, Ivan took them by elevator to the penthouse floor. The top two floors made up the presidential suite. It was divided into three mini-suites, and Ivan explained that they were named after former presidents of the United States.

The elevator opened directly into the massive lower lobby, which was connected to the upper floor by a glass staircase as wide as the Liebherr. Ivan gestured toward to the wall, also made of glass. The sun was setting, making the desert and mountains shimmer with a pink glow.

"As you can see, the views are spectacular. But let me show you the clock."

"Great," Thomas said.

Ivan led them to the end of the floor and pressed his remote. The blackout curtains parted and the floor to ceiling window revealed the Palm Beach Hotel and its two-story clock tower. The clock's face was made from mother of pearl, with hands of black onyx, outlined with diamonds. When it came into contact with the sun, it sparkled so much that it seemed to be pulsating. In the middle was a digital readout in gold script with minute, hour, day, month, and finally, year.

It read: "36. 17. 29. 12. 70."

Thomas did a quick translation in his head: Five-thirty p.m., December 29, 2070.

Eno, who obviously did the same translation, gave him a worried look.

And Thomas knew exactly what he was thinking.

Ajax had only told them that it was 2070, but now they could see that it was perilously close to the year's end. In three more days, Thomas would be born. If they arrived even a nanosecond after his birth, he'd occupy the world at the same time as his infant self, and as the invasive version, be blown out of time. Eno would no doubt use this to make a case for turning back. Not only would Thomas have to convince him otherwise but do so without telling him the real reason he wanted to keep going had to do with Elly and a vow he'd made to himself back in England.

"Wow," Elly gushed. "I know I said I could do without the clock, but that's the most amazing one I've ever seen."

Ivan nodded. "After it was built, it became the biggest attraction in the city, known to all as the doomsday clock. The hotel ran a daily pool for wagers to bet on anything from when the first shuttle would leave for Mars to where the next flood would strike. They bet on when the polar bears would become extinct and what would be the first country to go underwater. And of course nearly everyone made the ultimate bet: the day it would all be over."

"All?" Elly asked.

"Technically defined by the time the last-known human leaves the planet."

"Why would anybody make a bet like that?" Elly asked. "By definition, the moment that happened no one would be alive to collect their winnings."

"Of course, it makes no sense." Ivan shrugged. "My father used to say that people are obsessed with being right, and despite the consequences, would bet anything to prove it. That's the human race for you. Anyway, I'm available twenty-four seven for whatever you need. I keep the intercom on all night, in case one of the younger kids has a nightmare or takes ill."

"That's so thoughtful of you," Elly said.

"The number one task for a good hotel manager is to make sure his guests are happy. I hope you'll be."

"I'm sure we will," Thomas said. "Thanks for everything."

Ivan gave them a tip of his top hat and headed out.

"I don't know about you guys," Elly said, "but I'm going to find the nearest tub and soak myself into a prune. I have sand in my hair, under my nails, even between my teeth. See you post-bath."

"Go ahead," Thomas said. "I'll stay with Eno."

In truth, he would've preferred to find his own bathtub, but knew that he'd have to deal with Eno sooner or later. He might as well get it over with. The two of them stood facing the clock and the moment Elly was gone, Eno turned to him. But Thomas cut him off before he could start.

"I know what you're thinking. We only have two days to get to Colorado before I'm born and blown out of time."

"Your math is correct. But just as importantly, perhaps you could explain why you'd even consider undertaking that kind of risk?"

"Ajax said the trip would take nine hours, so if we leave in the morning, we'll be there by night. That still leaves a day to explore the area, maybe more, depending on what time I'm born."

"It's still not worth the risk—to you or the mission. And I hope you're not going to give me that mystical nonsense about being there for some mysterious reason known only to the tide of time."

Thomas had to admit, Eno was right. Not only would the trip incur personal risk, but potentially end the mission. It was only fair that he told him the truth. But to do that would mean betraying Ignatius's confidence. On the other hand, he felt he owed Eno some sort of explanation.

"Actually," Thomas said, "there's another reason."

"Well, are you going to tell me what it is?"

"I can't."

"Why not?"

"Because...it's a secret. A secret Ignatius asked me to keep."

Eno said nothing, but Thomas could see that he was hurt. While he understood Thomas had a special relationship with Ignatius, he believed that when it came to the mission, they were both privy to the same information, equals in at least that way.

"I'm sorry, Eno."

"No need to be. If Ignatius told you something in confidence, then I'm sure he had a valid reason. I'll prepare to leave for Colorado in the morning."

Eno turned and walked away.

The room was so quiet that Thomas could hear the big clock ticking from outside. Suddenly, the seconds seemed to be moving much faster.

He had the strange feeling that some sort of new countdown had begun.

CHAPTER 16

For the first time since the mission started, Thomas felt completely alone. He couldn't quite face Eno, but was equally anxious about seeing Elly. Ignatius was right, the secret he now carried was a burden, and was getting heavier by the minute.

He found an empty suite with a huge bed, pulled the sheets over his head, and fell into a deep sleep. When he woke up, the sun was beginning to lower itself over the mountains. He decided to take a shower. Counting the one earlier in the desert, it was his third since leaving Mars. It made him feel slightly better but he knew there was only one thing that might really help.

After a quick search of the presidential suite, Thomas heard Elly's voice. She was humming from somewhere at the opposite end of the floor. The door had the name George Washington written on it. He knocked three times.

"Come in," Elly shouted.

Thomas entered to find Elly in a fluffy white bathrobe that was so long it trailed behind her on the carpet. Her head was wrapped in a towel covered in blue stars and red stripes. As she dried her hair, he recognized the design of the American flag, flapping around her neck.

"How was your bath?" Thomas said.

"Incredible. You really should take one."

"I already took a shower."

"Good I hope?"

"Yeah, but I overshot your five-minute limit by thirty-one seconds."

Elly smiled. "I don't think we have to worry about wasting water anymore."

Thomas shifted his weight from foot to foot, then stretched his neck from side to side, as if trying to get comfortable in his own skin. Elly stopped drying her hair and put down the towel.

"Is everything all right?" she said.

"What do you mean?"

"I know something's been eating you since Shrewsbury."

"Eating me?"

"Meaning conflicted. It often feels like it's coming from the stomach."

Thomas instinctively reached for the knot in his stomach.

"I hope you're not upset that I spent so much time with Charles back in England. I wouldn't want you to think that I'm not completely focused on the mission."

"Why would I think that?"

"You shouldn't."

"I don't."

"Good," Elly said, tossing the towel on the bed. "So, now that we've got that out of the way, what is it?"

Thomas had no idea how to begin.

"The only way you're going to feel better is to talk about it." Elly pulled out a chair and Thomas sat opposite her. "Complete the following sentence. The problem is…"

Thomas took a deep breath. "The problem is…I've been told a secret. A secret I promised to keep. But I'm starting to feel I may not be doing the right thing by doing that."

"I see. Well, secrets are tricky things. People have them for all sorts of reasons. Some are toxic, and having them inside you is like a kind of poison. Some are just meant to make other people feel bad because they're not included, you know? But there are also good secrets, like ones meant to protect people, to avoid putting them in danger or causing them unnecessary pain."

"This is one of those."

"So, you should keep it then. Why wouldn't you?"

"Oh, I wouldn't tell the person the secret's meant to protect. It's just that...there's another person I think I should tell."

"Like Eno?"

Thomas hesitated.

"You don't have to answer that. Let's just say you want to share the secret with somebody *like* Eno, but aren't sure whether it's all right?"

"Right."

"Did the secret giver ask you not to tell that other person?"

"Not in so many words."

"Do you think the secret giver is concerned that by sharing the secret with this other person, you run the risk of having that person blow the secret?"

"Blow the secret?"

"Tell the person who the secret's meant to protect?

"He didn't really say, but I don't think so."

"Then I guess you have to ask yourself how trustworthy the person you're thinking about telling is. Can he keep a secret?"

"I think so. Actually, I'm sure of it."

"Have you considered going back to the secret giver and getting permission to share the secret?"

"I can't."

"So, we're talking about Ignatius here?"

Thomas hesitated again.

"You don't have to answer that. But let's say it's somebody *like* Ignatius, somebody you wouldn't want to disappoint. By keeping the secret, it might affect your relationship with somebody *like* Eno, who's easily offended. And now you're weighing one against the other."

"Yeah, and the scales are dead even."

"In my humble, non-professional opinion, I think you're waiting for the scales to reveal the answer so you don't have to take responsibility for making a decision you could later regret. But here's the thing: the scales are never really dead even. So I say forget the scales and do what you feel is best. You may be right, you may be wrong. Either way you have to live with it."

What Elly was saying made complete sense, but Thomas was still conflicted.

"Or maybe you just need more time," Elly said.

Thomas shrugged. "Time. It always seems to come down to that."

"Either way, sooner or later the answer will come to you and you'll know it. Now let me get dressed so we can go to dinner. I hear we're dining in Louie's."

"I have no idea what that is."

"Me either," Elly said, smiling. "But I'm sure it'll be an adventure."

✦✦

AN HOUR LATER, THOMAS and Elly arrived downstairs as Ajax entered the hotel. Like Thomas and Elly, she'd changed clothes, but was still wearing her captain's hat. "Hey, guys, how's the suite?"

"Amazing," Elly said. "I could easily spend a few weeks here."

"Tell that to Ivan. You'll make his day. C'mon, I'll take you to the dining room. Hope you're hungry."

"Starving," Elly said.

"Where's Eno?"

"I'm not sure he's coming," Thomas said.

"He's a very picky eater," Elly added. "Where's Duck?"

"Out on the wall. He sits up there at sundown and sunset, on the lookout."

"For cowboys?" Elly said.

"No, Chindi."

"Chindi?" Thomas said.

"Spirits. They're what's left behind after a person dies. They hide out in dust whirls. Or at least that's what the Navajos believe."

"I thought you said Duck was Shoshone," Elly said.

"His *father* was Shoshone, but his mom was Navajo. When the dust whirl spins clockwise it's a good spirit, but if it goes the other way, it's bad."

"Bad in what way?" Thomas asked.

"Last time he saw a wrong-way chindi we were comin' from the boat yard and got caught in the mother of all electrical storms. Hundreds of lightning bolts, like an alien attack."

"Hundreds?" Elly said.

"No exaggeration. Good thing Jack is lightning proof. Just the same, it was one wild ride back to the hotel."

Ajax turned toward a pair of glass doors with the name "Louie" stenciled across the front.

"Here's the dining room. Ivan's father named it after Louis Armstrong, the famous singer and trumpet player."

"Was he Ukranian?" Thomas asked.

"Ha, no. American, from New Orleans. 'What a Wonderful World,' was his dad's favorite song."

"Hey," Elly said. "It's my dad's too."

Ajax held the door for Thomas and Elly. Most of the tables and chairs had been pushed toward the walls, leaving only a single long table in the middle. Engaged in serious conversation were an Asian girl and a Muslim boy, each about thirteen years old.

"Hey, guys, meet Thomas and Elly."

They looked up and waved. Thomas and Elly waved back.

"This is Al-Jabr and Momoko. They met up in Tahiti, where their parents were working on the Mars Project. Al's our math whiz and Momo's our tech master. They keep the lights on around this place, and we were in the dark until they showed up. Believe me, you haven't seen dark until you've been in this place at night."

"I can only imagine," Elly said.

"Have a seat," Ajax said, taking the chair at the head of the table for herself. Thomas and Elly sat on either side of her, as Pooja joined them.

"Is it just us tonight?" Thomas asked.

"Yeah. Roos and Greet are in the weather center, and Thor and Muirin are still with the raft. I told them about you guys, and they were hopin' you were gonna join up with us, but I said you had to leave tomorrow."

"At least you'll be here for the signing ceremony," Pooja said.

"We're gonna autograph the flag," Ajax explained. "Thanks to your work in the boat yard today, the raft is officially complete. The ceremony's at midnight."

"But before that," Pooja added "we're having a little party in the casino. Ivan taught us all how to play roulette."

Ivan appeared from the kitchen. "But first, let me announce dinner."

He turned back toward the kitchen, where two ten-year olds, a boy and a girl, came out wheeling a pair of carts with serving dishes. The boy had huge brown eyes and the girl a mass of black curly hair that tumbled out of her chef's hat. They wore aprons with the hotel insignia.

"That's Zeffi and Sardinia driving the carts," Ajax said. "Zeffi's from Portugal, and Sardinia's from...well...Sardinia, an island off the coast of Italy."

"Wow," Elly said. "It's a regular United Nations in here."

In unison, everyone in earshot turned to her with the same question. "What's that?

But before she could answer, the boy parked the cart at the end of the table, and Ivan held up a water glass to make a toast.

"I'd like to officially welcome our new guests to the Armstrong Room. For dinner tonight, Zeffi's chosen one of my personal favorites, fried chicken, and Sardinia's serving her surprise pasta, which she makes on odd nights. On even nights, she makes a surprise pizza."

As Ivan began to serve the meal, Elly turned to Ajax. "So, they do most of the cooking?"

"Except for Friday nights, we do take-out from the hidden freezers."

"The hidden freezers?"

"Most of the ones in the hotel kitchens got cleaned out after the last flood, but if you look hard, you can still find some buried treasure. On Fridays we send out our freezer detectives, which is basically me and Duck. Last week we found an ice cream truck parked in somebody's garage."

"It still had ice cream in it?" Elly said.

"No, but we checked the basement in the house and the freezer was loaded."

"Just out of curiosity," Thomas said, "how are the jobs assigned?"

"They're not. It's an all-volunteer army. Everybody does what they think they do best."

"That's really smart," Elly said. "But there must be some bad jobs?"

"We have a system for those," Ajax said. "Everybody's got a number, starting with me, then Duck, Ivan, and on down the line. If you don't want the job, you're free to trade it with anybody who'll take it. Most of the time, that's also me."

When everyone was served, Ajax raised her water glass. "To the raft."

The kids echoed his toast. "To the raft!"

With that, they began to eat.

Elly took a bite of pasta. "This is really fantastic."

"Zeffi's dad was a chef for one of the hotels," Ivan said. "As for Sardinia, nobody knows where she got her skills, including her."

"What do you mean?" Elly asked.

"Amnesia. We found her in the desert, almost dead. She had a huge burn mark on her back and Pooja thought she might've been hit by lightning in the electrical storm. Anyway, every time we asked her a question, she answered 'Sardinia.' So that's what we call her. When we first got her, she didn't say much. But now you can't shut her up."

Elly glanced down at Sardinia, who was indeed talking up a storm to Pooja.

"She doesn't remember anything?" Thomas asked.

"Nothing," Ajax said. "Probably for the best. Whatever happened, my guess is it's not something you'd want stuck in your head."

"So, the raft is finished?" Thomas asked.

"Almost," Ajax said. "We're running our final test after dinner. You should come see it. Maybe you'll change your mind about joining us."

"As much as I'd like to, I don't think it's possible," Thomas said.

"Hey, we plan to spend the rest of our lives on planet ocean, so I like to think everything's possible."

"That's a great attitude," Elly said.

"Yeah," Thomas nodded. "Which reminds me, I should probably go check in on Eno. I'm sure he wouldn't want to miss your raft test."

Thomas found Eno at the window, staring at the clock tower. His face was reflected in the glass, and since it was six o'clock, the two clock hands formed a straight line from to bottom. On the left side of Eno's face was his good eye, while on the right he was wearing his eye patch.

"I haven't seen you wear your patch since Mars."

Eno kept both eyes glued to the clock, where the countdown continued to race toward 2071.

"My prosthetic was covered in sand, so I'm soaking it in one of those enormous tubs."

"Eno, I know you're not happy about my decision to go to Colorado."

"Let's just say that I'm as happy as I was with your decision to go to Washington, or plow a boat through a giant geyser, or zipline down a five-hundred-foot obelisk."

"I seem to have a knack for putting us in dangerous situations, don't I?"

"You've also managed to keep us alive and moving forward. That is your job."

"Thanks." Thomas smiled. "You missed dinner, but we've been invited to see Ajax do the last test on the raft. I thought you might be interested."

"Why? I couldn't care less."

"Maybe you could give Ajax the benefit of your technical expertise."

"What expertise? I don't know a thing about boats or water."

"But you know a whole lot more about everything else. I figured you'd be able to give them some feedback that might be helpful."

"Is this an order?"

"No, but I'd consider it a favor."

The clock continued its relentless ticking. Four more seconds whooshed by and Eno finally turned from the clock. "Very well."

✦✦

THE FISH TANK THAT Ajax referred to was actually a massive tube-shaped aquarium that snaked through the back of the hotel and once served as a major tourist attraction. It no longer held any of the dolphins for which it was originally intended. But several species of smaller, tropical fish still occupied its water, flashing by like tiny colored jewels.

Thomas and Eno found the tank, then followed it around until they spotted Ajax and Elly standing under the raft, which floated above them. Made from a motley collection of used boat parts, the raft was constructed in the shape of a rectangle, with a triangular section at the front, which acted as a crude bow. The ship was moored by four ropes, two on each side, which were draped over the tank and tied off to the huge pots that held indoor palm trees. On the other side of the tank stood Al-Jabr and Momoko, armed with handheld computers. Their faces rippled behind the water, making them look slightly unreal.

"Hey, Eno," Ajax said. "Glad you could make it."

"I wouldn't have missed it for the world," Eno said dryly, as he and Thomas took their places alongside Ajax and Elly under the raft.

Up close, Thomas could see that it was only half the size of the Star of the Sea. And from underneath, it revealed a patchwork of salvaged boat bottoms in so many colors it looked like a floating quilt.

"Ready everybody?" Ajax said.

From the other side of the tank, Al-Jabr and Momoko gave a thumbs up.

"Let the flood begin!"

Al-Jabr, who controlled the water flow, punched some keys on his computer. Almost immediately, a strong current began to flow through the tank. The raft, still moored to the palm trees, tugged against them, and after only a few seconds, the simulated flood became strong enough to make the mooring lines taut.

"All the way now!" Ajax shouted. "Superflood level!"

Al-Jabr hit a few more keys on his computer, and a huge wave began to build at the other end of the tank. Ajax turned to Thomas, Eno, and Elly.

"Better stand back if you don't want to get wet."

They retreated a few steps as the mini flood hit the raft. Small waves sloshed over the side, slapping at their feet. The mooring ropes snapped back against the pots like wild horses, pulling them across the floor. Meanwhile, the raft thrashed against the water's surface, but held steady.

"All right, Momoko—take it up."

Momoko hit some keys on her computer as Duck untied the mooring lines on both sides of the tank. A moment later, four miniature blue and white striped balloons, one at each corner, began to inflate. They slowly lifted the raft toward the hotel ceiling as the torrent of water rushed beneath.

Ajax held up her hand. "Test complete."

Al-Jabr and Momoko worked their computers to slow the current and deflate the balloons. The water became calm and the raft slowly returned to the surface.

Ajax turned to Thomas, Eno, and Elly with a big smile on her face.

"Well, what do you think?"

Thomas glanced at Elly. They were all thinking the same thing but were afraid to say it.

Eno had no such reluctance. "It's a clever concept—well executed, at that. And while I know nothing about living on the water, using the raft as a permanent home seems out of the question. The simple fact is that it's far too small."

Ajax looked to Duck, then burst out laughing.

Al-Jabr shouted from the other side of the tank. "What did he say?"

Ajax shouted back. "He said the raft is too…small!"

Al-Jabr and Momoka broke into laugher as well.

Eno glanced at Thomas and Elly. "What is so humorous?"

"This isn't the real raft, friend," Ajax said. "It's only a scale model."

"Then where is the real thing?"

"Up on the roof."

CHAPTER 17

AJAX TOOK THOMAS, ENO, and Elly up to the roof on the freight elevator. With only a sliver of moon to guide them, she turned on a handheld floodlight and beamed it at the six-foot-high wall that surrounded the roof. A pair of ladders ran up the side.

"Just follow me," Ajax said. "But be careful. We don't want anybody going overboard."

Ajax climbed the ladder and disappeared over the side. She shined the spotlight back over the wall so they could see where they were going.

Elly went up first, followed by Eno and then Thomas. As they got to the top, Ajax held out her free hand and guided them onto a wooden platform. The doomsday clock was off to their right, its digital read-out flashing in the dark like a warning light.

"Where's the raft?" Eno said.

"Right in front of us," Ajax said. "You just can't see it in the dark. Hold on."

Ajax shouted into the darkness. "Muirin?"

A girl's voice, in a thick Irish accent, echoed back. "Ya?"

"I've brought our guests to see the raft. Can you hit the lights?"

"One moment."

A second later, the roof exploded with brightness, radiating from a series of elevated spotlights around the perimeter.

Thomas, Eno, and Elly looked out in utter disbelief. The raft took up the entire roof and, on first glance, appeared to be at least ten times the size of the scale model.

"Whoa," Elly said. "It's huge!"

Ajax nodded. "One-hundred twenty-six-feet long, forty-nine-feet wide. You see why we laughed when Eno said it was too small."

"Can we see it up close?" Thomas asked.

"Right this way," Ajax said, as she led them down the stairs to the deck.

"How in the world did you get it up here?" Eno asked.

"Piece by piece, in the freight elevator. Took us almost five months."

"I gave my sticker sketch to Momo, who ran it through a computer program to make a real three-dimensional design, and Thor took it from there. His dad was a boat builder, so he drew an outline of the raft with chalk on the roof, then roughed out the frame with Muirin, who's the only one of us who's actually spent any time on a working boat. There she is."

A girl about fourteen crossed the deck toward them. She had a tangle of red hair, a round chin, and a face thick with freckles.

"Thomas, Eno, Elly, this is Muirin. Rhymes with marine."

Muirin smiled. "It means 'born of the sea,' after a sixth century pagan mermaid, who was rescued by local fishermen. I come from a family of them. Fishermen, that is, not mermaids. I was born on a Galway Hooker and spent half my life at sea, so I'm happy to be back on a boat."

"She and Thor have pretty much been livin' up here for the last few months. Without them, we'd be leaving on the raft in the fish tank."

"It's truly amazing." Thomas said, glancing at Eno.

"Remarkable, I agree," Eno said.

"You should be very proud," Elly added.

"We all had a wee part in it, yourself and yer two boys included," Muirin said. "Ajax tells me you were a godsend in the boat yard. Come then, I'll give you the tour."

Muirin walked them toward the stern, passing a series of bunk-houses that were made, like the raft itself, from sections of fiberglass cut from other boats. Each had a sea-facing window along with a retractable canvas top. In the middle of the raft were the pontoon lifeboats, along with a dining cabana, recreation area, and large wheelhouse. It contained a bank of computer monitors dedicated to navigation and boat operation, including six masts, three on each side of the raft. At each corner of the deck were four small bunkers, which held larger versions of the balloons, and in the middle was a lounge area, outdoor kitchen, and even a pair of inflatable swimming pools.

"Wow," Elly said. "You really could live on this thing."

"That's the plan," Ajax said.

At the very front of the bow, a boy Thomas's age was kneeling over a large sheet of blue silk, looping some rope through several holes along one edge.

"Hey, Thor, meet our guests."

Thor stood up. He was the biggest of all the kids, almost a head taller than Thomas. He had apple red cheeks and a thatch of blond hair so thick it looked carved out of marble.

"Thomas, Eno, Elly…Thor."

"I hope we're not interrupting your work," Thomas said.

"I was just finishing our flag, so it'll be ready to fly for tonight's ceremony."

"You're comin', I hope," Muirin said to Elly.

"You bet," Elly said.

"See you later then. We've got a good bit of work left to do."

With a wave, Muirin and Thor headed off toward the stern.

"So," Ajax said. "What do you think?"

"The raft's incredible," Thomas said. "But there's only one thing I don't understand."

"What's that?"

"How do you plan to launch it from up here?"

"Oh, that's the easy part. We drilled a bunch of holes around the wall so that when the flood hits, the water will come in, lift us up, and take us away."

Thomas, Eno, and Elly exchanged a look of surprise.

"But that would mean…" Elly started.

"I know," Ajax nodded. "The water will be twenty-six stories high."

"That can't be possible," Eno said.

"I'm no expert, but that's what the Dutch girls think. You can ask 'em yourself."

"I'd like to do that, if you don't mind," Eno said.

"Let's go."

Ajax took Thomas, Eno, and Elly back on the freight elevator down to the twenty-fourth floor and knocked on one of the doors.

A pair of voices answered in unison. "Come in."

Ajax opened the door to a large suite. The furniture had been removed except for two chairs and a small desk, while the walls were covered with banks of computer monitors and maps. Two girls, about Elly's age, were sitting in front of the monitors.

"Thomas, Eno, Elly…meet Roos and Greet, our in-house weather team. Back in Holland, their parents designed inflatable dams, so they're as close to experts as you can get."

The sisters waved. They both had fair skin, hazel eyes, and hair chopped at the chin. The only difference was that Roos had dyed hers red, while Greet's had the seven colors of the rainbow.

"Love your hair," Elly said.

"Thanks," Roos said. "Since we're twins, nobody can ever tell us apart, so we decided to make it easy. Roos mean 'rose' in Dutch."

Greet sighed. "Greet doesn't mean rainbow. My hair's a nod to our country's tulips."

"So," Ajax said, "I was telling these guys about your predictions for the next flood. They had a hard time believin' it was gonna come over the roof."

"We don't have a crystal ball," Roos said, "but you don't need one if you've been tracking the floods for a while and can read a weather satellite."

Greet gestured toward the largest monitor, which was hung on the wall directly above them. "Fortunately, one of the few things the flooding hasn't affected is transmission."

They looked up to see a massive swath of water moving toward a land mass somewhere in the upper northern hemisphere.

"Is that Alaska?" Elly asked.

"No, but close," Greet said. "Alaska went under in the last cycle. This flood's farther east, over central Russia. It's about to hook up with the Siberian Sea."

Roos went to a large world map plastered against the opposite wall. She picked up a blue sharpie and began to draw an arrow tracing the path of the flood.

"The superflood circles the Earth like water flushing a toilet. Las Vegas is three hundred feet below sea level, so it should already be underwater. But the Spring Mountains have its back, literally, and funnel the water south, toward the Colorado River, then down to Mexico and over to the Caribbean, before crossing the Atlantic to the Mediterranean, then back around the globe. Each time it goes around, it picks up more water, making it bigger and bigger." Roos continued the sharpie arrow across the Pacific Ocean through California toward Nevada then stopped. "As the water heads for Vegas, some of it sloshes over the mountains, like a bucket that's too full. It creates a waterfall twenty-miles wide, most of which drains into the desert. But over the years, the floods have finally left the desert saturated, and the last few filled up the valley like a bathtub."

Roos swiveled toward another one of the computers. "The most recent flood came up to the nineteenth floor. Unfortunately, the next one will be exponentially higher. Watch." She hit a few keys and the flood tides began to move, circling the globe, as Greet described. A series of numbers filled the bottom of the screen. "As you can see, the water is calculated by volume."

Eno leaned over the computer and studied the figures. They watched the digitized re-creation of the water coming over the mountain. As they did, Elly noticed that Greet put a hand over her eyes, unable to watch.

Roos hit another key to get a sidelong perspective of the city. They watched in silence as the water filled the valley up to the twenty-fourth floor, then proceeded to wash over the roof. "The only good news is that it's not a tsunami."

"A what?" Eno said.

"A flood caused by an earthquake under the ocean," Elly said. "We Californians know all about that stuff."

"So, you know that the water will be relatively slow moving," Roos said, "maybe only ten to twenty miles per hour, which is sufficient for our purposes. The important thing is that it will be our last chance to launch."

"The flood after that will be impossible to survive," Greet said. "Of course, there's always the chance this one might be the same. We won't know until it happens, at which point it'll be too late."

Thomas and Elly exchanged a concerned glance.

"Despite the fact that we're twins," Roos said, "we're not exactly alike. My sister is the pessimist to my optimist."

"Or as I prefer," Greet countered, "realist to idealist."

Thomas turned to Eno, who looked up from the screen. "Her equations are correct."

"When do you think the flood might hit?" Thomas asked.

"It depends on some variables we can't compute," Greet said. "We don't have data on the Thermohaline Circulation, otherwise known as the oceanic conveyor belt. And we know nothing about the saturation level east of the Sierras, let alone the status of the California coastal dam."

"There's a dam on the California coast?" Elly said, surprised.

"A big one, built in 2053," Greet said. "It runs from San Francisco to LA along the same route as the bullet train. It's four hundred feet high, so if it's still standing, it could delay the water flow. But it won't stop it. Best case, the flood will hit us sometime in the next forty-eight hours."

Ajax nodded. "That's why tonight's the deadline for finishin' the raft."

Roos turned off the monitor. "Starting at noon tomorrow, we're on official alert."

Thomas could feel the mood in the room darken with a seriousness he hadn't seen with any of the kids they'd met. But for some reason, Ajax was smiling mischievously.

"But first," Ajax said, "we party."

CHAPTER 18

At eight o'clock sharp, the kids began to gather in the casino. Pooja arrived first, along with Al-Jabr and Momoko, followed by Zeffi and Sardinia, Muirin and Thor, Roos and Greet. Ajax arrived last, along with Duck, Thomas, Eno, and Elly.

When they were all assembled, Ivan's voice boomed over the loudspeaker. "Welcome everybody…to our final soiree."

A groan of disappointment echoed from the kids.

"But because of that, the house will reward the first person at the cashier's window a bonus of…ten thousand dollars!"

The groan morphed into a squeal, as the kids sprinted toward the cashier's window.

"He does that every time," Ajax said. "Great way to kick off a party."

Ajax walked them toward the cashier, where Ivan, dressed in a blue tuxedo, was handing out money. Sardinia ran from the window with an armful of cash, screaming with excitement.

"That's not real money, is it?" Elly asked.

"Sure is," Ajax said. "We used to play with chips, but Ivan figured the kids would have more fun with actual cash. Pooja won a half million bucks three weeks ago."

"I didn't think paper currency was still used," Thomas said.

"You're right," Ajax said. "During the last few years, people only traded valuables. All the paper was locked in the vault, but Ivan found the combination."

By the time they got to the cashier's window, the line had already vanished. Ivan handed Ajax, Duck, Thomas, Eno, and Elly ten thousand dollars each in hundred-dollar bills, then appeared from behind the window. "C'mon, you can play at my wheel."

They followed Ivan to one of the three roulette tables. The rest of the kids gathered in small groups around two other wheels, run by Al-Jabr and Momoko.

"All right," Ivan announced, "time to gamble."

"I don't know how to play," Thomas said.

"It's simple," Ivan said. "Just pick a number or a color and lay down some money. I spin the wheel, the little silver ball goes round and round, then lands on a number from zero to thirty-eight. If it's the one you put your money on, you win."

Ajax looked to Duck. "What's the number, Duck? I lost track."

"Twenty-eight," Duck said.

Ajax glanced at Elly as Duck put a thousand dollars on the velvet layout. "That's the number of weeks since me and Duck met."

"Then I'm putting my money on number one," Elly said. "That's how many weeks I've known Thomas."

Thomas didn't need to think about it. "I'll bet on number eight, the number of days I've been on…"

"…the West Coast," Elly said, cutting him off.

"Right," Thomas nodded. "What about you, Eno?"

"I'll pass. I don't believe in the concept of luck and I'm not interested in games of chance. From a mathematical point of view, the field probability is quite low."

"Oh, come on," Elly said. "Be a sport."

"I have no idea what that means," Eno said. "But very well, I'll chose number thirteen."

"You do know that thirteen's not a lucky number?" Elly said.

"As I said, I don't believe in luck." Eno slid his entire ten thousand dollars on the number thirteen.

"Here we go," Ivan said, giving the wheel a hard turn.

Thomas and Elly leaned forward as the small silver ball dropped into the circular track. It bounced from number to number, and gradually lost momentum, as the wheel slowed down. On the final turn, it hopped from two to nine to thirteen to twenty-eight, and finally...thirteen.

"We have a winner!"

Ajax slapped Eno on the back. "Who says thirteen is unlucky!"

✦✦

THE HOURS PASSED QUICKLY as the kids moved from table to table, pausing only to eat from the dessert carts. There was an ice cream station, a chocolate machine, and several bowls of jellybeans. The floor was punctuated with howls of delight from the winners and the frequent roar of laughter.

At eleven o'clock, Ivan made an announcement. "Ladies and gentlemen, this is the final roll of the evening!"

After the roulette wheels went silent, everyone counted their take. Eno had amassed over a hundred thousand dollars, far and away the biggest total.

Ajax turned to Eno. "The night's winner gets to cut the cake."

Ivan appeared from the kitchen wheeling a cart holding a five-tier cake, each layer a different color and flavor.

"Wow, that's beautiful," Elly said. "Who made it?"

"Ajax and Duck found a bunch of frozen layers over at the Canary Hotel. Zeffi and Sardinia did the stacking and icing."

Pooja and Greet readied the plates.

Eno took the knife from Ivan as if it were a dead fish. "I've never cut a cake before. Or held a knife for that matter."

"Here," Pooja said, "let me help you."

She put her hand around Eno's wrist and made a triangular cut, then scooped out a perfect slice. Everybody applauded.

"Who wants milk?" Momoko asked, and several hands shot into the air.

"Milk?" Eno said, glancing at Elly. "Have I had that?"

Everyone laughed, assuming it was a joke.

As soon as they were finished, the kids filed into the freight elevator and made their way to the roof for the signing ceremony. The celebratory mood suddenly turned serious. It was as if the party had officially ended the moment the elevator doors shut.

The elevator stopped. Ajax and Duck held flashlights to guide everyone to the wall ladder. Thomas, Eno, and Elly brought up the rear. Duck held a spotlight on the ladder while Ajax led the group up and over the wall to the viewing platform. They huddled under the glow of the clock tower, which revealed that only nine minutes were left in the day.

"Hold on," Muirin said. "Let me get the lights."

Thor helped her down the stairway onto the deck of the raft.

"Ready?" Muirin shouted from the darkness.

"Anytime," Ajax shouted back.

Instead of the floodlights, the deck was illuminated by strings of smaller lights draped around the vessel. Against the night sky, it made the raft seem as if it were floating through the stars. For a few moments, no one spoke.

Finally, Zeffi shouted. "Extraordinario!"

And everyone broke into wild applause.

Ivan, who was standing with Thomas, Eno, and Elly, seemed in shock. "It's more amazing than we could've ever expected."

"But you've seen it before, right?" Thomas asked.

"Not the finished product," Ivan said. "I supervised the living quarters, but the rest of the prep was done downstairs and Ajax asked that we not tie up the freight elevator unless absolutely necessary. So, while we've all seen various parts of the raft, only Thor and Muirin have seen the entire thing. The whole raft-on-the-roof concept was a bit crazy to begin with, and I suspect Ajax thought it would be helpful for us not to see it before it was ready."

One by one, they stepped onto the deck of the raft, and Ajax waved them all toward a large table. Draped over it was the blue silk flag that Thor was working on earlier.

"Time to sign up for the voyage of a lifetime," Ajax said.

Duck brought out a can of white paint, along with a small brush.

"Tonight, we go in reverse order," Ajax said. "Last shall be first."

Zeffi stepped forward, took the paintbrush, and signed his name in a corner of the flag with a slashing Z. Sardinia was next, followed by Pooja, Al-Jabr, and Momoko. When it was Muirin's turn, she painted a large shamrock next to her signature, while Thor drew a large hammer and Roos and Greet sketched a Dutch windmill. Thor was followed by Ivan, who painted a top hat, and Duck drew an arrow flying around the globe. Finally, Ajax took the brush, and wrote: Captain A. Jax along with a small pair of angel wings in tribute to her given name.

Thomas and Eno had the same thought at the same moment.

"You don't think she could possibly be related?" Eno started.

"She's too young to be Dr. Jax's daughter," Thomas said. "Beside, he only mentioned that he had a son, though for all we know she could have been born after he evacuated to Mars."

Eno nodded. "The math works. You think we should mention it?"

"What would we even say?" Thomas said.

"You're right, of course. Explaining the future to someone in the present is one of the most difficult challenges of time travel."

When Ajax was finished, Thor picked up the rope attached to the flag and handed it to Zeffi. The others gathered on alternate sides.

"All hands on deck, everybody," Thor called.

They each put a hand on the rope and hoisted the huge flag into the air. As if on cue, a gust of mountain air swept across the roof and unfurled it for all to see. The names of the twelve passengers fluttered to life, accompanied by a boisterous cheer.

In the middle of the circle was a single word: SURVIVOR.

✦✦

Moments after the signing ceremony, the breeze that arrived during the flag raising died, as if mother nature had declared the raft off limits. An eerie calm settled over the roof and everyone wandered off in small, silent clusters. It was as if each person was occupied with the same thought: the fun around building the raft was finally over and the journey of their lives was at hand.

Thomas, Eno, and Elly stood off by themselves, suddenly feeling like outsiders.

"So?" Ajax said, approaching.

"It's beyond amazing," Thomas said, as Eno and Elly nodded.

"I still can't get over the fact that you built it by yourselves," Elly said.

"Not like we had a choice," Ajax said. "Like I told everybody when we started, there's nobody comin' to save us. Us kids are on our own."

"You're right," Elly said. "If we want to save the world, we better do it ourselves."

"I don't know about savin' the world," Ajax said. "But we'll settle for staying alive."

"Speaking of which," Eno said, "we have an early start tomorrow."

"I'll be up early to see you off," Ajax said.

"Tomorrow then," Thomas said.

Ajax waved and returned to the raft to join her fellow travelers. As Thomas watched, a part of him felt disappointed that he couldn't join them on the adventure of a lifetime. But they had their own adventure to continue, and it would begin again first thing in the morning.

Thomas, Eno, and Elly got off the freight elevator outside the presidential suite.

"I don't know about you two, but I'm wide awake," Elly said. "Anyone up for nightcap? I found the most delicious organic soda in my refrigerator."

"I'll take you up on that," Thomas said.

"I'm going to sleep," Eno said. "See you in a few hours."

Eno walked off, leaving them alone.

"Why don't we sit on my balcony?" Elly said. "It faces away from that awful clock."

"Sounds good," Thomas said.

They entered Elly's suite, and she opened the balcony doors, which revealed the mountains, now gently outlined by moonlight.

"Give me one sec," Elly said, as she disappeared into the kitchen area.

Thomas looked out to the unknown landscape they were about to cross. He was relieved to be away from Eno and the dilemma that continued to consume him.

Elly came back with a bottle of purple soda and two glasses. She poured them each a glass and held hers up for a toast.

"To a safe journey. For all of us."

Thomas clinked her glass and drank. "Sometimes I wish we could just put the mission on hold for a few days and travel."

"Where would you go?" Elly said.

"That's the thing," Thomas said. "I don't know enough about Earth to really say. I'd just find the nearest train and go wherever it took me. How about you?"

"Well, Darwin's home would be number one, but we've already done that."

"So, what's your second choice?"

"Tibet."

"Where's that?"

"About as far from here as you can get, in the Himalayas."

"Why there?"

"I've always imagined it to be the most peaceful place on Earth. If the world had a soul, it would be Tibet."

Thomas wanted to hear more, but the thought of what was now in front of him with Eno was too pressing to put off any longer. He downed the rest of his soda and put down his glass.

"I guess we should both try to get some sleep. We have to leave early if we want to get to Colorado by nightfall."

Elly smiled. "I'll take that as a marching order."

By the time Thomas got back to his suite, Eno was in the bedroom with the door closed. The ticking of the doomsday clock outside was barely audible through the triple-pane glass, but somehow the ticking managed to seep into his head.

A voice startled him. "There's no way to stop it, you know."

Thomas turned to see Eno, standing in the bedroom doorway, a blanket over his shoulders.

"The clock?"

"The brain. It won't let me sleep. It keeps me thinking."

"About what?"

"Their raft, for one. Don't get me wrong, it's an extraordinary accomplishment. But I still don't see how they can survive this next flood."

"We might not survive it either if we go to Colorado now."

"I chose not to mention that. What would be the point?"

"The point would be that I can't ask you to risk your life without knowing why."

"What do you mean?"

Thomas drew a deep breath. "Eno, sit down. I have a secret to tell you."

CHAPTER 19

After he'd revealed the startling truth of Elly's real parentage, Eno had spent nearly an hour going over every detail, trying to find some inconsistency that would render the story false. But with each retelling, Eno's disbelief slowly ebbed away, leaving him in a state of mental exhaustion. Thomas couldn't face the giant clock for another second and moved to the window overlooking the hotel entrance. He spotted Duck sitting on the wall, no doubt watching for Chindi.

"Are you having second thoughts about telling me Ignatius's secret?"

Thomas answered honestly. "No. It's only fair that you know why I think going to Colorado now, and giving Elly the chance to meet her mother, is so important. She was responsible for my meeting mine, so it's only fair I do the same for her."

"How do you know she even cares?"

"Back in Washington, she told me it was always her dream."

"There's only one problem. She won't know it's her mother."

"I thought about that. But it's still better than never meeting her at all. And at some point in the future, she'll discover the truth."

Eno let out a sigh of resignation. "I assume your decision is final?"

Thomas nodded. "I made a promise to myself before we left England. If I was going to take Elly with us and risk her life, the very least I could do is give her this chance."

"Even if it meant putting yourself at risk by being timeblown?"

"Yes," Thomas said. "When we started this mission, Elly was a stranger. But now, she's much more than that, even to you."

"To me? Why do you say that?"

"You once told me how you were designed using some of Ignatius's own DNA, his loyalty genes in particular. And since Elly turns out to be his biological daughter, she's naturally got some part of his DNA, too. That makes you partly brother and sister."

Eno's face went slack. "I suppose that's true," he finally conceded, "technically speaking."

"There's also one factor we may have overlooked," Thomas said.

"What?"

"The issue of time—in the Ignatius sense. As something with its own mysterious purpose. I know how you feel about that, but why do you think we landed here six months early? If we were to get to Colorado after I'd left for Mars, Elly's mother would've been on the same shuttle as me and not even there. As it turns out, this is their only opportunity to meet."

"All right, you have a point. But we need to get there as quickly as possible and get out. No stopping for helpless animals, drowning children, or points of geographic interest."

Thomas put out his hand to shake. "Deal."

✦✦

THOMAS PASSED OUT ON the couch in a state of relative contentment. With the issue of Elly's secret resolved—at least with Eno—there was nothing to prevent a good night's sleep. That's why the urgent knocking at the door startled him even more than it might have under normal circumstances. He glanced at the doomsday clock to see that it was almost three in the morning. The knocking came again, faster and louder, and he hurried to open the door. He was surprised to find Ajax standing in the hallway, with Roos in tow. The looks on their faces said that something was wrong.

"Ajax, Roos…is everything…?"

"Roos's sister, Greet, is missing."

"Missing, as in…?"

"Out of her room, out of the hotel, nowhere to be found," Ajax said.

"I woke up to find her gone," Roos said. "She packed up her things, so I know she's not just wandering around, like she sometimes does in the middle of the night."

"What do think happened?" Thomas said.

"She's freaked out about the flood and the raft and well… everything. It's been building for a while now, but I think the official alert put her over the top. I should've said something about how she was feeling," Roos said.

"Not your fault, Roos. It's just the way of the world right now," Ajax said. "I thought we could put together a search party but didn't want to alarm the kids. I figured you might help us."

"Of course," Thomas said

A voice came from the hallway. "What's going on?"

Elly was standing outside her door and Roos turned to her.

"My sister's gone."

"Oh no," Elly said. "I guess she didn't think she could go through with it?"

"How did you know?" Ajax said.

"After our session with the satellite map, I had a strange feeling."

"Elly's instincts are never wrong," Thomas said.

"Why don't you come into my room and we can talk?" Elly said, and the four of them reconvened in Elly's room.

"First off," Elly said, "you don't think she'd do anything crazy, do you, Roos?"

"She wouldn't harm herself deliberately, if that's what you mean."

"I take it you've searched the hotel?" Thomas said.

"All the usual spots," Ajax said. "She likes to hang out sometimes in the bowling alley."

"And outside?" Elly said.

"It's not like she could've gone far on foot. She does have an old bike she rides around the hotel when she wants some air, but it's not in the arcade, where she usually parks it."

"Okay, the bike is missing so she obviously went somewhere," Elly said. "We just need to think out of the box. Has she said anything suspicious lately?"

"Not really," Roos said. "She's been homesick, and I know how much she misses the Netherlands."

"Anything in particular?" Thomas said.

"The weather, the food, our parents..."

Elly nodded thoughtfully. "What about the flowers?"

"The flowers?" Ajax said.

"Yeah, she said that's why she dyed her hair so many colors. As a tribute to the tulips."

This seemed to spark a reaction in Roos.

"Now that I think about it, she did mention the tulips a few times the last couple weeks. But it seemed normal. Like most of us Dutch girls, she loves them."

"I don't guess there are any in Las Vegas?" Elly said.

"You could search the place in every direction and not find a single flower," Ajax said.

"Nothin' much grows here. Anythin' that tries gets flooded out."

Elly's expression changed, and Thomas could see the telltale sign she had an idea.

"What?" he said.

"Didn't Ivan say that the hotels were named after special places all over the world that were lost in the floods?"

"Yeah?" Ajax said.

"Is there one from the Netherlands?"

"I don't know," Ajax shrugged. "Maybe we should ask Ivan."

"We don't have to," Roos said. "There's an old hotel called the Keukenhof, named after the famous Gardens in Lisse. I wanted to check it out when we first got here but Greet thought it would bring back too many sad memories. It's supposed to have a great mural of the—"

Roos stopped short and shook her head with exasperation.

"The what?" Thomas, Elly, and Ajax said.

"Tulip fields."

✦✦

THOMAS DROVE ONE OF the complimentary cars belonging to the Odessa, while Ivan sat in the passenger seat and gave directions. Elly was in the backseat, between Ajax and Roos. The Keukenhof was in the old section of the city, stuck in a group of broken-down hotels that were built after the second superflood. They were part of the golden age of Las Vegas, according to Ivan, when most people thought the floods couldn't possibly continue. The streets themselves were decrepit and, despite the fact that the city was deserted, felt slightly dangerous.

"Here, Thomas," Ivan said. "Pull over."

Thomas stopped in front an unlit ten-story hotel. Its only distinguishing characteristic was the fact that the ground floor was double the width of the nine on top of it. The search party jumped out of the car and hurried toward the entrance.

They entered the darkened lobby and stopped to get their bearings. Roos shouted Greet's name, but it faded into the silence of the musty reception area.

Ivan brought his high-powered flashlight and scanned the reception desk toward the back wall, which was covered with a serpentine mural of thick stripes in every color.

"This is the one I was talking about," Roos said, as they walked closer, where they could see that the stripes were actually made up of flowers, like a rainbow. It curved toward the adjacent hallway as if directing the visitor to follow its path.

"The mural looks like it continues into the next hallway," Elly said.

They hurried toward the end of the wall, where it continued through a passageway, covering the elevators doors. Led by Ivan's flashlight, they entered a large circular room, where the floor-to-ceiling mural of the Keukenhof gardens swirled around them. Even in the low light, the fields of colored tulips sparkled with life.

"Greet?" Roos shouted. "Are you here?"

Again, there was nothing but silence.

They shuffled toward the middle of the room, and Roos turned her body in a circle to take it all in. But something caught her eye and she stopped.

"Ivan, can you put the light down there," she said, pointing to the area where the wall mural met the floor.

The flashlight revealed a border of white wood about two feet high that ran around the entire room. Roos went over and knelt down.

"It's filled with dirt," Roos said.

Elly came over to look. "It's a flower bed. With no flowers."

"They must've grown them when the hotel was still operational," Ivan said.

Roos scooped up a handful of soil. "It's damp." She stood up, and called out, "Greet?"

Still, there was no reply. She raised her voice slightly. "If you're here, I want you to know I didn't come to try and change you mind about leaving on the raft. I came to say goodbye."

A hush fell over the huge room for several moments, until the silence became almost unbearable. Finally, there was a creak in the wall, and a door-sized panel slowly opened. Greet emerged, framed by the tulips, as if she was standing in the legendary gardens themselves. She was holding a large object in her hand.

"I'm sorry to cause you such trouble, Roos. I'm sorry to all of you."

"No, Greet," Roos said. "I'm the one that should be sorry. I didn't understand just how bad things had gotten for you."

"You've had more important things on your mind."

"Nothing's more important than you. What have you been doing?"

"Taking care of the bulbs," Greet said, holding up her hand to reveal a watering can. "Most of them were dead from lack of water, of all things. I've been coming over the last few weeks, trying to bring them back to life. I've got four so far. I believe they wait for me."

"It's a wonderful thing you've been doing. Our parents would be very proud of you."

"You really think so?"

"Yes. They can rest in peace knowing the Jansen van Beek girls didn't give up when the world needed them the most. So whatever decision you make about going on the raft is good with me. You've done more than your share to help us prepare, isn't that right, Ajax?"

Ajax nodded. "We couldn't be doing it without you, Greet."

Greet put the empty watering can on the floor and sat on the edge of the wooden border, eyes cast downward in a mixture of sadness and shame.

"I'm just not as brave as you, Roos."

"You're certainly a lot smarter. And your hair looks much better."

Greet couldn't help but smile.

"Nobody's getting any medals for bravery around here," Ajax said. "Including me or Ivan. We're all afraid of what's coming."

"But even with all the danger, we have one thing on our side," Roos said.

Greet looked up.

"Each other."

Greet stood up slowly, walked toward her sister, and threw her arms around her. They stayed that way for a long minute. Finally, she released her and turned to Ajax.

"Is there still room for me on the raft?"

"Only if you bring your tulip buds," Roos said. "So we can watch them bloom together."

CHAPTER 20

By the time Thomas got into bed, it was almost four in the morning, though he couldn't sleep. At exactly five fifty-five, he watched the sun peek over the Spring Mountains. At the Doomsday Hotel, an orange glow lit up the big clock. Time was running out for him to get to Colorado. But he didn't want to wake Eno early and went to Elly's room first.

He found her in a deep sleep, so he only opened the curtains a little to let the morning creep into the room gradually.

Without opening her eyes, Elly pulled the big white robe she'd slept in around her face.

"Thomas?" she said with a muffled voice. "What time is it?"

"About six o'clock."

"Didn't we just go to bed?"

"Yeah, sorry about that."

"We helped Roos find her sister, right? I didn't dream that."

"Nope. But we have to get going."

Elly groaned. "I was having such a nice dream."

"You can tell me about it while you get ready."

Elly climbed out of bed and went into the bathroom, talking as she went. "You and me were shipwrecked on a desert island, and rescued by Ajax and the kids on their raft. We were so happy to be rescued, but even happier to see that they made it."

Thomas smiled. It was just like Elly to be happier about the fate of someone other than herself.

"You do think they'll make it, don't you?" Elly said.

"Yeah, I do," Thomas said. "But they're going to need some luck. Just like us."

“I don’t suppose there’s anything we can do to help them?”

Thomas thought about it for a moment.

“Now that you mention it, maybe there is one thing.”

Elly poked her head out of the door, smiling. “I knew you’d think of something.”

Thomas, Eno, and Elly arrived in the lobby to find Ajax and Duck having breakfast with Ivan at a buffet table filled with cereal, eggs, strawberries, melon, and orange juice.

“Mornin’, kids,” Ajax said. “Help yourself to breakfast. It’s the last of the real thing. From here on out, we’re on the frozen food and canned goods plan.”

“Care for some coffee?” Ivan said. “It’s my high-octane brew. There’s enough caffeine in it to get you to Colorado without blinking. We also have some of my signature tea, made from a mixture of orange, cinnamon, and cloves.”

“That sounds great,” Thomas said.

Ivan pushed a large glass pitcher toward Thomas. “I’ve also packed up enough provisions to get you to Colorado. Let me get them.”

Ivan headed into the kitchen as Elly and Eno went to the buffet table, leaving Thomas alone with Ajax. He poured himself a cup of tea and let the steam rise into his nostrils and over his eyes. “I could get used to this stuff.”

“Sure you don’t want to join us?” Ajax said. “Even with Greet’s tulip buibs, we have room for you three. After everything we’ve been through, you’re one of us now.”

“I wish we could, Ajax, but we have to move on. Thanks for your hospitality, not to mention your truck. We were honored to be invited to your party last night. I’ve never actually been to one, but I can’t imagine anything better.”

“The kids deserved a celebration. They’ve been workin’ nonstop for months, and between us…” Ajax lowered her voice. “I don’t know how long we can make it on the raft.”

“I’m no expert on boats, but it looks pretty well made to me.”

"Muirin and Thor saw to that. But sooner or later, we'll need to make repairs, restock the food supply, find terra firma. The Dutch girls tell me there'll only be a few mountain tops in the whole world where we can do that. And if we don't find one, it's pretty much the end of the line."

Thomas suddenly realized what Ajax was saying.

"Do the kids know that?"

"Sure, we've talked about it a lot. They've seen the floods up close, lost friends and family alike. If it all goes bad, they're prepared for the end. That's why we wanted those first aid kits. They have those deep sleep pills, and thanks to your help we finally got enough to go 'round."

"I hope it never comes to that."

"Me too. But it'd be a lot worse to starve, or for those megalodons to have us for lunch."

Elly and Eno returned from the buffet table with take-out containers of breakfast food as Thomas drained the last of his tea. Ivan was right behind them with large coolers in each hand.

"I brought you enough for breakfast, lunch, and dinner."

"Thanks, Ivan," Thomas said.

"You sure you don't want to sit down and have a relaxing breakfast?" he said.

"Afraid we have to hit the road to stay on schedule," Thomas said.

"We'll walk you out," Ajax said.

Their little procession went out the door to find Jack parked in front. Thor and Muirin were getting out of the back of the truck with some power tools and two large buckets.

"How'd it go?" Ajax shouted.

"It's as close as it can be to an amphibian vessel now," Muirin said.

Thomas looked at Ajax, somewhat puzzled.

"Muirin and Thor said if you hit any floodwater, that transport of yours would sink like a rock. So, I got them to work some of their nautical magic."

"We molded the front of your cable car with urethane foam, so it acts like the bow of a real boat, to lift you above the water line," Thor said. "While we were at it, we rigged you up with one of our back-up rudders, since you seemed to be missing one."

"We also filled in the cavities and bolted flotation pods around the sides," Muirin said. "They're not quite as strong as the ones on Jack, but they should do the trick. It may list a bit in a strong wind, but she won't sink. You've got yourselves an eight-ton cork."

"Amazing," Elly said.

"Quite," Eno added.

"It's the least we can do for fellow travelers," Ivan said.

He put the coolers in the back of the truck as Eno and Elly got into the cab.

Finally, Ajax handed Jack's keys to Thomas, then pulled a folded map from her pocket. "You'll be on sand for the first ten miles or so, then pick up what's left of Route 15, which'll take you to what's left of Route 70. The highways come and go, but Jack couldn't care less. He'll drive over just about anything. And remember, if you hit a flood, his flotation tubes will kick in automatically."

"Thanks, Ajax. I have something for you too." Thomas climbed into the back of the truck and grabbed his sleeping bag from the cable car. He jumped back down to the ground. "If you do happen across any of those megalodons we talked about, there's only one way to scare them off."

Thomas unrolled the bag to reveal the Sonic Inducer he carried on the Acqua Stella, tucked in its holster. He handed it to Ajax, along with the dozen new cartridges Matt had given him.

"A Sonic Inducer?"

"You know what it is?"

"I heard about 'em, but never saw one up close. Where'd you get it?"

"Actually my father gave it to me."

"That's mighty generous, Thomas. You sure you won't need it?"

"We're headed to the mountains," Thomas said, "so unless the Megs have learned to climb, we'll be fine. But you guys will be out on the open water."

"Hey, just havin' this thing on board will help us sleep at night. Right, Duck?"

Duck nodded as they all shook hands.

"Well, I guess this is it," Thomas said.

Duck whispered something to Ajax.

"Hey Thomas, one more thing." Ajax said. "Don't mean to alarm you, but when Duck was on the wall this morning, he saw some Chindi spinnin' in the wrong direction. He says it's a warnin,' maybe for us, maybe for you, maybe for all of us. He thought you should know."

"Thanks, Duck," Thomas said, and shook the boy's hand. When he was finished, Duck didn't let it go, and pulled himself toward Thomas's ear as if he had a secret of his own to share.

"We meet again."

"I sure hope so, Duck."

"No. We meet for sure. Shoshone time doesn't travel straight, like an arrow. The arrow of *time* bends in a great circle. And when it comes around, we meet."

Something about the way Duck said this gave Thomas a chill.

"Then I'll see you when it does, Duck. I look forward to it."

Duck released Thomas's hand and stepped back into the shelter of Ajax's arm, which circled his small shoulder.

Thomas climbed into the driver's seat and addressed the truck.

"Okay, Jack, take us to Colorado."

The truck started and pulled toward the front gate as Eno disappeared in the back seat, preparing to go back to sleep. Thomas and Elly glanced in the rearview mirror to see Ajax and Duck, along with Ivan, Muirin, Thor, Sardinia, Zeffi, Pooja, Al-Jabr, and Momoko. Roos and Greet ran out of the hotel at the last minute and joined the pack, now huddled so tightly together they seemed like a single organism. Their arms flew into the air with a farewell wave as if lifted by a sudden gust of wind. Thomas felt a surge of hope that Duck was right, and they'd meet again.

As Jack made its way down the road, Thomas couldn't keep his eyes off the Survivor raft, sitting on top of the Odessa hotel. It soon took on the appearance of an ornament, with its tiny blue flag flying in the wind. But as much as he tried to hold on to the image, it soon disappeared entirely, a mirage in the desert heat.

CHAPTER 21

Two hours later, Thomas drove across the state line from Nevada into Utah and entered an endless field of debris. A town of small homes sat on their sides, rotting in the sun, in a sea of sand. The only sound was the whoosh of Jack slipping through the still air at eighty miles an hour.

"You know," Elly started, "I've been thinking…"

"Should I tighten my seatbelt?" Eno said, still lying unseen in the back.

"Something weird just occurred to me. We're going in different directions, time wise."

"Why exactly is that weird?" Eno said.

"Well, I've been living on Earth in 2023 and you guys traveled from Mars in 2086. We're now on the road in 2070, which for me is the future, but for you it's the past."

"And your point is?" Eno said.

"Don't you see? We're going backward and forward at the same time. That must be some kind of paradox, right?"

Thomas flashed back to his conversation with Ignatius at the Mount, about Elly's spells being caused by her living in her past. "You're right, Elly."

"So, if it's a genuine paradox it probably has a name," Elly said.

"Maybe not," Thomas said. "Because of the time travel element, we're probably the first people to do it."

"If that's true, and I think it is, then we have the right to name it," Elly said.

"The very last thing time travel needs is another paradox," Eno said. "But if it makes you feel better, go right ahead."

"What about 'the destination paradox'?" Thomas said.

"Or 'the destiny paradox,'" Elly said.

Eno popped into view from the back seat. "The problem is, it makes no difference which direction we're coming from as long as we're going to the same place. May I suggest 'the pointless paradox.'"

"Hmnn," Elly said. "I like that."

Thomas nodded. "Me too."

Eno laid back down, satisfied he'd resolved the issue.

"Yet another example of the pointless paradox," Elly said, imitating the tone of a teacher.

"The pointless paradox strikes again," Thomas said, imitating his professor back on Mars.

Elly startled laughing, triggering Thomas to do the same. For the next twenty minutes, they continued coming up with examples of how to use the phrase 'pointless paradox,' each time breaking out in spasms of laughter. Finally, they settled into an exhausted silence.

A few minutes after that, Thomas looked around the cabin to see that both Eno and Elly were sitting up, tilted against their respective windows, napping. The cab was bathed in sunlight, which seemed to make it even more quiet. Even though they'd only been been gone from Las Vegas for a couple hours, Thomas already missed the Survivor kids and their enthusiastic spirits. He had to admit, some part of him wished he could experience the thrill of being on the raft when it was lifted off the hotel roof to begin their incredible adventure. He wished he could've spent a few more days with them, maybe even getting Duck to teach him how to shoot a bow and arrow.

Thinking about Duck made him wonder about the boy's prediction that they'd see each other again. But given the fact that they were time travelling while the Survivor raft was making its journey in real time, it was highly unlikely.

The thought was suddenly interrupted by a strange sight a mile or so ahead of him. A large object was curled across the highway like a mechanical snake.

He leaned over to Elly, who had just opened her eyes. "Can you tell what that is up ahead?"

Elly checked her binoculars. "It looks like a train."

"Really?" Thomas said, unable to hide his excitement.

"Make that a train*wreck*," she said, putting down the binoculars.

Thomas slowed as they approached the sleek white locomotive, which was tilted to one side, barely upright. The passenger cars were each tilted slightly more, making it look like the train had been twisted from end to end by some strange force.

"It's a Triple Bullet," Thomas said.

"How do you know that?" Elly asked.

"I told you, he's obsessed with trains," Eno said, waking up.

"I read about them in the Information Archives," Thomas said. "The Triple B's could go three times the speed of the original. They started making them in 2038."

"Wow," Elly said.

Thomas sat up. "Would anyone mind if we stopped and took a look?"

"I don't see why not," Elly said. "I wouldn't mind seeing it myself."

Eno tapped his wrist pod. "Three hours and forty-eight minutes to Colorado."

Thomas glanced at Eno in the rearview, mindful of his promise to get there without any unnecessary stops. "On second thought," Thomas said, "we should probably keep moving."

Without waiting for Elly to object, Thomas drove around the train.

A half hour later, they reached the junction to Route 70 and turned toward Colorado. From that point on, the highway was more or less intact as far as they could see. Thomas had just finished his second cup of Ivan's tea from the thermos he prepared, when they passed a freshly painted billboard. It was all black, with a single orange word: THIS.

"This what?" Eno asked.

Elly shrugged. "Your guess. Probably an advertisement of some sort."

About twenty minutes later, they saw a second billboard, with the word IS, and after another twenty minutes, a third, with the word YOUR.

Eno glanced at his wrist pod. "The billboards are spaced exactly twenty-three miles apart. I wonder whether there's some significance to that?"

"I guess we'll know in another twenty-three minutes," Elly said. "What do you say we eat lunch in the meantime?"

"Do we have to stop?" Eno said.

"No," Thomas said. "I can put Jack on automatic so we can keep going."

As Thomas gave Jack instructions, Elly served lunch from one of the coolers, passing around cold pizza and red velvet cake from the previous night's dinner. They'd just about finished eating when they passed a fourth billboard, with the word LAST.

"This is your last?" Eno said. "I have to say, that's a bit unsettling."

"Probably the last rest stop," Elly said. "But under the circumstances, it is kind of creepy."

Thomas drained the remainder of his tea. "How much farther to Colorado, Eno?"

"Ninety-one miles to the border. And nineteen miles to our next billboard."

They drove on in silence. Fourteen minutes later, they saw the fifth and final billboard. The word was no longer in orange, but electric blue. It read: CHANCE.

"This is our last chance?" Eno said. "For what?"

"A bathroom, I'm hoping," Elly said.

In the distance, a tower of some sort jutted out from the flat landscape.

"What's that up ahead?" Thomas asked.

Elly checked Ajax's map for the location.

"I don't know. I can see some buildings. Maybe a small town."

As they drove closer, they could see that the "town" was merely a compound made of low wooden structures, some without roofs or windows. A sign appeared, faded from the sun and floodwater. Several of the letters were impossible to read, but Elly sounded out the words as best she could.

"U…Laun…plex. Whit…and…sil."

"That makes no sense," Eno said.

Thomas slowed the truck to a crawl as Elly got out her binoculars.

"Okay I can see most of the letters now. It says…Utah Launch Complex of…the White Sands Missile Project. Wow. That big wooden tower must've been built to hold missiles. This is where we tested them during the Cold War."

"What's a cold war?" Eno said.

"A war without the physical warfare part. We were in one with the Russians, years ago."

Thomas drove toward the tower, which was built with vertical planks over a thick slab of concrete. But up close, they could see that the wood didn't have the weathered look of the surrounding buildings.

"It looks new," Eno said. "Which doesn't make sense if it was built to test missiles a century ago."

"You're right," Thomas said. "I think it was built for something else."

"Like what?" Elly asked.

"Look," Thomas said, pointing to a large trailer that was sitting at the end of the property. It was several times longer than the truck, and practically new. Its steel frame glistened in the sun, with no sign of rust.

"Three guesses what was on that trailer," Thomas said.

Eno and Elly had no idea.

"One of our shuttles," Thomas said.

"The one that brought you to Mars?" Elly asked.

"No. The one I was on launched from a pad in the Colorado mountains."

"This one was the next-to-last shuttle to leave Earth," Eno said. "Shuttle 94."

"How do you know?" Elly asked.

"I have a list of them."

"You do?" Thomas said, slightly surprised.

Eno nodded. "It was in my background package on the final days of Earth."

He scrolled through his wrist pod. "Here it is. Shuttle 94. It was the only one launched in the state of Utah, on November 28."

"That was over a month ago," Thomas said. "I wonder if they left behind any information about the Science Alliance that could be helpful."

"Let's check it out," Elly said. "We have to stop anyway."

"Why?" Eno asked.

"I don't know what kind of bladders you have on Mars, but ours only last about six hours."

"I wouldn't mind stretching my legs," Thomas said, pulling over.

Elly jumped out and hurried toward the wooden buildings.

"I suppose I should avail myself of the bathroom as well," Eno said.

While Eno followed Elly, Thomas used her binoculars to check out the mountains. He felt a ripple of excitement knowing that in a matter of hours, he'd be nearing his birthplace. Even if they weren't able to locate Elly's mother or spot the Biosphere, they could at least explore the area and maybe even see the lake from Ignatius's photos. If landing on Earth was phase one of his mission, reaching Colorado would be the beginning of phase two.

For the first time since they left England, he felt that he was making real progress.

But the feeling was abruptly broken by a muffled scream.

He turned around and shouted. "Elly? Eno?"

They didn't answer.

Thomas turned and sprinted past the shuttle tower toward the nearest building. The interior was empty, except for a pair of broken couches. He continued down a hall lined with small offices, littered with paper files, broken lamps, and overturned furniture. There was no exit at the end of the hall, and he hurried back toward the entrance. He froze when he saw a man sitting on the couch, his hands calmly folded across his lap. His hair was silver white and touched his shoulders, along with a short beard. Both had a greasy sheen, as if he hadn't bathed in days. Despite the heat, he wore a long gown. It was the same color of electric blue as the word on the last billboard.

"Looking for something?" the man said, in a strangely disembodied voice.

"My friends are here somewhere. We stopped to find a bathroom."

"But I know why you're really here."

"What do you mean?"

The man smiled, as if he knew everything and had no reason to explain. "They call me Silver Man. Who are you?"

"I'm Thomas."

"Not a doubting Thomas, I hope? Because you're among the faithful here."

"Have you seen my friends?"

"I have. Come, I'll show you."

Silver Man stood up and led Thomas outside. He pointed toward a nearby structure.

"Your friends are inside."

Thomas couldn't help feeling that he was being led into some sort of trap, but he had no choice in the matter. As Silver Man watched, he entered the building. Inside, the walls were lined with folding chairs, occupied by thirty or so adults of all ages. They were wearing robes identical to Silver Man's, though none in the same vibrant shade of blue. Sitting on the far wall were Eno and Elly. It was clear by the expression on their faces that they were being held captive.

Silver Man appeared at the doorway, along with two large men who blocked the entrance. "Are these your friends?"

"Yes," Thomas said. "And we have to leave now."

"We've already tried," Elly said. "They won't let us."

"You can at least tell us why you're keeping us here," Thomas said.

Silver Man held out his open palms. "All will be explained in due time. The only thing you need to know is that you're one of us now."

CHAPTER 22

The adults followed Silver Man out the door, leaving Thomas, Eno, and Elly behind. When the last person was gone, the men at the door locked it. There were no windows in the room, and nowhere to avoid the sun that leaked through the broken roof, filling the space with unescapable heat.

Elly sighed. "I'm sorry, guys."

"For what?" Thomas said.

"If I hadn't made us stop…"

"It's not your fault," Thomas said.

"I agree," Eno said. "Who could have imagined something like this would happen?"

"Who are these people anyway?" Thomas asked.

"I think I have an idea," Elly said. "You remember when Ajax told us that Sardinia escaped from some cult out in the desert? This is probably them."

"What do you think they want with us?" Thomas asked.

"I don't know," Elly said. "But it can't be good."

"I guess we'll know sooner or later," Thomas said.

Eno checked his wrist pod. "It can't be too much later. We're supposed to be in Colorado in two hours, which would leave us the rest of the day until—"

"Right," Thomas said, not wanting Eno to slip into the subject of his being timeblown. "We've got to get out of here as soon as possible."

"Any idea how?" Elly asked.

"No," Thomas said, "but I think our best shot is to wait for it to get dark."

✦✦

An hour later, the sun began to disappear behind the mountains. Thomas, sweat beading on his forehead from the heat, stacked several of the folding chairs against the wall, then climbed up to look outside.

"Can you see anything?" Eno asked.

"Just Silver Man," Thomas said. "He's standing at the top of the shuttle tower."

"What's he doing?" Elly asked.

"Just looking up at the sky."

Suddenly they heard the door being unlocked. Thomas jumped down as it opened. The two men guarding the room parted to allow a middle-aged woman with white hair to enter. She held a tray with a pitcher of water and three glasses. "You must be thirsty," she said.

"We are," Elly said, wiping her forehead with the back of her hand.

The woman poured them each a glass of water.

Elly took one but hesitated. "How do I know you didn't put something in it? To drug us?"

"The water is pure. We don't believe in consuming anything unnatural, particularly now, as we prepare ourselves."

"Prepare for what?" Thomas asked.

The woman didn't answer. "Drink up. I'm not allowed to leave the glasses."

Thomas took a small sip. "Can I ask what we're doing here?"

"It's not my place to explain. Silver Man will do that."

"Can you at least tell us your name?" Elly asked.

"I am Alcyone, one of the seven sisters."

"Daughter of Atlas and Pleione?" Elly said.

The woman looked at Elly, surprised. "You know the Greek gods?"

"A little. People call me Elly, but my birth name is Elpis."

"Spirit of Hope."

"Yes," Elly said. "And I was *hoping* me and my friends could get to Colorado by tonight. We're on a very important mission."

"I wish I could help you, child, but we have a mission of our own."

She glanced back at the door, where the two guards were in the hallway talking.

"Alcyone, did you by any chance know a girl named Sardinia?"

Alcyone didn't respond, but her eyes betrayed her.

"She was here, wasn't she? Did you help her escape?"

Alcyone lowered her voice to a whisper.

"As adults, we've chosen our destiny. Children have no choice."

"Can you help us?"

"Finish your water now."

Thomas, Eno, and Elly drained their glasses and put them on the tray. Alcyone glanced at the guards, who were still talking to each other. She slipped a folded cloth napkin from her gown and pressed it into Elly's hand, then hurried out of the room. The door closed and locked behind her.

Elly unfolded the napkin to reveal a small pair of bolt cutters.

"I think she just gave us our ticket out of here," Elly said.

She folded the napkin over the bolt cutter and slid it into her pocket.

As she did, the door opened, and the two guards entered.

"Silver Man wishes to see you."

✦✦

THE MEN LED THEM outside. It was only minutes past dusk, and a faint purple light bathed the desert. They walked toward the shuttle tower, where two more men guarded the entrance. They were ushered into the tower, where Silver Man sat on the concrete slab floor. A strip of sunlight flared across his eyes, giving him an even stranger appearance.

"Welcome, my little stars," he said. "You've been summoned here by a higher power."

"To be your captives?" Thomas said defiantly.

"Nothing could be further from the truth. Unconsciously, you came here of your own volition because you're meant to be here."

"Actually, we're meant to be someplace else," Thomas said. "And we're really late."

"This is the most important place on your planet right now."

"Why?" Elly asked. "We have a right to know what this is all about."

"We are Pleiadians, children of the star cluster Taurus."

Elly glanced at Thomas and Eno and widened her eyes.

"So, you're…aliens?" Elly said.

"The Pleiades gave birth to humans with solar DNA, so we're of both worlds. The last of the pure humans abandoned Earth weeks ago from this very site. Your arrival proves you're Pleiadian children, like us, summoned for the final journey. My calling is to deliver you home."

"Home?" Eno said.

Silver Man looked to the top of the shuttle tower, where a small platform had been constructed along with several spotlights. Above it, stars began to appear in the night sky.

"To the heart of the Milky Way. The humans think it's merely a black hole. But we know it as our galactic heaven."

Elly glanced at Thomas and Eno. "That's what they're *preparing* for."

"But you have no transport," Eno said, glancing up at the empty tower.

"The cosmos itself is our transport. There will be an awakening of the Galaxy's Nucleus. A thousand bolts of light will signal us when the time has come, and the force of its energy will deliver us. You can feel it in the air. It will happen tonight."

"And if we refuse to go along?" Thomas asked.

"You have no choice. It is the will of the cosmos."

Silver Man nodded to the men standing behind them. The largest grabbed Thomas around the chest, pinning his arms.

"Hey, what are you doing?" Elly shouted as two others grabbed her and Eno, while a third snapped thick metal bracelets on their wrists. On the outside of each bracelet was a circular clasp about two inches wide.

Silver Man smiled. "You will thank me in paradise."

✦✦

THOMAS, ENO, AND ELLY were taken to a structure at the farthest end of the property. They sat in the dark, the only light coming from the boys' wrist pods. After a few minutes, the adults began to arrive. They ignored their new guests, talking quietly among themselves in small groups.

Elly watched Alcyone enter, but she refused to make eye contact. Thomas gestured for Eno and Elly to follow him to the back of the room, as far from the others as possible, where there was a gaping crack in one of the walls.

"Eno, look outside," Thomas whispered.

"What for?"

"Jack."

"The truck?"

"On the walk from the tower, I triangulated the distance to be about six hundred steps away. I figured you might be able to see it with the night vision in your new replacement eye."

Eno slid behind Thomas and peeked outside. "It's still where we parked it."

"Good," Thomas said.

"Are you thinking we make a run for it?" Elly asked.

"It's too far," Thomas said. "We'd never get there without being caught."

"Well the truck can't come to us," Eno said.

"Actually, it can," Thomas said. "I've still got the keys, so I can use the remote to start the ignition. If I can get close enough, I can voice command Jack the rest of the way."

In the distance, the faint rumble of thunder sounded. They turned to see that the adults were lining up, single file, at the door.

Alcyone stepped out of line and approached them. "It's time," she said, ushering them into the back of the line.

Thomas went first, followed by Eno and Elly. The line moved slowly, as each adult paused at the door before moving into the hallway. Something was happening, but Thomas couldn't see what. Finally, he reached the doorway where one of the guards held a roll of thin steel cable, which he'd attached to everyone who passed. He grabbed Thomas's wrist and threaded the cable through the ring on his cuff. Thomas glanced at Eno and Elly as the cable was attached to them. When they finished with Alcyone, the guards attached it to their own wrists.

Outside, Thomas could see that they were headed toward the shuttle tower. He counted the steps, trying to confirm the distance to the truck. It was two hundred and twelve steps, exactly the same number he'd counted on the way from the tower. That left another three hundred and sixty to the truck, making a total of five hundred and seventy-two.

When they reached the tower, the group formed a huge circle around its perimeter and watched solemnly as Silver Man ascended the tower platform. When he reached the top, he held out his hands and gestured for the Pleiadians to sit. In unison, they dropped to the ground, as the cable that held them together dragged Thomas, Eno, and Elly down as well.

Silver Man raised a battery-operated bullhorn to his mouth. "Welcome, children. This is the night you return to the place of your birth. Turn your eyes upon the great star cluster of Taurus."

The adults looked up to the seven stars of the constellation as Elly used the distraction to slide her free hand into her pocket for the bolt cutters Alcyone had given her.

A single slash of lightning flashed in the sky.

"Behold! Taurus speaks!"

A cheer went up from the Pleiadians as a second flash lit up the sky, followed in short order by several more. With each spasm of lightning, the sky became a frenzy of sound and light.

"Whoa," Elly said. "This looks like the kind of lightning storm Ajax was talking about in Las Vegas. She said it was like an alien attack, remember?"

Thomas nodded as a roar of thunder passed over the tower, and a light rain began to fall.

Silver Man adressed the sky. "We await you, Pleiades. Come to us!"

The Pleiadians repeated his words, chanting them like a prayer, as the rain became stronger and stronger, quickly turning into a torrent.

Eno leaned over to Thomas. "What do they think is going to happen?"

"I'm not sure. But hopefully we'll be out of here before it does."

Elly glanced at Alcyone, who shifted her body toward the two guards and began talking.

Elly could tell she was distracting them and slid the bolt cutters out of her pocket as Thomas did the same with Jack's remote. In the distance, the truck's headlights popped into view, but between the constant barrage of lightning, no one seemed to notice. A gust of wind suddenly hit the tower, rattling the wooden planks and nearly throwing Silver Man off the platform. As he tried to steady himself, the bullhorn dropped over the side, leaving him voiceless, shouting silently into the night. The rain began to fall so strong that the Pleiadians were forced to lower their heads. As the wind grew stronger, Silver Man dropped to his knees and held onto the platform.

Thomas nodded to Elly, who applied the bolt cutters to the cable and snapped it off. Eno pulled the end through his cuff, then passed the cable to Thomas, who did the same.

They were suddenly free.

Several lightning bolts joined together in a braid of electricity directly in front of the tower as the wind howled like a burst of anger. Thomas used the noise as cover to trigger Jack's remote, starting the ignition. On that, the three of them jumped to their feet and ran, unnoticed by the children of Taurus, who had all they could to protect themselves from the storm.

They barely got out from beneath the tower when a lightning bolt made a direct hit on the structure, starting a small fire on the platform. As Silver Man tried to avoid the flames, several burning planks broke off, sending airborne torches spiralling onto the crowd. They tried to run but were held back by the cable that still bound them together. In the screaming commotion, Thomas, Eno, and Elly ran through the deep mud, and Thomas shouted into the rain.

"Jack! Over here!"

For a moment nothing happened. But then the big truck kicked into gear and began to move. Thomas sprinted ahead of Eno and Elly, toward the driver's side of the truck. With a perfectly timed leap, he opened the door and swung himself into the driver's seat as a bolt of lightning landed on the cab roof. Thomas instinctively ducked, then remembered Ajax telling him that Jack was lightning proof. He closed the door and swung around to pick up Eno and Elly, who jumped into the back. But as Thomas tried to pull out, the truck only managed a few more feet before sliding to a stop in the thickening mud.

Thomas pumped the accelerator to no avail. A larger bolt of lightning crackled behind them and they turned to see that it hit the middle of the tower, nearly cleaving it in half. The fire quickly devoured the wood, leaving the top of the tower without support, and it began to sway, threatening to topple directly on top of them.

"Hurry, Thomas!" Elly said.

Unable to get the truck to move forward, Thomas put it in reverse. The twelve big tires squealed, sending mud flying in every direction, as the middle of the tower began to disintegrate. Thomas put the truck back in drive, and the shift finally provided enough traction to move. Behind them, the tower slowly began to tilt and as they drove out, it fell down in flames.

Thomas steered them onto the main road, where Jack gripped the hard asphalt and quickly picked up speed. Eno and Elly flopped against the seat, dripping water and mud.

In the rearview mirror, they could see the tower fire jump to the rest of the compound, quickly consuming the entire property. The crowd, free of the cable that bound them, ran in every direction as the inferno filled the mirror with flames.

Elly shook her head in amazement. "Now that's what you call a bonfire."

CHAPTER 23

As they drove, the fire that engulfed the Launch Complex shriveled to the size of a candle then finally went dark. Eno anxiously checked his wrist pod at regular intervals. Twenty-eight minutes and forty-one miles later, they crossed the Utah border into Colorado, where the storm disappeared in favor of a clear, starry night.

Elly leaned over to Thomas. "Can I borrow your laser?"

Thomas reached into his backpack and handed her his Tetrascope.

Elly turned it on and used it to cut through the clasp that held her metal wrist cuff together. It flopped open, and she tossed it out the window.

"Anybody else?"

Thomas held out his arm. Elly cut off his cuff, then did the same for Eno.

"What time is it?" Thomas asked.

"Almost midnight," Elly said. "How much farther do we need to go?"

"One hundred seventy-nine miles to Grand Junction," Eno said. "Then another thirty-four to the base of the mountain. After that it's anybody's guess."

"That's almost three hours," Elly said. "We won't get to the Rockies until the middle of the night. Think you can make it, Thomas?"

"Yeah. If I get sleepy, I can always put Jack on autopilot and take a break before heading into the mountains."

"Well," Eno said, "at least we've left the disastrous weather behind."

A muffled boom echoed from somewhere behind them.

"Was that thunder?" Elly asked.

"It sounded like an explosion," Eno said. "Perhaps something at the Launch Complex blew up. If they used to launch missiles on site, there were probably combustible chemicals on the property."

"After a hundred years?" Elly said.

Eno didn't respond and Elly stayed silent.

"So, nobody's thinking what I'm thinking?" Thomas said.

Elly sighed. "That it was the sound of Greet's cosmic waterfall coming over the mountains behind Vegas? No, nobody's thinking that."

"Even it if were," Eno said, "we're now four thousand feet above sea level. It would be unlikely to climb to our current elevation."

"Right," Elly added, "It would also be hundreds of miles behind us, traveling a lot slower than us. Hopefully we'll be long gone before it ever catches up."

Thomas had his doubts. It was one thing to evade the FBI or even the Mastership, but another thing to be chased by a force of nature. But there was nothing he could do about it now other than continue to a higher elevation and hope for the best.

"Hey," he said, nodding to a road sign in the distance, "at least we're in Colorado."

✦✦

IN ANOTHER TWO HOURS the Rocky Mountains came into view, and shortly afterward they spotted the town of Grand Junction. Thomas was forced to make several detours around disabled roads to reach the abandoned town center, pushing their arrival back another hour. When they pulled into the empty parking lot in front of a deserted cluster of small shops, it was 3:26 in the morning.

Thomas stretched and Elly yawned.

Eno, who had crawled into the rear seat and fallen asleep, lifted his head. "We're here?"

Elly nodded. "Time to get some serious shut eye."

"How long do we have?" Thomas asked.

Eno checked his wrist pod. "We lost five hours to the Pleiadians, so we need to time jump no later than sundown, which is fifteen hours from now. If we awake at sunrise, that would give us about ten hours of daylight to accomplish whatever it is Thomas hopes to accomplish."

"What exactly is that, by the way?" Elly asked.

Thomas and Eno shared a quick look.

"I'll let Thomas explain," Eno said.

Thomas knew he had to come up with a sensible plan or Elly might get suspicious. "I'd like to find the site of the Biosphere so we could at least map a potential route."

"Won't that be tricky? Elly said, "since it doesn't get built for another few months?"

"I'm not exactly sure when it was built, but the shuttle site should already be here, along with the Science Alliance. And since we might get back when everybody's evacuated and everything's covered in snow, any landmarks we could locate would be helpful."

"Good point," Elly said. "You'd think the shuttle site would be hard to miss."

"I can check my father's map in the morning. But right now we need to get some sleep. Let's set our alarms for sunrise."

"Why don't we bunk in the cable car?" Elly suggested. "It's much more comfortable."

"Somebody should stay at the wheel," Thomas said. "Just in case."

"In case of what?" Elly asked. "We've already run into cannibalistic cowboys and half-aliens from Taurus, so what could possibly be left?"

"You never know on this bizarre planet," Eno said.

"I don't mind sleeping in the truck, really," Thomas said.

"Elly can have the cable car," Eno said. "It's much safer, and I'm sure she'd prefer the privacy."

Thomas opened the door. "I'll get our sleeping bags, Eno."

Thomas and Elly got out and went to the back of the truck.

Elly inhaled through her nose. "Mmmm. Smell those Evergreens. That's one thing the floods couldn't destroy."

They climbed into the back of the truck and into the cable car.

"Feels like we haven't been here in weeks," Elly said, patting the cabin affectionately.

"Good to see our old friend," Thomas said.

"Don't let Jack hear you. He might get jealous."

Thomas pulled out the duffel with the sleeping bags. "You sure you'll be all right out here by yourself?"

"I'll be inside a cable car, which is inside a truck. A grizzly bear couldn't get to me."

"See you in a few hours then."

Thomas jumped off the back of the truck.

"Hey, Thomas?"

"Yeah?"

"Is it my imagination, or is Eno being especially nice to me lately?"

"What do you mean?" Thomas said, feigning ignorance.

"He went out of his way not to blame me for stopping at the Launch Complex, which was totally my fault. And when has he ever been concerned about my safety, let alone privacy?"

"Uh…"

"Never, that's when. He's starting to treat me like I actually belong on the mission."

"Maybe he's finally getting used to it," Thomas said, anxious to change the subject. "Hey, be sure and let me know if you spot a grizzly. I'd give anything to see one up close."

"Oh, you'll know," Elly said. "I promise."

Thomas closed the door and returned to the cab. Eno unzipped his sleeping bag and got inside. Thomas lay on top of his, using it as a mattress.

"Are you sure Elly's going to be all right back there?" Eno asked.

"She'll be fine. But maybe you shouldn't act so concerned in front of her."

"Why?"

"She noticed you've been treating her much better. What's up?"

"After you reminded me that we share some of Ignatius's DNA, I did a little computing and determined it was nearly thirty-six percent. I don't think I need to tell you of all people how jarring it is to realize you're related to someone by blood, that you have a—what's the word?"

"Sister?"

"Yes. But the facts are the facts, and I have no choice but to act upon them."

"Let me get this straight. You're treating Elly nicer because you share thirty-six percent of your DNA?"

"Well, I'm only treating her thirty-six percent nicer."

Thomas saw the hint of a smile on Eno's face. "Eno, you made a joke!"

Eno shrugged modestly."I suppose I did. Goodnight, then."

✦✦

THE ALARM ON THOMAS's wrist pod buzzed at 6:30. He opened his eyes, but the windows of the truck were so fogged he couldn't see outside.

"Morning, Jack. Please roll down the window on the driver's side."

The window came down, revealing a glorious view of the mountains, the sun sitting at the very top, as if waiting for Thomas before rising farther. The sky was crystal blue with brilliant white clouds and green-brown mountains. Crayon colors, he instantly thought. It brought back the memory of the moment he got out of the time shuttle in Muir Woods and saw the Earth in all its vivid glory for the first time. And in a way he couldn't explain, the sense was even more overpowering this time. Perhaps it was not simply the beauty of the landscape, but some basic connection to his birthplace.

He got out of the truck and took a deep breath of mountain air. If anything, the smell of evergreens was even stronger than the night before.

A voice echoed from above. "Breathtaking, huh?"

Thomas looked up to see Elly sitting on top of the truck cross-legged, her sleeping bag wrapped around her shoulders, binoculars in hand.

"It's so incredible, it doesn't seem real," Thomas said.

"It's not, in a way."

"What do you mean?"

"It's the end of December and there's no snow on the mountains. They should be covered in the stuff by now. It looks more like what they used to call Indian summer."

A knock came from inside the truck cab and they turned to see Eno's face in the rear window, wiping away the fog. "What's the plan?" he said in a muffled voice.

"We should get moving," Thomas shouted.

"Shouldn't we eat something first?" Elly said.

"Any ideas?" Thomas said.

"I'd kill for a donut right now," Elly said.

"A donut?"

"Thick circle of cooked dough. My secret obsession."

"I had one on the ferry the day we arrived," Thomas said. "But where would we get some?"

"Over there," Elly said, pointing to the cluster of stores across the parking lot. Most were boarded up, but one was adorned with a three foot plastic donut that still dangled from above. The bottom half was broken off, which made it look like a giant bite had been taken out of it. "I spotted it with the binocs. It's probably empty but can't hurt to check it out."

"Let's go," Thomas said.

Thomas, Eno, and Elly walked across the parking lot to the shop.

Elly tried the front door to find it unlocked. They entered to see the tables and chairs sitting in a huge pile-up in the back, no doubt courtesy of the floods. But the refrigerator case that held the donuts was propped up on a wooden pallet to protect it from flooding.

Elly put her hand on the outside. "We're in luck. It's still cold."

Eno pointed toward the back of the freezer, where an electrical cord ran into the hallway. "It must be connected to a power source somewhere."

Thomas went into the hallway and wheeled out a portable generator. "Looks like somebody plugged it in after the last flood."

"Maybe somebody from the Science Alliance," Thomas said hopefully.

"Whoever it was sure had their priorities right," Elly said.

She lifted the case and pulled out a donut. "Wow, these are still fresh. I don't think they'd mind if we bought a few. What's your pleasure?"

"I've only ever had one kind," Thomas said.

"And that was your basic plain," Elly said. "Good place to start, but the bottom of the donut chain. It looks like we've hit the jackpot here. Glazed, chocolate, cinnamon, sprinkles, jelly-filled, and my personal favorite: powdered sugar. Why don't we take a half-dozen mixed."

"Sounds good," Thomas said.

Elly pulled out a twenty-dollar bill, left over from her casino winnings, and left it on the counter. She grabbed a box and carefully began to fill it. "Now if we could just make some coffee."

Eno looked puzzled. "Why can't we use the generator for that?"

"Gotta hand it to you, Eno," Elly said. "Always thinking."

Back at the truck, Elly cut the donuts in half and passed them around as Eno poured the coffee that she made into some paper cups he found near the machine.

They sat at the small five-seat counter as Thomas studied his father's map. "According to this, we're in the town center at an elevation of fifty-three hundred feet. We need to get to the junction of Route 29, about three miles north, which will take us up to the shuttle pad. It's at the base of a *sky* area," Thomas said, hesitating over the pronunciation of the unfamiliar word.

Elly leaned over the map. "Actually, it's pronounced *ski.*"

"What's that?" Eno asked.

"It's a recreational activity, where you put two narrow boards on your feet and slide down a snow-covered mountain."

"How bizarre," Eno said. "What happens when you reach the bottom?"

"You go back up and do it again."

"Doesn't that get boring?"

"Not at all. It's actually very—"

"Elly, Eno?" Thomas interrupted. "Maybe you could talk about this later. It looks like we have a ways to go."

"Yessir," Elly said, pretending to zipper her mouth.

"According to this map," Thomas said, "there's only one little road that goes up to the town, and it cuts back and forth over the mountain."

"They're called switchbacks," Elly said. "Roads cut into the mountain to make the ascent less steep. The downside, no pun intended, is that you have to drive really slow, because if you happen to go over the side, it's a long way—"

Elly abruptly stopped talking and put a finger in the air.

"You hear that?"

"The rumble," Thomas said. "It's like the one we heard last night."

"That's definitely not thunder," Elly said.

Thomas threw open the door and the noise, louder now, continued. He glanced at Elly.

"I'll grab the donuts," she said. "Let's go!"

They ran for the truck, and while Elly found her binoculars, Thomas jumped on the roof. She handed them up to him. He gave quick look, then stopped.

"No need for these," Thomas shouted. "You can see it coming."

"See what?" Eno said.

"The flood."

Eno and Elly joined Thomas on the roof. On the horizon, they could make out what seemed to be a wall of muddy brown water.

"How far away do you think it is?" Thomas asked.

Elly shook head. "Hard to say. Ten miles, maybe less?"

"The more critical question is whether it has enough acceleration to reach this elevation," Eno said.

"Let's not wait around to find out," Thomas said.

He hopped down and jumped into the driver's seat of the truck as Eno and Elly scrambled into the rear, with Elly behind Thomas. They pulled out of town onto a small two-lane road, some of which had already washed away in the last flood. Huge chunks of asphalt were missing, creating potholes the size of small craters. While Jack was able to navigate them safely, Eno and Elly had to hold on to keep from hitting the ceiling or slamming into each other.

They kept their eyes on the water as it reached the beginning of the mountain's incline, sloshing against it in a jumble of foam. But after a few seconds, it began to charge upward.

"How we doing back there?" Thomas asked.

"Not good," Elly said. "It's chasing us."

Thomas pushed Jack to his top speed, and they began to bounce wildly over the potholes. Eno and Elly held onto the stabilizing bars in the back of the cab while Thomas gripped the steering wheel with all his strength. In the background, they could see the flood hit the town center, instantly transforming it into a watery stew of homes, cars, and utility poles.

"Looks like we liberated those donuts none too soon," Elly said.

"We're only a couple miles from the junction," Thomas said. "Once we make the turn up the mountain, maybe we can outrun it."

A sign for the junction appeared ahead, but they could suddenly hear the sound of trees being broken and smashed. Behind them, the huge mass of floodwater was being funneled into a raging river in the valley beneath the steep mountain.

"Thomas!" Elly shouted.

He glanced at the rearview mirror just as the river hit the truck with a soft thud, lifting it like a toy and causing the steering wheel to go slack.

The road, along with everything on both sides of it, disappeared under the water.

CHAPTER 24

THE FLOOD TILTED THE truck sideways, sending water gushing into the front and back seats and forcing Eno and Elly to grab onto the safety straps to avoid being swept out the opposite window.

Thomas shouted, "Close the windows, Jack!"

The windows closed, but not before the three of them were soaked. Jack started to rotate, but its big flotation tubes quickly managed to stabilize the truck. Even though they were in no danger of sinking, a greater threat came at them from all sides. Cars, trees, telephone poles, and roads signs clanked loudly against each other, elbowing each other for space in the narrow tunnel of water. Any one of them, let alone a combination, could do serious damage.

Out of the corner of his eye, Thomas saw a small suspension bridge break free and float toward them. On the passenger's side, a bicycle rack—complete with a dozen or so locked bikes —drifted past. The bridge and rack collided, their metal tentacles twisting into each other with a loud clatter. On the driver's side, a moving van with furniture pouring out of its rear doors lumbered along beside them.

"Hold on," Thomas said. "I'll get us turned around." He located the switch on the steering wheel that activated the rudder. With the steering reengaged, he turned the truck toward the mountainside, barely missing the van, which clipped the door, knocking Eno into Elly. She held him upright as something caught her eye in the rearview mirror.

"Guys, look! Behind us!" Elly shouted.

Thomas glanced at the rearview expecting to see more danger, but instead glimpsed a blue flag rippling in the wind about a mile away.

“That can’t be what I think it is, can it?” Thomas said.

“It sure looks like it,” Elly said, as she pulled up her binoculars. “I think I can see Ajax!”

With its sleek bow, the raft was moving much faster than the truck, and quickly gaining on them. In a few moments, Survivor was only a hundred or so yards away.

“Jack, roll down the windows!” Elly shouted.

The windows came down and Elly leaned out to her waist. She waved frantically toward Ajax and Duck as they pulled closer. Several of the kids—Pooja, Ivan, Muirin, and Thor—shouted to them as the raft caught up and floated beside the truck. Suddenly Ajax and Duck were face to face with Thomas and Elly, no more than a few yards between them. Next to them were Roos and Greet, waving furiously. Thomas held onto the steering wheel but leaned out the open window.

“You were right, Duck!” he shouted. “We meet again!”

“Sure you don’t want to come along?” Ajax shouted. “It’s not too late!”

“We can’t,” Thomas shouted back. “But good luck!”

“You too!” Ajax yelled as Duck gave them a thumbs up.

And with that, Survivor zipped past them, quickly moving out of sight.

Thomas made eye contact with Elly and saw the wistful look on her face. He could guess what was going through her head. He was wondering the same thing: if the Survivor kids could possibly survive the floods. Their time in Vegas was short but magical. More than that, it was the first time since they’d been on Earth that they’d made friends who were also alone, and on a mission of their own. It was the bond that connected them. But right now, he had more immediate concerns. At the speed they were moving, they’d be past their destination point at any time.

“I think we better try and make land,” Thomas said, “or we’ll never make it back here.”

"Can you get us over to the mountainside?" Elly said.

"I can try."

"The steering seems to be working again," Eno said with uncharacteristic optimism.

"Yeah," Thomas said. "The only problem is we don't have any brakes, so it'll be a crash landing. We can hit the rocks or the trees, take your pick."

"I vote for the trees," Elly said. "You know what they say, bend don't break."

"Never heard that one," Eno said, "but I concur."

"Buckle up," Thomas said.

As they fastened their seat belts tighter, Thomas turned the wheel sharply to the left. The churning water caught the back of the truck and, despite the stabilizers, spun it sideways.

"Lemme try that again," Thomas said.

This time he turned the wheel slowly, trying to find an angle that would hold in the roaring water. When the truck was diagonal to the mountain, the steering wheel vibrated so strongly that a jolt of pain shot through Thomas's arms. But he held on and they began to move toward the mountainside, which rose at a steep angle. The flood had already lifted them hundreds of feet higher than the town, and the landscape was now more rugged, thick with rocks and trees.

"I'm gonna try to find a parking place. Better get down in case the windows break."

Eno and Elly slid to the floor and put their hands over their head. Thomas pointed Jack toward a pair of huge trees with just enough separation to accommodate the big truck. But at the last moment, a floating gas pump sideswiped them, sending the truck sideways and causing it to hit the trees broadside. A branch smashed through the front windshield and Thomas ducked to the side just in time to avoid being decapitated. Jack thrashed against the trees, shearing off one of the flotation tubes, and leaving the rudder dangling like a broken tail. With a final groan, the trees surrendered to the weight of the truck and were pushed to the ground, leaving Jack leaning to one side, as if he were taking a nap. Twenty feet below and behind, the flood, having established a high-water mark, continued on its way, oblivious to the damage it caused. Thomas brushed off the splintered wood and shattered glass that covered the lower half of his body.

"You guys all right back there?"

Thomas turned to see Eno and Elly jammed against the door. "Hold on," he said.

He climbed through the passenger window, opened the rear door, and pulled them out one at a time.

"Whew," Elly said. "Nice landing."

"You can thank Jack," Thomas said. "Though it doesn't look like he'll be doing much more driving anytime soon."

Elly glanced at the forest surrounding them on three sides. "He'd need a road for starters."

"Fortunately that's not something required for time travel," Eno said. "I suggest we check on the cable car before we do another thing."

"Good idea," Thomas said, as he reached into the driver's seat for the remote and triggered the hydraulic lift. With a clanking sound, the rear doors opened and the metal prongs delivered the cable car out of the back of the truck. But like Jack, it was tilted sideways and lodged in the trees. "Do you think we'll still be able to time jump from that position?" Thomas asked.

Eno walked around the cable car for a closer inspection. "At this angle, we'll only have mirrors fully functioning on one side and the rear, so it might take a bit more time to gather enough dark matter, but there's no reason it shouldn't work."

"Great," Thomas said.

The three of them walked to the front of the truck to survey the terrain. They were at the bottom of a steep hill with no path in sight.

Thomas pulled the map out of his pocket. "I have no idea where we are, or how far we came."

"Well, we need to go *somewhere* fast," Eno said. "We only have six hours of daylight."

"We'll give ourselves three hours," Thomas said, folding up the map. "That way, if we don't find anything, we can get back in time to make a jump."

"That actually sounds like a reasonable plan," Eno said, as if it were a surprising development.

Elly checked out the area with her binoculars. "There has to be a trail up there somewhere," Elly said. "I think I can see a sign."

"I'll set my wrist pod," Eno said. "Three hours and counting."

✦✦

THEY STARTED UPHILL, AND after ten minutes or so, found a walking trail. In a short time, they came upon a wooden cutout of a fisherman with a rod over his shoulder, pointing west toward a small stream. Someone had tied an inflatable pink fish at the end of his line.

"This is at least…something," Elly said.

"That remains to be seen," Eno said, checking his wrist pod for the time.

They hiked for another few minutes, and when the trail crossed a small stream, it split in two directions, each with a separate sign. The first pointed to a campsite farther along the same trail and the other straight up the mountain to a lake at the end of the stream.

"Which way?" Eno asked.

"I say we follow the stream," Elly said.

"Uphill?" Eno sighed.

"Maybe we should take a short break first," Thomas said, dropping the backpack on the ground. "We could all use some fuel."

Elly pulled out the food that Ivan had packed. A brown bag was labeled "breakfast," a second "lunch," and a third "dinner." She said, "We've got egg sandwiches for breakfast, ham sandwiches for lunch, chicken sandwiches for dinner."

"Can I have half lunch and half dinner?" Thomas said.

"Sure," Elly said. "I'm going with full breakfast myself. Eno?"

"Did any of those donuts survive the trip?"

"You kidding?" Elly said. "I guarded them with my life."

She pulled out the box and handed it to Eno. They sat and began to eat. The soft bubbling of the creek competed with the hum of the floodwater, nearly drowning it out. The sun had come out and the temperature had risen to seventy-five degrees, almost drying their clothes.

"On the plus side, you couldn't ask for a more beautiful day," Thomas said, looking up at the trees. "Or more beautiful scenery."

Elly nodded. "Hard to believe this was the end of it."

"Six months, almost to the day," Eno said. "That's when the last shuttle leaves, along with you-know-who."

"So, when exactly will Thomas be born?" Elly said.

"Sometime tomorrow," Eno said. "We don't know the exact hour, but…"

A loud crack echoed in the distance. Thomas wasn't familiar with the sound and looked to Elly for an explanation.

"Either a big firecracker or a gunshot."

A second crack echoed louder.

"Gunshot, definitely," Elly said.

It was followed by a voice. But they couldn't make out the words. They jumped to their feet, ready to run, when a third shot rang out, much closer.

"Hello?" the voice called out. "Anybody there?"

Thomas shouted back in its direction. "Down here!"

They heard the sound of a car motor, and moments later a jeep appeared on the hill above.

The driver, a dark-skinned woman in her mid-twenties, pulled over and jumped out. Her hair, a shorter version of Elly's, was tucked under a baseball hat, and a rifle was under her arm.

"It's a woman," Elly said.

She bounced down the hill, deftly sidestepping trees and rocks. As she came closer, Thomas recognized her immediately. While her skin was darker than Elly's, their features were so similar he was surprised she didn't notice it.

Thomas turned to Eno, who clearly did.

The woman approached, careful to keep the rifle pointed at the ground.

"Name's Gabriela, but I go by Gabby," she said with a melodic sing-song in her voice.

"My name's Elly. These are my friends, Thomas and Eno."

"Nice to meet you all. Sorry about the rifle, but we still get the occasional loose screw out here. I take it you got caught in the flood that just came through?"

Thomas, Eno, and Elly nodded in unison.

"Where'd you come from?"

"Nevada," Elly said. "We were driving through Colorado when the flood caught up to us. We barely managed to make it to land."

"So, you weren't with those other kids? The ones on that big raft?"

"No," Elly said. "But they're friends of ours."

"I spotted them from our outpost up the mountain. I came down in case they ran into trouble, but amazingly enough, they made it. So far, anyway."

"So far?" Elly said.

"They're going where we came from, and trust me, there's nothing but water from here to god knows where."

"They plan to live on the raft permanently," Thomas said.

"Brave bunch. Speaking of which, what the heck are you guys doing out here?"

"We're looking for my father," Thomas said, trying to stick to the truth as much as possible. "He built a cabin up in the mountains, though I'm not exactly sure where."

Gabby looked puzzled. "Huh. We've been here for weeks, but I haven't seen another person since we set up camp."

"My guess is he's at a higher elevation, above the tree line," Thomas said. "We were planning to hike there."

Gabby looked Thomas up and down. "Our outpost is at eight thousand feet. Anything much higher and you need climbing gear, which I notice you're not wearing."

Thomas and Eno exchanged a glance.

"Don't worry, we're camped right outside the ski lodge, which has a bunch of shops with everything you could want. They're abandoned, so it's all yours for the taking."

"That's very generous," Thomas said. "How far is it?"

"About twenty minutes up the mountain, give or take."

"We wouldn't be able to stay for long," Thomas said.

"Eleven hours and sixteen minutes exactly," Eno added, checking his wrist pod.

"No explanation required," Gabby said.

"In that case," Thomas said, "we'll take you up on your offer."

"Right this way," Gabby said, as she turned and started up the hill.

Elly took the food, along with the donuts, and hurried after her. Thomas and Eno followed Gabby to the jeep, which had no top, exposing a pair of fishing rods sitting in the rear well. Thomas nudged Eno toward the back seat so that Elly had to take the front.

Gabby put on her seat belt and glanced over at Elly.

"I see you got the last of my donuts."

"These are yours?"

"Not legally," she smiled. "But I made friends with the owner when we first got here, and she evacuated a few days ago, so I've been goin' down ever since to keep the generator going. The end of the world is one thing, but the end of the world without donuts is completely unacceptable."

"Do you happen to like the ones with powdered sugar?" Thomas asked.

"You kidding?" Gabby said. "They're my favorite."

CHAPTER 25

Gabby guided the jeep to a gravel road and followed a sign for the ski area. In the distance, one of the lifts was still operating with several people in the chairs on their way up the mountain.

"What are those people doing?" Eno asked.

"That's the shuttle crew, going to work. The fuselage came in on a Crawler a few weeks ago, but it takes weeks to prep it for the five-month trip to Mars. One of the first things we did when we got here was get the lifts going again. They hadn't been used in years, but it cut the time up to the launch pad in half."

"You said you've been here for weeks?" Elly said.

"Yeah, but we've been traveling across the country for the last fourteen months, like a modern-day wagon train, only with mobile science labs. We move up to a higher elevation before each flood, but this looks to be our last stop."

"How do you know?" Elly said.

"The alliance climatologists can predict the timing down to the week, so we can alert towns to evacuate along the way. The next big flood will take out pretty much everything."

"That's so sad," Elly said. "Where do all the people go?"

"Nobody knows exactly, but it's been that way for a few years now. It's one of the great mysteries of the superfloods, how people just seem to disappear. I think most folks get together with friends or family and decide how to wait out the end. As far as I know, the owner of the donut shop and her girlfriend were the last people in town to go, so now it's just us."

"How many of you are there?" Thomas asked.

"Eleven full-time members of the Science Alliance, and another fourteen on the security team or shuttle crew."

Eno leaned forward. "That only makes twenty-five people. I thought the shuttles were equipped to handle several hundred."

"Normally, they are. But this isn't your normal shuttle. As the last one out, it was built for our group plus storage for scientific equipment."

"So, you're a scientist?" Elly asked.

"A lepidopterist actually, which is the study of—"

"Butterflies," Elly said.

"Wow," Gabby said with surprise. "Most people don't have a clue. I'm with the Alpine Butterfly Project, the only one of us left. I'm trying to find a species that might be adaptable to life on Mars."

"How many have you found?"

"Exactly one. Truth is, with all the habitat loss, there are barely any butterflies alive on Earth." Gabby reached over and pulled a glass jar out of her backpack and handed it to Elly, who examined the butterfly inside. It was brown with yellow trim.

"What a beauty. Dakota Skipper?"

Gabby looked even more surprised. "How'd you know?"

"I'm a naturalist, too, in training."

"Too bad you didn't show up earlier. I could've used you."

"For what?"

"I've been trying to find him a mate. I managed to collect a few of these males every day, but the females seem to have vanished."

"Maybe they know what's coming," Elly said.

Gabby laughed. "Yeah, even the butterflies aren't thrilled about going to Mars. But I'm still hoping she's out there somewhere."

"Maybe you should let him fly around for a day or so, see if he can find his own lady."

"I'd love to, but like all of us, these guys are running out of time."

"So, you've finished your project?"

"There's not much left to do, actually. When I'm not looking for Miss Dakota or tending the donut shop, I spend my time fishing.

There's a beautiful lake a few minutes from here. Usually at this time of day I head over there and try my luck. Since there are no lakes on Mars, I figure there won't be any trout."

"I see you have two rods," Thomas said.

"Ignatius normally fishes with me, but he's been too busy lately."

"Ignatius?" Elly said.

"My fiancé."

Elly glanced at Thomas in the rearview mirror.

"Where is he now?" Thomas asked.

"Back at headquarters, holding down the fort for Matthew, who's the head of the alliance. His wife's about to give birth, so they took the chopper over to the valley for a babymoon. The last couple days, I've had to fish alone."

"I'll fish with you," Elly said.

"Yeah?" Gabby said, glancing at Thomas in the rearview. "You sure you have time?"

"We have time for that," Thomas nodded.

"All right, hang on."

Gabby made a sharp turn into the woods. After fifty yards, they came out onto a dirt road that took them on a steep downward path. Ten minutes later, they pulled off the road.

"We have to hoof it from here."

She grabbed the fishing rods and slipped her arms through a lightweight vest. On the back was a small handheld net and an aluminum frying pan. They came through the woods and into a meadow covered with sunflowers. Gabby put a finger to her lips, signaling for quiet. At the edge of the lake a small mountain goat was taking a drink. It looked identical to the one in the picture Thomas had seen in his mother's room.

"It's Wild Bill," Gabby whispered. "We have a loose arrangement. He gets the place until noon, and I take over at lunchtime."

She pulled out a small camera and took a few quick shots. Wild Bill finished drinking, then sauntered back into the woods.

"Okay," Gabby said. "Our turn."

They approached the edge of the lake.

"You done much fishing, Elly?"

"A little. My dad took me to Yellowstone a few times."

"You must've been pretty young. Yellowstone's been gone for over a decade. I always wanted to fish it, or at least see it."

"It was spectacular," Elly said. "But so is this."

"Yeah, the mountain is filled with these glacier lakes, but this one's the jewel in the crown."

Gabby handed Elly a rod and kept one for herself. "So, you know the drill," Gabby said. "Keep your eye on that little red popper. When it dips under the water, pull back, and start to reel."

Gabby cast her line into the lake. A tiny red-and-white plastic ball landed on the water, causing a few ripples. Elly followed and her popper landed about ten feet from Gabby's. For a moment, they bobbed next to each other as if they wanted to stick together.

"You sure you boys don't want to give it a shot?" Gabby asked.

Thomas was desperate to try but wanted to let Elly enjoy the experience alone with her mother. "Maybe later," he said.

Thomas and Eno wandered over to a pair of boulders and sat down. They were far enough away that they couldn't hear what Elly and Gabby were saying, but close enough to see they were talking nonstop, making the exact same gestures with their hands.

"We got lucky," Thomas said.

"You mean finding Elly's mother? Luck had little to do with it. There are only twenty-five people on the entire mountain, so the probability was quite high."

"Still, we could've spent all day looking. Now at least they get to spend the time together."

They glanced over to see mother and daughter, standing in front of a perfect lake, under a perfect sky. In spite of the near disaster of the morning's flood, it had turned into a perfect day.

Suddenly Elly's popper disappeared under the water. She let out a squeal of delight, pulled back her rod, and reeled in her line. Gabby put down her own rod, and netted a medium-sized trout.

"It's a rainbow."

Gabby and Elly exchanged a high five.

"Hey, Thomas," Elly shouted. "How about a picture?"

Thomas jumped up and ran toward them. Elly pulled out her cellphone and handed it to him. But he suddenly realized that he'd never actually taken a picture before.

"I'm not really familiar with your phone," he said, trying to cover his ignorance.

"Yeah, it's an ancient model," Elly said. "Just press the little red dot."

He focused on Elly and Gabby and took the picture, knowing that whatever happened from here on out, the two of them would be frozen in time together.

✦✦

IT WAS ALMOST TWO thirty when Thomas built a small fire. Gabby and Elly caught a half-dozen trout, two of which would be consumed for lunch while the other four were designated for dinner. Gabby built a pyramid of sticks and placed the frying pan at its center. She then slid two of the fish into the pan and sat around the fire as it sparked and crackled.

"So, Thomas, you said your father's building a place above the flood line?" Gabby said.

"I sort of lost contact with him years ago, but that's what a friend of his told me."

Gabby glanced up at the mountains. "Anything that high would be near the Blue Bells."

"The Blue Bells?" Thomas said.

Gabby pointed up to a patch of clouds that resembled a rumpled pillow. "Those three peaks just under the clouds. Up close, they look like bells. There's a glacier right underneath, and the ice is blue, so they reflect the color when the sun rises and sets. Hence the Blue Bells."

"You've been there?" Elly said.

"No, but it's supposed to be a brutal hike over a treacherous glacier. From what I hear, more than a few climbers have died trying. But Ignatius and Matt have been over there in the helicopter a bunch of times to check the stability of the ice."

Thomas and Eno exchanged a quick glance.

"Stability?" Eno said.

"I don't know how much you know about glaciers," Gabby said, "but they're basically rivers of ice. If the Blue Bell glacier ever came down, it would be the mother of all avalanches."

"What makes it so difficult to climb?" Thomas asked.

"For starters, it's at fourteen thousand feet, so it's hard to breathe without oxygen. Because of the unpredictable weather, it's melted and re-frozen so often it's filled with bumps and crevices. One wrong step and you slide to your death or get swallowed by the mountain. On the plus side, as your father must know, it's one of the few places the flood won't reach for a couple more years."

"So, you could survive up there?" Elly said.

"Assuming you had enough oxygen, you could eke out a barebones existence. You'd never see a butterfly, and you couldn't even go outside for more than a few minutes at a time during certain times of the year. But I guess you could live with that, given the alternative."

"You mean resettling to the Red Planet," Eno said.

"Or as I call it, the dread planet. Dark, desolate, and donut-free."

"Don't you have a choice?" Elly asked.

"Sure. But I can't really face life without Ignatius. We've been together since we met in science camp at the age of twelve. We bonded over the fact that we were both from Portland, even though mine was in Oregon and his in Maine. So, at the end of every summer, we went home to opposite coasts, three thousand miles apart. We were star-crossed from the start."

"Star-crossed?" Thomas said. "I don't know that expression."

"Kept apart by forces beyond our control. In our case, geography. By the time we got together, we were both in our early twenties. We vowed we'd never separate again."

"That's sweet," Elly said.

"So, Ignatius wants to leave?" Thomas asked.

"I wouldn't go that far," Gabby said. "But he believes we owe it to the Earth."

"I don't understand," Eno said.

"If we stay, we die. But if we leave, we live, and maybe solve some of the problems we caused on Earth. Ignatius has this crazy idea we might even be able to come back someday."

"How does the head of the Science Alliance feel about that?" Thomas asked.

"He's not happy about leaving Earth either. And his wife feels even stronger. She told Matt she wasn't stepping foot onto the shuttle until their baby was at least six months old. She wants him to start life breathing Earth air, seeing Earth sky, eating Earth food. Speaking of which, these fish look done."

Gabby pulled a pair of plastic plates and utensils from her vest. "Sorry, I wasn't expecting company, so I've only got two forks. But Elly and I can share if she doesn't mind."

"Good by me," Elly said.

"Eno and I can share," Thomas said.

Gabby divided the fish and passed one of the plates to Thomas and one to Elly.

Thomas took a bite of the trout as Eno looked on, slightly revolted.

"I know you don't eat fish, Eno, but you really have to try this."

Eno took a small bite. He closed his eyes and swallowed in one gulp, as if he were trying to put a painful experience behind him as quickly as possible. "I have to say, it's quite interesting."

"Compliments to the chef," Elly said.

"Compliments to the fish," Gabby said. "I'm just an amateur, but you should see what our cook does with it. It's a whole other level of delicious. He also makes a mean hot fudge sundae. You're all welcome to stay, by the way."

"We really do have to get going," Eno said, glancing at Thomas.

"I understand," Gabby said. "But if you're going to do any hiking, we'll have to get you outfitted."

"Thanks," Thomas said. "From what you say, it sounds like getting to the Blue Bells could take a few days. Maybe while Elly stays for dinner, Eno and I can do a short hike to get the lay of the land, then we can all head back to our truck for the night."

"What do you think, Elly?"

"This trip is for Thomas, so it's up to him," Elly said.

"But dinner is up to you," Thomas said firmly.

Elly's eyes immediately lit up. "Well, if it's up to me, I vote hot fudge sundae."

Gabby and Elly exchanged a smile, as if it had been their secret plan all along.

Gabby threw an arm around Elly's shoulders. "So, it's settled then."

CHAPTER 26

It was just after three o'clock when the alliance outpost came into view. As Gabby had said, it was little more than a collection of mobile trailers circling the ski lodge, which housed a variety of shops, a cafeteria, and a sun deck. Wire lines were tied between many of the trailers with clothes hanging out to dry, a strange contrast to the armed security guards who patrolled the perimeter.

"Why do you have guards?" Thomas asked.

"A lot of people would kill to get on the last shuttle, literally." Gabby said. "Just last week, a bunch of International Security thugs tried to storm the outpost."

"I take it they weren't successful?" Elly said.

"Most of them ran when the shooting started. We took in the wounded and patched them up. They're working for us now. One is the cook I told you about."

"What happens to them when you leave?" Thomas asked.

"Oh, we're taking them along."

"But I thought you had limited space?" Eno said.

"We do. But we carved some extra room by retrofitting the library pod."

"You're taking books to Mars?" Elly said.

"Each scientist is allowed three cubic feet of personal storage. I'm bringing some framed photos, my spice rack, and family keepsakes, but Ignatius is only taking a few cannisters of lemon tea and his time travel books. He thinks they might be the ultimate solution to saving Earth."

Thomas, Eno, and Elly exchanged a look.

"I know, time travel is crazy, huh? At least that's what everybody thinks. But I wouldn't rule it out for the future. He's done a lot of reseach on the subject and he really is brilliant."

She pulled the jeep up to the lodge. "C'mon, I'll take you in so you can do some shopping."

As Gabby and Elly walked ahead, Eno pulled Thomas aside.

"What are we doing?" he said, unable to hide his exasperation.

"C'mere, I want to show you something."

Thomas dropped his backpack on the ground and pulled something out.

"What's that?"

"My father's map. Remember when Gabby was talking about Blue Bells being the place to build something?"

Eno nodded as Thomas unfolded the map.

"Look, here's the ski lodge at the bottom left corner, right where we're standing. And here's where we need to go…"

Thomas traced his finger on a diagonal line to the top right corner, where the Biosphere was marked with a large blue bell. It was in the middle of the three peaks Gabby had mentioned.

"The Blue Bells," Eno nodded.

"If we hike in that direction, we should at least be able to scope it out."

"All right," Eno said. "But remember, we have to time jump before midnight, which means we need to leave by ten at the latest. No delays, promise me?"

"Promise."

✦✦

Twenty minutes later, Gabby held the lodge door open for Thomas, Eno, and Elly as they walked out wearing new all-weather jackets, pants, knit hats, and hiking boots and carrying enough dehydrated food for a week, in case they got lost.

A jeep pulled up in front, and the driver, a young man in his late twenties, got out with the aid of a walking stick.

"Hey, Ignatius, meet some new friends."

Ignatius limped toward them with an outstretched hand.

Thomas, Eno, and Elly exchanged a smile. Having only seen Ignatius as a wounded boy and a damaged older man, it was great to see him now, in the prime of life, happy and healthy.

"Meet Thomas, Eno, and Elly."

Ignatius's expression changed slightly. "Your name is Thomas?"

"Yes. Is something wrong?"

"No." Ignatius said. "It's just that the boy who saved my life when I was a kid was also named Thomas. I was in a medically induced coma for most of it, but I have a hazy memory of him, and you could almost be his brother."

"Well," Gabby said, "this Thomas is looking for his father, who's living up the mountain."

"I see," Ignatius said. "They'll be staying the night, I assume."

"Actually, they have to leave right after dinner and get back to their truck. They're going on an exploratory hike while Elly stays for dinner."

Gabby glanced at Elly. "But before that, Ignatius and I are going off to our daily sunset butterfly release if you're interested."

"I'd love to," Elly said, "if you're sure you don't mind a third wheel."

"We'd love the company," Ignatius said. "Sure you boys don't want to join us?"

"Thanks," Thomas said, "but we're anxious to check out the route to the Blue Bells."

Ignatius nodded. "There's a good walking trail that will take you up to the Mountain Patrol Cabin at 8,600 feet," Ignatius said. "It has a great view of the bells."

"Sounds good," Thomas said.

"It shouldn't take you more than a couple hours to get up there and back," Gabby said. "We'll meet you in the lodge. They'll still be serving dinner if you're hungry."

"I'm sure we will be," Thomas said.

Elly got into the jeep with Gabby and Ignatius, and they drove off, waving.

"Well, that's a bonus," Thomas said.

"What do you mean?

"It's probably the only time in Elly's life she'll be able to be with her whole biological family, even if she isn't fully aware of it."

"Let's just hope this trip is worth it."

✦✦

Thomas and Eno left the outpost and found the walking path up the mountain. Forty-five minutes later, the trail disappeared in front of a steep hill. They climbed it slowly as the air continued to get thinner. Breathing heavily, they reached the top, which was marked by a massive boulder. A blue bell, similar to the one on Thomas's map, was painted on its front. Thomas wandered over to a small clearing, which overlooked the lake where they had lunch. From their vantage point, it looked like a shiny silver coin.

Eno plopped on the boulder and checked his wrist pod. "We're at eighty-four hundred feet. Do we really need to go farther?"

"Yeah," Thomas said. "It's only a couple hundred more feet to the Mountain Patrol Cabin Ignatius told us about. C'mon."

Thomas started up the hill while Eno reluctantly followed. Twenty minutes later, a three-story structure came into view. It looked like a miniature lighthouse, only built of stone. Near the top was a catwalk, which circled the exterior like a big wooden belt.

Thomas opened the door to a stairway that led up to the second floor. "Almost there," he said, starting up the stairs.

"I'm not climbing another step. You can tell me all about it."

Thomas walked out onto the catwalk and came face to face with the Blue Bells, which were partially obscured by a bank of clouds that made them look vaguely mysterious. The sun had begun its descent, illuminating the glacier below. It looked like a giant tongue made of ice, daring them to ascend any farther.

"Hey Eno, you have to see this for yourself!"

Eno trudged up the stairs and joined him. He looked at the Blue Bells and shook his head.

"How did your father possibly get it up there, not to mention with seventeen children?"

"No idea," Thomas said. "But that's a mystery for another day."

"The sun's going down," Eno said. "We better start heading—"

But before he could finish, a gunshot echoed overhead.

"Is somebody shooting at us again?" Eno said.

A second shot took out a chunk of the wooden catwalk, directly beneath them.

"Looks that way," Thomas said, ducking down and pulling Eno with him.

A woman's voice rang out. "Stand up so I can see you, hands over your head."

"What is it with the women around here?" Eno said. "Are they all armed?"

"Better do as she says," Thomas said.

They stood with their hands in the air but couldn't see anyone.

"Now come down the stairs and walk outside, backsides first. Try anything funny and I'll fill your butts with lead."

They did as she ordered and backed out the door. Thomas glanced out of the corner of his eye to see if they could see the shooter, but she was hidden by the trees.

"All right," the voice shouted, "sit down on the ground."

They sat. A moment later, the shotgun barrel emerged from the woods followed by the woman who held it. She was wearing a ragged dress under a tattered green ski jacket and seemed to be about ten years older than Gabby. A little girl, no more than four, walked behind her. She was holding a stuffed animal with one missing ear. As they got closer, Thomas could see that the woman's face was filthy, and from the gaunt look on her cheeks, she hadn't eaten in days.

She stopped and pointed the rifle at their heads. "You with the shuttle people?"

"No," Thomas said. "We're looking for my father."

"You alone then? Don't lie to me."

"We're with another friend. She's with some of the alliance people."

"Then you'll do."

"Do for what?"

The mother cradled the shotgun under one arm and pulled her daughter next to her with the other. "You're our ticket out of here."

CHAPTER 27

The mother tied Thomas and Eno's hands behind their backs with some old fishing line, then marched them through the woods to an abandoned cabin with no water or electricity. From what Thomas could gather, they'd lost their home, along with the rest of their family, a father and two boys, in the last flood. When the mother overheard some people in town talking about the alliance shuttle, she was determined to get passage.

"We don't have much left in the way of food," the mother said, "but you can share what we got. Crackers and canned beans."

"Actually," Eno said, "we can't stay for dinner. We have to be out of here by midnight. We can't really explain, so you'll just have to trust us on this."

The mother lit a small fire in the wood-burning stove. She didn't seem to hear a word Eno said. Thomas tried another approach.

"I'm sorry you've had such a rough time," Thomas said. "But we're not your enemy, and we don't have a say about who goes on the shuttle."

"I guess we'll just have to see about that," the mother said.

She opened a large can of beans and emptied them into a pan on the stove.

Thomas and Eno exchanged a look of concern. "Can you at least tell us what your plan is? We came up here with a friend, and she'll be worried."

The mother glanced at Thomas and then at her daughter, who was gripping her stuffed animal tightly. "The plan is to give the shuttle people the night to worry. When we show up in the morning, they'll know we're serious."

"We've been gone since this afternoon," Thomas said. "By midnight they'll know something must've happened to us. And if they send their security guards looking for us, you may never get to talk to the right people."

The mother turned to Thomas, sensing he might have valuable information. "And who are the right people?"

"Gabby and Ignatius. They're scientists with the alliance. They helped us, so maybe they can help you."

The mother used a wooden spoon to move the beans around the pan.

"*Maybe* ain't gonna cut it."

After dinner, the mother lit a fire in the fireplace and laid out a sleeping bag for her little girl. She covered her with a child's blanket as ragged as the clothes on her back. Thomas could see that all their worldly possessions were jammed into a single cloth bag.

The mother put a few more logs on the fire and sat down, propping her back against the cabin wall. She cradled her daughter's head in one arm and the rifle in the other. "Don't think about doing anything crazy. I have nothing against you boys, but I have nothing left to lose, so if you try to run, you leave me with no other choice than to shoot at least one of you."

The sun was now down, and the temperature dropped. Thomas and Eno sat with their backs against the opposite wall, facing the fire. Exhausted from the hike, Eno nodded off, his mouth slightly ajar, snoring loudly.

Thomas noticed the little girl watching.

"He does that a lot when he sleeps. I usually use ear plugs, but I forgot to pack them."

The little girl gave him a half smile.

"My name is Thomas. What's yours?"

"Luna."

"How old are you Luna?"

"The little girl held up four fingers."

"I like your stuffed animal. Is it a boy or a girl?"

"Boy."

"Rabbit?"

"Sloth."

"Wow. I've never seen one of those before. But I bet he helps you sleep at night."

The little girl nodded.

"And I bet he doesn't snore."

She let out a giggle.

"Enough talk now," the mother said. "Time for shut eyes. Been a long day."

Thomas nodded, and the mother pulled the little girl closer.

As night descended, the flames in the fireplace became hypnotic, poking the darkness in every direction. At some point Thomas was jarred by a strange object, and woke to feel the barrel of the mother's rifle tapping him on the shoulder. A flashlight was tied on top of it and the light was in his eyes. She had a knife in her other hand. The fire had burned to embers, leaving the room with only shadows.

"Thought about what you said, and maybe you're right. It's near midnight, and they've had plenty of time to worry about you. No sense putting it off any longer."

Eno suddenly woke up. "What's going on?"

"We're leaving," Thomas said.

The mother turned him around, and while still holding the rifle under her arm, used the knife to cut the fishing line that bound his hands. "You can carry our stuff, but your friend stays tied. If you try anything funny he gets a bullet. It's that simple."

"I understand," Thomas said.

He picked up the bag while the mother held her daughter, now sound asleep. She marched the boys outside and pointed the gun barrel into the woods, so that the flashlight lit the way.

"All right, start moving."

They walked silently in the frigid mountain air. It was almost an hour before they saw the outpost lights shimmering through the woods. Thomas guessed that most of the alliance scientists were now asleep. Three guards sat near the lodge, talking to each other.

"Drop the bag here," the woman said.

Thomas did as she said.

"Now go find whoever you said I need to talk to. If one of those guards so much as looks in our direction, the next thing you'll hear is a gunshot, got it?"

"Yeah," Thomas said. "I'll say we got lost and that my friend is up here hurt."

"Say whatever you need to. Just come back with the right people. And make it quick. Ten minutes go by and it's all over for your friend."

Thomas nodded. "I'll be fast—okay, Eno?"

Eno nodded and Thomas took off, sprinting down the hill toward the outpost. He went up to the guards, who pointed him toward the lodge.

Thomas ran into the lodge to find Elly huddled with Gabby and Ignatius.

"Thomas!" Elly said. "What happened to you? Where's Eno?"

"We were just about to organize a search party," Gabby added.

"I'm fine, but Eno's in trouble. A woman shot at us and then took us back to her cabin. She's got a daughter and they want passage on the shuttle. She wants to talk to somebody but if a guard comes near, she says she'll shoot Eno."

"I'll go talk to her," Gabby said to Ignatius. "Woman to woman."

"I'll be right behind you," Ignatius said,

"I'm going, too," Elly said.

Without speaking to the guards, the four of them hurried past the trailers and back through the woods to where the woman was waiting, her rifle at Eno's back.

Gabby held up her hands to show she was unarmed. "Hello. I'm Gabby and this is Ignatius. We both work with the Science Alliance. I understand you want passage on the shuttle for you and your daughter."

"The boy got it wrong," she said. "I want passage, but just for my daughter. I'll give you back the boy if you take my little girl. An even trade."

Gabby glanced at Elly, both of them clearly surprised at the request.

"I need to talk to my friend here for a second," Gabby said. "I'll be fast, promise."

The mother nodded as Gabby pulled Ignatius aside and whispered. Thomas couldn't hear what they were saying, but after a few moments, Gabby turned back.

"I'm sorry," Gabby said. "There's no place for a motherless child on the shuttle. Either you both come, or nobody does."

The woman was stunned. "You can make room for both of us?"

"Yes. But it's a one-time offer. You have to put the gun down and come with us now."

"How do I know I can trust you?"

"I'm not a mother, but I hope to be some day, and when that time comes, I hope I'll have the courage to do what you're doing right now."

The woman looked at Gabby for a few moments, then lowered the shotgun. Even in the darkness Thomas and Elly could see the tears on her face. "Bless you," she said, holding out the knife to Thomas, who quickly cut the fishing line around Eno's wrists, freeing him.

"Why don't you give her to me," Gabby said. "Your arms must be about to break."

The woman handed over her daughter and the child woke up, slightly puzzled.

"Her name is Luna," Thomas said.

"So we'll be taking the moon to Mars," Gabby smiled. "That should brighten things up. Now come on. You and Luna look like you could use a hot meal and some new clothes. We've got plenty of both in the lodge."

Ignatius took their duffel bag, and the woman followed them toward the outpost.

Thomas and Elly stayed with Eno. "You all right?"

"Yes," Eno said. "But it's well after midnight. We have to get out of here."

"Can I at least say goodbye to Gabby and Ignatius?" Elly said.

"Can you make it quick?" Eno said, checking his wrist pod.

"Back in a flash," Elly said, running to catch up with Gabby, while Eno turned to Thomas.

"I know and I'm sorry," Thomas said. "As soon as she says goodbye, we can leave."

Eno was about to protest, but Thomas beat him to it.

"They did just save your life."

By the time they reached the lodge, Ignatius was escorting everyone inside.

Elly waved to Gabby. "I came to say goodbye."

Gabby handed Luna to Ignatius and turned back to Elly.

"You're leaving now, at this hour? Why don't you wait until morning?"

"I wish I could, but I promised the boys."

Gabby turned to Thomas and Eno for confirmation. "You sure? Matt just called and said that his wife went into labor. They're on their way back now."

Thomas, Eno, and Elly exchanged a look of panic.

"Under normal circumstances, I'd love to," Elly smiled," but…"

Thomas finished her sentence, "it's just not possible."

"I understand," Gabby said. "I hope you find your father, Thomas. But if you don't, please come back. We can always make a little more room on the shuttle."

Thomas had to smile at the invitation. In a bizarre twist that could only happen in the realm of time travel, it was the same shuttle he'd been on fifteen years ago.

"On behalf of Eno and myself, thanks for everything you've done for us," Thomas said.

"At least we got to share a beautiful day on Earth, and who knows how many more we'll have," Gabby said. "Hold on Elly, I've got something for you." Gabby disappeared for a few moments, then came back with the glass jar that held the Dakota Skipper. "He's my last one, and I was thinking about your idea of letting him do the job. I think you may be on to something. So, whenever the instinct strikes, let him go."

She handed the jar to Elly, who cradled it like a precious gift.

"Thanks," Elly said. "I'll consider it a sacred trust."

"I know you will."

Gabby gave Elly a quick hug and then turned to Thomas and Eno. "Anything else I can do for you guys?"

"Yeah," Thomas said. "It's getting late for another hike, so could we borrow your jeep?"

"Of course. It's right outside, keys inside. Just leave it near your truck. I have a locator on my phone, so we'll drive down in the morning and pick it up."

"Thanks again," Thomas said.

They climbed into the back of the jeep and Thomas started the motor.

As they pulled out, Elly turned and gave Gabby a wave goodbye. "Now that's the kind of woman I want to be when I grow up."

Thomas nodded. "I think you have a really good chance."

They drove down the mountainside with the high beams on. Thomas followed Gabby's tire tracks, and they soon arrived at the juncture where they met earlier that morning.

"Almost there," Thomas said. "Shouldn't be more than another ten minutes or so."

Suddenly they heard a noise above and looked up to see a helicopter in the distance, framed by the moonlight. It was heading toward the shuttle pad.

"That must be your mother and father coming back," Elly said.

Eno leaned forward anxiously. "I don't suppose Ignatius ever mentioned the exact time you were born?"

"No."

"Then perhaps we should go a bit faster."

Thomas hit the gas and turned down the path where they'd left Jack. Above them, the helicopter reached the shuttle pad and hovered in mid-air, about to land.

"Are we at least close?" Eno said.

"I can hear the floodwater," Thomas said, as the sound echoed faintly in the background.

He drove through the woods, dodging trees and bouncing over rocks as the helicopter began to descend. Thomas hit the brakes and the jeep skidded into the thicket of downed trees where they left Jack. He turned off the ignition but left the keys.

They jumped out of the jeep and jogged down the hill toward the area where they'd crashed. In the background, the helicopter disappeared from view.

Thomas broke into a run with Elly right behind and Eno bringing up the rear. When they reached the cable car, Thomas turned and looked back the mountain. It was a strange sensation to know that somewhere above, his mother was about to give birth to him. Then he looked at Elly and thought about how happy Ignatius would be to know that she met his wife, her mother. He was looking forward to being able to tell her the truth, so the memories of the day, along with the pictures she took, would become precious keepsakes.

Suddenly Elly came to a dead stop.

"What are you doing?" Eno said.

"I almost forgot…" she said, sliding off her backpack.

She quickly removed Gabby's butterfly jar and pulled off the top. The Dakota Skipper rose from its glass enclosure into the air. It hovered for a few moments, then looped past Thomas and shot up toward the moon. As it did, Thomas could see that what had appeared as plain brown wings concealed an explosion of yellow dots, each uniquely rendered by nature. The Skipper seemed to freeze in mid-air, its wings becoming orange, blue, and silver all at once, blending into the moon itself. Thomas turned toward Eno and Elly to see if they were seeing the remarkable transition, but his voice had suddenly disappeared. A numbness ran through the soles of his feet and he looked down to see that they were no longer touching the ground.

Thomas could make out Elly's mouth, distorted with urgency, as well as Eno's eyes, exploding with panic. They were holding his arms and legs to keep him from floating away as some unknown force sucked him toward the sky.

Somehow they managed to pull and push him into the cable car as the night was shattered by a piercing scream coming from the mountain above.

The sound was unmistakeable. It announced the arrival of a new life on Earth.

In his last lucid moment, Thomas knew what it meant.

He was out of time.

PART 3

CHAPTER 28

THERE WERE NO TIME-FLIES.

There was no sound or movement of any sort, just silence and stillness.

And darkness.

Finally, a faint thump sounded in the cable car, followed by a second and third in perfect rhythm. His heartbeat slowly became louder, each throb like a hammer inside Thomas's head. His eyes forced themselves open, as if to let the pain escape. All he could make out were shadows.

"Eno?"

"I'm right here in front of you," Eno said, his voice reverberating as if coming through a sound machine. "How do you feel?"

Thomas winced. "My ears, nose, and mouth are throbbing and my eyes burn."

Eno turned on the small light from his wrist-pod. Thomas shielded his face with his hand.

"I can't speak to your head," Eno said, "but my eye feels like that after a replacement. The burning doesn't last long, but you'll be sensitive to light for a short time." Eno held out two pills and a bottle of water. "Elly said to give you these when you woke. They should dull everything."

With his eyes clenched, Thomas took the pills and swallowed them. "What happened?"

"In Colorado? You froze, and then started to lift off."

"Lift off?"

"Elly said you looked like a human kite, whatever that is. We were only able to keep you from levitating by holding your ankles. We dragged you into the cable car moments before you were completely timeblown."

"Timeblown?" Thomas repeated as if it hadn't occurred to him.

"You don't remember? The helicopter with your pregnant mother? She must've given birth moments after they landed. By the time we started the time jump you seemed dead. We've been here an hour but could only detect a heartbeat about ten minutes ago. Fortunately, Ignatius told me what to expect if it happened. It turns out you were lucky."

"Lucky?"

"When it happened to Ignatius, he couldn't make it back to his transport and wound up a on an island off the coast of Maine in the middle of winter. It took him months until he could find a local to ferry him back to the mainland."

"Are you and Elly all right?"

"Perfectly fine. We weren't timeblown ourselves so we didn't experience any of your symptoms. But since we were all together in the cable car we were thrown out of time with you. As Elly correctly observed, we were along for the ride."

"Where are we now? And where is Elly?"

"We didn't have time to program the globe obviously, so no idea about our location. But as soon as your breathing returned to normal, Elly left to investigate."

"Have you looked outside?"

"Yes, but there's not much to see, except for a small mountain, which looks like a miniature version of the Mons. We could almost be on Mars in fact, except for the weather. Elly said it was like a summer day."

"Can you open the door for me?"

"Yes, but you better shield your eyes."

Thomas slowly lifted himself onto one of the benches and held his palms over his eyes.

Eno pushed the platform door open with his foot. Indeed, a small volcano sat at the end of a massive lava field. "It's like the view from our portal back in our cell on the Station."

Suddenly there was a rhythmic beeping sound.

"What's that?" Eno asked.

"The cell phone Elly gave me. It's in my backpack."

Eno pulled out the phone. "Hello? Yes, he's up and around, more or less. Talking, not walking." He put down the phone. "Elly's on her way. We should be able to see her any second."

Outside, a small figure was visible on the barren landscape. An arm waved.

In less than a minute, she was at the the cable car. "Thomas! Welcome back to the almost living. How are you?"

"I feel like something turned my body inside out. But other than that, not so bad."

"Did you find out where we are?" Eno said.

"Yes," Elly said. "Turns out the globe has a wicked sense of humor. It sent you home."

"To Mars?" Thomas said, confused.

"No, Iceland. Also known to you natives as the Land of Fire and Ice. That volcano behind us is the Snaefellsjokull, which is still active, hence the fire. The glacier on top is the ice."

"How do you know all this?" Eno said.

"After you became fake citizens, I followed Thomas's example and did some research. I thought it might come in handy."

Eno's face fell with disappointment. "So once again we're in the middle of nowhere?"

"Actually, we're only thirty-one miles from the capital, Reykjavik. I saw the sign on the Ring Road, which goes around the island. We can hitch into the city."

"Hitch?" Thomas said.

"Beg for a ride. It's an internationally recognized custom. All you need is a thumb."

"Why would we go into the city?" Eno asked.

"We need to find out what year it is, for one thing. And I think we should get Thomas to the local hospital so he can be examined. He might have a concussion."

"I'm all right, really," Thomas said unconvincingly.

"You don't look all right," Eno said.

"What I could really use is some food."

"One more reason to go into town," Elly said. "In the race to leave Colorado, we left the dehydrated stuff behind, though we do have Mrs. Teasely's poached eels, now three days old."

"Are your eyes any better?" Eno said.

"Not much," Thomas said.

"Hold on," Elly said. "I think I may have something that will help."

She rifled through her backpack and pulled out a pair of sunglasses. She carefully slid them onto Thomas's face.

"There. Now you look like a real man of mystery."

✦✦

It took almost a half hour to reach the road. Thomas, who normally set the pace, lagged behind, walking stiffly. They took up position on the gravel shoulder and Elly extended her thumb. But the first few cars whizzed past them without slowing.

"Perhaps you should use both thumbs," Eno suggested.

"That's not the way it works," Elly said. "We don't want them to think we're weirdos. We are, after all, two boys from Mars and a half-Jamaican girl from San Francisco."

Several more cars passed, when an open-air truck carrying sheep, pulled over. The driver, in his late twenties, leaned out the window. He had long hair, a whispy blond goatee, and a friendly smile.

"Need a ride?"

"Yeah," Elly said. "We were biking and got flat tires on the lava rock. We need to get back to the rental shop in Reykjavik so somebody can come out and fix them."

"I'm on my way to the City Hall to get my truck permit renewed. If you don't mind the company of sheep, you're welcome. They're cool with humans if you're cool with them."

"We're cool with sheep," she said.

The young driver jumped out and met them at the back of the truck, where he unlocked the gate that held the sheep.

"You guys coming from the Center of the Earth?"

"The what?" Elly said.

"The volcano, from the Jules Verne book. *Journey to the Center of the Earth*?"

"Oh, that's what that was." Elly said. "Should've known."

"It's a big tourist attraction. You're Americans, right?"

"Yeah," Elly said. "We're from San Francisco."

"My name is Dufgus."

"I'm Elly. This is Thomas and Eno."

Dufgus studied Thomas closely. "Have I given you a ride before? You look familiar."

"We've only been in the country since this morning," Elly said.

"Sorry then, my mistake," Dufgus said, opening the gate and stood back.

Elly climbed in first, then held out a hand for Thomas. Eno reluctantly followed, making sure to stay as far from the sheep as possible.

"Excuse me, Dufgus," Elly said. "Do you happen to know the date?"

"Fifth of July," he said without hesitation.

"I assume it's 2023?" Eno said.

"It better be," Dufgus said, "My permit expires today, and I'd get a fine for being late."

Dufgus got back in the driver's seat and started the truck as Thomas turned to Eno, puzzled. "How did you know what year it was?"

"Just a working assumption. Ignatius said that in the event you were timeblown it would send us back time to our first jump on

Earth, which was July 4, 2023. According to my research, the time difference between San Francisco and Iceland is eight hours, which would make it the morning of the fifth."

"Amazing," Elly said. "After all this time, I've still only been gone overnight?"

"Exactly," Eno said.

Elly smiled. "You really do have to love time travel."

"But why Iceland? Thomas said.

"Regarding location," Eno said, "Ignatius admitted complete ignorance on the subject."

And with that the truck pulled out.

The drive took only ten minutes to reach the city, but to Thomas it seemed much longer. His head cleared after ten minutes or so, and he began to feel much better physically and much worse in every other way. In the aftermath of being timeblown, he suddenly felt a heightend sense of risk about the mission. Not so much for himself and Eno, but for Elly. If being timeblown proved anything, it demonstrated that there were forces beyond his control, some life threatening. If anything were to happen to him, there was a good chance Elly would wind up stranded in some random time or place forever. As that unsettling realization sank in, the truck slowed and they entered the city center. A minute later, they stopped in front of a pair of matching modern buildings separated by a long footbridge that crossed a small man-made lake.

With the truck still running, Dufgus appeared at the back and opened the gate. "I need to find a parking spot in the neighorhood, so I'll let you off here. There's an information desk inside, so you should be able to get directions to your bike shop. If you're hungry, the café in back has the best lobster soup in the city."

"Thanks for everything." Elly said.

"My pleasure," Dufgus said, then paused to glance at Thomas one last time. "You sure you've never been to Iceland? I could've sworn I've seen you before."

"Sorry," Thomas said. "This is my first visit."

"I hope it's a good one then," Dufgus waved.

Thomas nodded, though he wasn't looking forward to the conversation he needed to have with Elly.

The three of them walked into the city hall, past a giant 3D map of Iceland, and onto the outdoor café, which occupied a large open terrace overlooking the water. It was early for lunch so only a few people were eating.

"Let's grab that table over there," Elly said, gesturing to one near the railing. "Somebody left a newspaper on it."

They sat down, and Elly picked up the paper. "July 5, 2023."

"Looks like your theory was right, Eno," Thomas said.

"Though I'm not sure what that does for us," Eno said.

Thomas saw his opportunity, took a deep breath, and spoke up.

"For one thing," Thomas said, "it means Elly could get a flight home."

This caused an immediate reaction from both Eno and Elly, thought not the same kind.

"And explain why she was missing overnight?" Eno said.

"Yes," Elly nodded, "there would be that."

"Well," Thomas said, "we might not get another chance to be in Elly's time zone. So maybe time is trying to tell us something."

"Like what?" Elly asked, a bit suspiciously.

Thomas nervously fingered one of his Q-Rings and glanced at Eno. "I hate to say this, but after what happened in Colorado, I think things have gotten much more dangerous for Elly."

"Uh, excuse me," Elly said. "I wasn't the one who was timeblown."

"I know, but…if something happened to me, you might be stranded and never get home. Let's face it, the mission's become too unpredictable."

Elly gave Thomas a puzzled look. "Hasn't it always been? After all, I went to another *planet* on a rescue mission in the middle of an *armed rebellion.* Besides, if anything were to happen to you, I have complete faith that Eno could always get me home."

Eno couldn't help smiling at the compliment.

"So nothing's really changed," she said. "Unless there's something you're not telling me?"

Eno avoided looking at Thomas, who didn't know what to say. He couldn't bring himself to lie to Elly, but he couldn't tell her the truth either.

Fortunately, a young waitress appeared to interrupt the conversation.

"Welcome," she said, smiling. "Can I get you something to drink?"

"Water's fine, thanks," Elly said. "And we'll have three orders of the lobster soup. Oh, and some crackers please. My friend here hasn't eaten in days. It seems to be affecting his mind."

"I'll get it right away," she said, and hurried off.

Elly looked out at the water where a family of ducks glided past. At the table nearest them, two men sat down. Both were in their forties and dressed in similar dark suits.

Elly stood up, slightly annoyed. "Excuse me, I need to wash my hands."

As she left, Eno turned to Thomas. "Well, that didn't go very well."

"No, it didn't," Thomas sighed.

"Just out of curiosity, what were you thinking?"

Thomas sighed. "After seeing her with her parents in Colorado, I just don't know if I can look her in the eyes anymore knowing what I know."

"You're not considering telling her the truth?"

"No, but…"

Thomas suddenly noticed that the two men across from them were staring at him. A moment later, Elly reappeared from the building.

"That was fast," Eno said.

"I didn't make it to the bathroom. I only got as far as the bulletin board."

"What bulletin board?" Thomas asked.

Elly lowered her voice. "The one that said 'WANTED' with the big picture of you underneath, asking anybody with information about your whereabouts to call the local authorities."

"Are you serious?" Eno said.

"See for yourself," she said, sliding the copy of Thomas's photograph toward Thomas and Eno. "I took the liberty of taking it down."

The boys examined the photo. It showed Thomas wearing his hoodie and walking down the darkened street at night in San Francisco.

"One has to admit," Eno said, "you do look quite menacing."

"That's my house in the background," Elly said. "The FBI must've taken it the night you brought me home from New York. I told them you went back to Iceland, so they must've sent the photo here on the chance somebody could identify you. That must be why Dufgus said you looked familiar. There aren't many fifteen-year olds wanted by the FBI. Speaking of which, and don't look now, those two men a few tables away keep looking in our direction. Those sunglasses probably aren't helping, Thomas. It looks like you're in disguise."

Thomas took off the glasses as the waitress appeared with a tray and served the three bowls of reddish liquid, along with a basket of cellophane wrapped crackers.

"Will there be anything else?" the waitress said.

"No, thanks," Elly said. "Just a check, please."

The waitress put the check in front of Elly and walked away.

"What now?" Thomas said.

"Given the fact that your photo has been in the lobby for who knows how long, it's probably not wise to linger here much longer. Good thing about soup is that you can drink it."

Elly lifted the bowl to her lips and took a huge gulp. Thomas followed suit.

Eno looked at the soup suspiciously. "Dare I ask what 'lobster' is?"

"A large aquatic insect with oversized claws."

"I think I'll stick with the crackers," Eno said, taking a package from the basket.

As Thomas and Elly finished their soup, Elly took a fifty dollar bill from her casino winnings and put it on top of the check.

"What's the plan?" Thomas said.

"You and Eno get up and walk out slowly, over the footbridge," Elly said. "I'll follow just in case I need to distract our friends over there."

"If I remember correctly," Eno said, "this is what happened on our first time jump from San Francisco. When the police arrested you?"

"This time it's different. Worse case, they'll just put me on a flight back home. That should make everybody happy."

Thomas grabbed several packages of crackers and stuffed them into his pocket. He and Eno stood up and walked toward the bridge.

Elly opened a package of crackers and sauntered over to the railing, pausing to feed the ducks while she kept an eye on the two men at the restaurant. As Thomas and Eno started over the footbridge, one of the men got up and headed after them while the other made a call on his phone.

Elly screamed at the top of her lungs. "Thomas, Eno! Run!"

CHAPTER 29

THE BOYS SPRINTED OVER the footbridge and into the street. Elly quickly caught up and pointed toward a neighborhood of small, box-like houses with colored roofs. She turned at the first corner and came to an abrupt stop, scanning the area in every direction as if looking for something.

"Where are we going?" Eno panted.

Elly suddenly pointed. "Over there!"

Dufgus's truck was parked about fifty feet away.

"He said he was looking for a parking spot," Elly said, as they hurried to the back gate, where the sheep turned to meet them.

"Hey, guys," she said, "you remember us?"

Thomas and Elly climbed over the gate and pulled Eno up after them, as a police siren wailed in the background.

"Hopefully that's not for us," Elly said, "but we should lay low just in case."

Thomas and Elly crawled to the middle of the truck bed and dragged Eno to the floor. The sheep huddled around them, one nuzzling Eno's neck.

They could hear voices yelling in the street as a second police siren got louder.

"What do we do now?" Eno asked.

"Make yourself comfortable," Elly said. "We may be here for awhile."

They did their best to stretch out on the truck bed, though Eno wound up with his head between the feet of one of sheep. After about ten minutes the sirens began to fade.

"Can we go now?" Eno said.

"I don't think it's safe yet," Elly said. "The police are probably still around and it'll be tricky getting through this neighborhood without them seeing us."

"I don't think I can stay this way much longer," he said.

Suddenly they heard footsteps approach.

"You think it's the police?" Eno said.

"Sshhh," Elly whispered.

The truck door opened and closed. The engine started, and the truck began to move.

Elly raised her thumb. "Dufgus to the rescue."

They waited until he drove several blocks before Elly got to her knees and looked out, her head swiveling like a periscope. They were on a busy commercial street filled with people.

"Coast looks clear."

The truck came to a stop at a red light. Elly stood up.

"Let's go."

They had just enough time to climb out before the light changed to green. As the truck pulled away, they stood at the curb.

"Where to?" Thomas said.

"I don't know," Elly said. "But we need to get off the street."

She scanned the area and pointed to a small shop with a sign that read "Te and Kaffi." She said, "I don't speak Icelandic but I'm willing to bet that means tea and coffee."

They hurried across the street and ducked into the shop, which had long coffee bar with a dozen or so tables. They worked their way toward the back and found an empty one. Elly ordered them a pot of chamomile tea and a plate of Icelandic pastries filled with vanilla custard.

"I'm not sure the tea helps with the effects of being timeblown, but I've heard chamomile is good for anxiety, so I figure we could use some of that right now."

Thomas gobbled a pastry while Eno examined the custard that leaked over his fingers.

"What now?" Thomas said.

"I say we get back to the cable car," Eno said. "We need to get on with the mission."

"Does that include me, Thomas, or do you still think things have gotten too *unpredictable*?"

Thomas wanted to make it clear that he wanted Elly to continue, but also be honest about the jeopardy involved. "Obviously, you're as critical to what we're doing as Eno—right, Eno?"

Eno didn't hesitate. "No doubt about it."

"But because of your past with the police, there's a real possibility that..."

Elly nodded knowingly. "That I might be what, a liability?"

"No. That if we did get caught by the FBI, you'd get in even more trouble than us. What would your father say?"

The mention of Elly's father finally gave her pause, but she still resisted the idea of quitting the mission. "He'd understand that what I was doing was important for the planet. I hope."

"Unfortunately, you can't tell him," Eno pointed out, "without also getting into the whole time travel conversation."

Elly sighed with frustration. "You're right."

"I hate the idea of splitting up as much as you do, probably more," Thomas said. "But I really don't see any other way. At least for now. It's in your best interest, Elly."

Elly nodded. "All right, no use beating a dead horse. Let's figure out how to get back to the cable car before the FBI puts out an APB for both of us."

"APB are initials for what esactly?" Eno said.

"All Points Bulletin, which means they alert everybody in the country to be on the look-out. And this is a very small country. We'll have to wait until night to head back to the cable car."

"We need to find a place where we don't stand out so much," Thomas said. "Is there somewhere where lots of young people gather?"

Elly glanced around the coffee shop. At a nearby table, a woman just a few years older than them was reading a book. "Maybe that girl over there can help," Elly said. "Her sweatshirt says University of Reykjavik. I assume you have them on Mars?"

"No," Thomas said. "Anyone who's really smart, like Eno, gets assigned to a research group. The rest of us get sent to the water mines or mirror factories or one of the terrafarms."

"But you at least get your choice?"

Thomas laughed.

Elly smiled. "Well, at least I made you laugh again. I was starting to worry that getting timeblown killed your sense of humor. Sit tight while I see if I can get directions."

Elly got up and approached the young woman. Thomas and Eno watched as they shook hands. After a few moments of conversation, Elly came back.

"Good news. The school's not far from here, close enough to take a bus. The kids will be a little older than us, but we can definitely blend in for a few hours."

"And how will we get back to the cable car?" Eno asked.

"We'll cross that bridge when we come to it," Elly said.

"Hopefully we won't be chased over it like the last one," Eno said.

✦✦

THE WEARY TRIO TOOK the number five bus to the University of Reykjavik, a modern three-story structure with a series of wings built in a circular pattern around a glass reception area.

Elly found the directory, which had a diagram of the campus. "Hey, look at this. Each wing is named after one of the planets, and they all revolve around the Sol, which we're in now. The cafeteria's in Venus. We could hang there for a while, then hit the study area, which is in Pluto."

"What's in Mars?" Eno asked.

"Classrooms. But we can stop by, if you're feeling nostalgic."

“No thanks,” Thomas said.

“Okay,” Elly said. “The cafeteria it is. Maybe we can eat in peace this time.”

By the time they got there, it was almost four o’clock and the cafeteria was almost empty. Elly got a smoked salmon sandwich and an apple while the boys lingered in line, overwhelmed by the variety of food. Eno was still deciding when Thomas arrived back at the table with a large bowl of spaghetti and meatballs, three sandwiches and a pair of bananas. He stuffed the sandwiches into one pocket, the bananas into another, and went to work on the spaghetti.

It was nearly five o’clock when they left the cafeteria and walked through Mercury and Neptune to the study area, adjacent to the school library. As they moved through the corridors, they checked the school bulletin boards for “Wanted” photos of Thomas but didn’t see a single one. They settled on a table near the exit in case they had to make a fast escape.

“We’ve got a few hours to kill before sunset,” Elly said. “What else can you tell us about your home country, Thomas?”

Thomas leaned back and looked out the floor to ceiling windows at the coastline.

“Reykjavik’s a peninsula, so almost everything has a water view. You see that beach over there?”

“Yeah?”

“It’s geothermal, the only one in the world.”

“On the planet Earth, you mean,” Eno said.

“Well, it’s the only one where there’s actually water, and you can swim without getting incinerated.”

Elly smiled. “But why quibble.”

Thomas smiled too, happy that Elly no longer seemed upset. The disappointment she had over having to go home seemed to have passed, at least for now.

Suddenly her phone began to buzz.

"That's weird," she said, pulling her phone out of her backpack. She looked at the phone screen. "It's Rosario's number."

"Maybe she's trying to find you," Thomas said.

Elly answered. "Rosario? Hold on, let me get somewhere I can hear you."

Elly jumped up and hurried out the exit door.

"Well," Eno said, "this is going better than I thought. I think you actually managed to convince Elly it's in her best interest to go home. I know it's hard to imagine going on without her. But as you said, it would only be temporary."

"Maybe, maybe not. If the FBI's watching her, how long you think it'll take before they stop? And how will we even know?"

Before Eno could answer, Elly came back inside, looking dazed.

"Is everything all right?" Thomas asked.

She sat down, on the verge of tears. "No. My father had a heart attack last night. He's in the hospital."

"That's terrible," Thomas said, putting a hand over hers.

"He's alive, but they wouldn't give Rosario any more details because she's not family."

"I'm sorry, Elly," Eno added.

"What can we do?" Thomas asked.

"I need to go to the airport right away and get a flight home." Elly threw up her free hand. "What am I talking about? I don't have a passport!"

Elly shook her head with exasperation.

"I should never have left without even a note. It was so thoughtless of me. My father must've been worried sick when I didn't come home. I probably caused his heart attack!"

"Elly, listen to me," Thomas said. "We're going to get you home, as fast as possible, even if we have to turn ourselves in to the FBI."

"You can't do that, Thomas. I won't let you."

"Perhaps we should cross that other bridge now?" Eno said. "We can't wait for night. We need to go back to the cable car as soon as we can and get Elly back to San Francisco."

"Leave that to me," Thomas said.

He pulled out his chair and stood on top of it to address the room. "Can I have your attention everyone? It's an emergency!"

The fifty or so students in the study stopped talking and turned toward him.

"We need a ride to the Snaefellsjokull volcano, but don't have any local currency. However, I'm willing to pay in gold, which I brought with me from Mars."

The room, sensing that Thomas was joking, erupted in laughter.

"No, really," Thomas said, stepping up onto the table. "My friend Eno and I grew up on a station in Tharsis near the end of this century after the Earth became uninhabitable due to the superfloods. In 2086, we were sent here via time travel to try and save your planet." Thomas gestured to Elly. "Our friend Elly is actually from Earth and has been helping us, but her father is sick back in San Francisco. All we're asking is for a ride to our transport so we can take her home."

The laughter slowly subsided, replaced by a hum of curiosity as Elly climbed up next to him. "I know this is all hard to believe. But every single word Thomas just said is true."

A female student, her hair shaved in a circular patter with the fringe dyed blue, stood up. "How do you know?"

"Because I've been time traveling with them. We've been to New York in 2051, England in 1825, and Las Vegas in 2070. I've even been to Mars. And trust me, you don't want it to be your future home."

A heavyset boy with thick black glasses shouted from the very back of the room. "If you've been to Mars, then perhaps you can tell us how you solved the water problem? I assume you didn't bring along the bottled variety?"

There was a burst of laughter from his friends, when Eno stood on his chair.

"I'll answer that. Our water is mined using advanced deep drilling techniques that cut through the permafrost. We've also constructed mirror fields in areas receiving direct sunlight in order to warm the regolith. Our orbital mirror project will commence later this year, yielding an additional twelve percent of our water by the centennial in 2100, with a plan to be fully sustainable a hundred years from now."

The student who asked the question glanced at his friends, speechless.

"Look," Thomas said, "Eno could answer all of your questions and then some if we had time. But if there's one thing you should know about life on Mars is that it bears no resemblance to what you have here on Earth. In sixty-three years, almost everything that makes your life worth living—the air, the food, the animals, and most of all your values—will be non-existent on Mars. So, I'm not exaggerating when I say the fate of your planet is at stake, right now."

"All we're asking for is a ride," Elly added.

A hush came over the room, and the students began to look around to see how others were reacting. A young couple, about nineteen years old, stood up in the back. "We'll take you."

The rest of the students broke out in applause.

✦✦

IN FORTY-FIVE MINUTES, A beat up Volkswagen turned off the Ring Road and onto the bumpy lava field that led to the volcano. Elly was uncharacteristically quiet during the ride, so Thomas was left to explain to Falki and his girlfriend, Gunnborg, everything that happened from the time they evaded the FBI in San Francisco to the moment they were timeblown in Colorado. The two Icelanders were spellbound. Occasionally, they glanced at each other in disbelief, but Thomas relayed the story with such detail that it was hard not to believe him.

"This is us up ahead," Eno said.

Falki pulled off the Ring Road and headed toward the famous volcano. In a few minutes, the cable car came into view.

"Incredible," he said. "You really do travel in a cable car."

"And it's covered in mirrors, just like you told us," Gunnborg said.

"Can't time jump without them," Eno said. "You should pull over here and stay in the car while we walk the rest of the way. You don't want to get too close to the negative energy."

They pulled over and Eno jumped out of their Volkswagen.

As Thomas helped Elly out of the car, Eno ran into the cabin and reappeared holding a gold bar. He handed it to Gunnborg through the front window.

She weighed the heavy bar with disbelief. "Wait a minute…this is real gold?"

Falki was even more stunned. "We didn't think you were serious."

"So why did you give us a ride?" Elly asked, confused.

"We figured you were part of a theater group doing a piece about global warming."

"We thought the whole thing was a performance," Gunnborg added. "Including the car ride. I was half expecting you to fess up when we got here."

Falki nodded. "We just wanted to see how long it would take you to get a group of students to believe your story. And we wanted to be here at the end of it."

Gunnbord smiled. "The stuff about water on Mars was impressive, but the real turning point was your speech about the fate of our planet. We all know the Earth is in trouble. We see it every day. But to hear it put in such dramatic terms was really inspiring—right, Falki?"

"Our generation has to stand together if we want to save the planet."

"You don't know how right you are," Elly said.

"We can't thank you enough," Thomas said.

"Oh," Eno said, "as a bonus for your good faith, I suggest you stay until we leave. That way you can witness time travel in the works."

"Thank you," the couple said, amazed at their good fortune.

Thomas, Eno, and Elly disappeared inside the cable car while the couple held hands, filled with excitement at the possibility of what might happen next.

A minute later, a small tornado of dust gathered around the cable car and they watched as it disappeared from sight in a blast of redshift. It lit up the lava field and shot through the mouth of the volcano, all the way to the center of the Earth.

CHAPTER 30

IT WAS DARK WHEN they landed somewhere high above the city lights. The time-flies were back, buzzing urgently against the platform door as if trying to help open it.

Thomas and Elly woke at the same moment.

"We're here," Thomas said.

Elly jumped up, her eyes filled with nervous energy. "I need to hurry."

"Hold on," Thomas said. "Let me just make sure it's safe."

He opened the front door and stepped out on the platform. The sound of light traffic came from somewhere below.

"Please tell me we're back in San Francisco," Elly whispered under her breath.

"I can see the Golden Gate Bridge," Thomas said.

"Are we in Muir Woods?"

"No, we're in the city, near Chinatown I think."

Elly rushed out to see that the cable car was sitting on the observation deck of a skyscraper, which towered over the surrounding buildings.

"You were close," she said. "We're in the Financial District." She looked up to the glass pyramid that rose above them. Inside was a yellow beacon. "On the Transamerica building."

"Isn't that the place I asked you about when we first saw the city?" Eno said from the darkness of the cabin.

"Yeah. You wanted to know if I lived there. Seems like years ago, doesn't it?"

"Indeed," Eno said, amazed at how naïve he had been on that first day.

Thomas was silent. Elly had been their guide on Earth from the moment they landed, and bringing her back home now felt even more final than when they returned from their first time jump. But the look of relief on Elly's face undercut any sadness at their impending separation.

"Nice work with the Time Globe, Eno," Elly said. "My father's at Saint Francis Hospital, which is only a few blocks away."

"I can't take all the credit," Eno said. "Time obviously knows the city better than I do."

"I think it knows Elly too," Thomas said.

They grabbed their backpacks and hurried across the observation deck to a pair of elevators, located on the forty-eighth floor. In seconds, they reached the lobby and hurried out the back door. It was a few minutes before midnight, and the streets were deserted.

"C'mon," Elly said. "I know a shortcut."

She led them across the street to Redwood Park, a tree-filled oasis surrounding a large pond, complete with a fountain that shot jets of water into the air. On the surface were several metal frogs designed to look as if they were leaping into the pond. Thomas started counting the steps in his head, knowing that he and Eno would soon be coming back without Elly.

They hurried through the park to the street where Elly hailed the first cab that appeared. It took only five minutes to reach the hospital, but Elly kept her eyes out the window the whole time, keeping her thoughts to herself. The reception area was deserted and Elly stepped up to the information desk, where an older African-American woman looked up from her book.

"Can I help you sweetie?" the woman asked.

"My name is McAllister. My father is here, recuperating from a heart attack. I was out of the country when it happened and I just got back."

"Let me see," the woman said, checking her computer.

"Alfred McAllister."

"Yes. I'm his daughter, Elly."

"Visiting hours are over, but under the circumstances I think we can give you a pass. He's on the fourth floor, in the cardiac care unit."

She handed Elly a yellow stick-on badge along with a felt tip pen. Elly quickly printed her name and pressed the badge to her sweatshirt.

"Would be all right if my friends come along?"

The woman gave Thomas and Eno the once over.

"If it wasn't for them," Elly added, "I would never have even gotten here."

The woman could hear Elly's voice crack and patted her hand gently. Her fingernails were painted in orange and black tiger stripes. Without answering Elly's question, she slid two more badges across the counter, and Thomas gave them over to Elly, who suddenly remembered the boys didn't know how to write. She grabbed the pen and quickly printed their first names.

"Thank you so much," Elly said to the woman at the desk.

On the fourth floor, they got out of the elevator and hurried past a small waiting area on their way to the nurse's station. A nurse in his late twenties was watching a movie on his computer.

"Can I help you?"

"I'm Elly McAllister."

"Fred's daughter?"

"Right. I was out of the country, but I came back as soon as I heard what happened."

"Wow, you got here fast."

"As fast as humanly possible," Elly said, glancing at Thomas and Eno.

"I don't know if you're up to speed, but your dad's out of danger. He did have a pretty serious heart attack, and may need surgery down the line, but his cardiologist wants to observe him for a few days before making any decisions."

"Can I see my father?"

"He got some sleep meds about an hour ago, so he may be a little out of it, but let me check."

The nurse hurried down the hall. Elly turned to the boys.

"This could take a while. There's no reason for you to stick around."

"I don't agree," Thomas said. "You've been missing overnight. You might have some explaining to do. We can help with that."

Elly smiled. "And where would you start? With our trip to Mars? Or maybe our visit to nineteenth century England? What about our stay in 2070 Last Vegas and Colorado, not to mention the fact that we were in Iceland ten minutes ago?"

"But I'd leave out the part about Thomas being timeblown," Eno said. "Too preposterous."

The nurse came back down the hall.

"Thanks for the offer guys, but probably best to let me handle it."

"Good news, Miss McAllister," the nurse said. "Your father's awake, and you can go in. Room 411."

Elly turned to Thomas. "On second thought, would you mind staying until after I see him?"

"Of course not."

She hurried down the hall as Thomas and Eno went to the waiting area.

Eno plopped down on the couch while Thomas remained standing.

"Regardless of her father's condition," Eno said. "we really have no choice but to—"

"I know," Thomas said. "The mission, the mission, the mission."

He stood up, went to the window, and looked out at the bay toward Muir Woods, even though it was far too far to see it at night. He flashed on the image of Elly appearing out of the forest that first day. He thought of their first ferry ride, their first trip into the city, their first night in the tree house. "Elly's right. It feels like years since we got here."

"It seems as if we've been through several lives together," Eno said.

"The best ones, by far," Thomas nodded.

"Perilous though they've been, I'd have to agree."

More images flashed through Thomas's mind, snapshots in spacetime. Coney Island, New York, Washington, England, Death Valley, Las Vegas, Utah, Colorado, Iceland. It felt unnatural that they might go anywhere without Elly. "It doesn't seem right," he muttered out loud.

Eno knew very well what Thomas meant. "No, I have to admit, it doesn't."

Thomas looked up to see Elly hurrying toward them and turned to meet her.

"I just talked to my father," she said. "He's in good spirits. I said you had a chance to go hiking in Colorado, and I decided on the spur of the moment to go with you. But then we got stuck in the mountains without cell phone service until today but by that time he was in the hospital."

"Is he upset?" Thomas said.

"Not at all. He said he totally trusts my judgment but that the next time I go off like that I should leave a note."

Eno shook his head in disbelief. "Your father's a very understanding man."

"You're right. Oh, and Thomas, he wants to see you."

"Me? What for?"

"I don't know. He wouldn't explain why."

Thomas glanced anxiously in the direction of the cardiac hall.

"Go ahead, I'll stay here with Eno."

Thomas went past the nurse's station and down the hall to Mr. McAllister's room. He opened the door and peeked inside the room. Elly's father was sitting up, with a book in his lap. When he noticed Thomas, he waved him in. "Thomas, so good to see you again."

Thomas entered tentatively and stood at the foot of the bed, not quite sure how much he should say, if anything, about what Ignatius had shared with him. Perhaps Ignatius had promised Mr. McAllister that their arrangement about Elly would remain a secret. And the last thing he wanted to do was upset him, particularly in his current state.

"I think it's time we had a heart-to-heart. Are you familiar with that expression?"

"No, I'm not."

"It means an honest conversation. Our planetary mythology has designated the heart as the seat of our strongest emotions. While mine's a bit damaged at the moment, I think it's still functioning well enough to get the job done. The simple truth is that I know who you are, how you got here, and why."

Thomas felt a wave of relief wash over him. "How did you figure it out?"

Mr. McAllister lifted the book from his lap. "Some of it's in this incredible book I'm reading. Or should I say re-reading. I think you're familiar with the author."

Mr. McAllister flipped over the book to reveal the cover. It was blue with four words written in bold white letters: *The Tide of Time.* The author's name was written below in small gray letters: Ignatius Huxley.

"It was first published in 2068, forty-five years from now. Ignatius gave it to me as a present when he brought Elly to Earth. He told me all about you and your father's grand plan. Over the years, I wondered if it would ever really come to pass."

"But how did you know I was my father's…?"

"It was actually very simple." Mr. McAllister removed a photograph from the back of the book. Ignatius and Thomas's father were standing at the top of the glacier, directly under the Blue Bells. "The resemblance between you and your father is striking."

"Ignatius said I was his spitting image."

"I assume he told you about our arrangement before you came to Earth?"

"No. I only learned about it a few days ago, when we were in England."

"England?"

"Ignatius was in bad shape on Mars and we took him there to hide and recuperate."

"Is he going to be all right?"

"I think so. Doctor Darwin's taking good care of him."

"Would that be *the* Darwin?"

"His father, actually. Charles is still my age. It was all Elly's idea."

Mr. McAllister shook his head. "What an extraordinary world you live in. There's so much I'd love to talk to you about, but unfortunately now isn't the time. I take it you've kept the true circumstances of Elly's paternity to yourself?"

"Yes. I promised Ignatius I wouldn't tell her."

"Thank you for that, Thomas. I know it would upset her terribly. Of course, someday she must know. But hopefully after I'm gone, when it will be easier to understand."

Thomas nodded, filled with conflicting emotions. While Mr. McAllister had cleared the air about some things, there was one thing he was still curious about.

"So, you knew who I was as soon as you met me?" Thomas said.

"Your story about Iceland was quite convincing. But when I heard about your shuttle being discovered in Muir Woods, I knew for sure."

"Is that why you let Elly go with me?"

"Yes. I was prepared that you might show up someday, though I was hoping it was still a few years off. I was happy for the world's sake that your father's mission was beginning. But selfishly, I knew I'd be losing my daughter."

"You shouldn't worry, Mr. McAllister; she's not coming with us this time. She wants to stay with you, and I think it's for the best."

"I'd be lying if I said I wasn't relieved, Thomas. My ticker has rudely reminded me that my time on this planet is nearing an end, so I'd hate to lose her now. But I'm also saddened by the thought of her being alone after I'm gone. I trust you'll come back for her when the time is right?"

"I will. I promise."

"Thank you, Thomas. Oh, and for what it's worth, you needn't worry about those FBI agents, at least for now. I contacted their office and found out that they're on a plane to Iceland, where you were spotted earlier today." Mr. McAllister laughed, and Thomas was happy to see that their recent adventures had given him some pleasure. "You should go see Elly now. She might start to become suspicious."

"Thank you, Mr. McAllister. And good luck."

"Good luck to you as well, Thomas."

✦✦

THOMAS WALKED BACK TO the waiting area in a daze. He had to fight the urge to tell Elly everything that just transpired with her father. Instead, he now had yet another secret to keep.

Elly stood up as she saw him coming. "Well? What did he want to talk to you about?"

"He just wanted to thank me for bringing you back, and wish me good luck in my travels."

The nurse approached Elly and held up a finger to interrupt. "Sorry, but will you be spending the night, Miss McAllister? If so, I can arrange for a cot in your father's room."

"That would be great, thank you."

"No problem."

The nurse gave her a quick wave and disappeared down the hall.

"Where were we?" Elly said.

"Getting ready to say goodbye," Eno said, anxious to get the difficult leave-taking over.

"We could always wait until morning," Thomas said. "Eno and I can spend the night and come back in—"

"No, Thomas, you can't," Elly said regretfully. "By morning, people will be coming in to work at the Transamerica building and see the cable car sitting on the observation deck. Besides, it would only postpone the inevitable. Back in Iceland you said things were getting too unpredictable for me on the mission, and you were right. But now they're really simple. I only have one father after all, and for now I belong with him."

Thomas and Eno didn't respond. There was nothing left to say.

"Eno, would you mind if Thomas and I had a moment alone?"

"Of course not. I have to find the bathroom anyway. That lobster soup didn't quite agree with me."

Eno disappeared down the hall.

"Before you leave," Elly said, "I want to give you something." She lifted her backpack and put it on the couch. "Do you remember me telling you that my birth name was Elpis?"

"Yeah."

"In Greek mythology, she was the last thing in Pandora's box, which history tells us was actually a jar." Elly reached into her backpack and removed the butterfly jar Gabby had given her in Colorado, the one that held the Dakota Skipper. "It was probably something like this one. Anyway, Elpis was the spirit of hope. So even when the jar looked empty, hope was always there. I don't know where or when you'll wind up next, but as long as you have it, you'll have my spirit. You'll have hope."

Elly handed it to Thomas.

"Thanks, Elly." Thomas carefully put it into his own backpack, "I have something for you, too."

"Back at Stinson Beach, you told me a ring meant that a boy had a relationship with a special girl. Well, you're the most special girl I've ever met, so I want you to have this."

He removed the Q-Ring from his left hand and held it out.

"But, Thomas, you may need this."

"I've still got one. Anyway, I'm not leaving until you take it."

Elly took the ring and slid it onto her finger. It was a few sizes too large, but Elly held in place with her thumb.

"Thank you, Thomas. I'll always cherish it."

"I want you to know, whatever happens, I'll come back for you."

Elly threw her arms around Thomas and he put his around her. As they tightened their grip on each other, Thomas felt as if they were suspended in time and he wished they could stay like that forever. But a shadow soon appeared in his eyeline to break the moment.

"Sorry to interrupt," Eno said. "but a pair of policemen just got off the elevator. I don't mean to be paranoid, but given recent history…"

"Eno's right," Elly said. "You better go. Here, take these." She dug into her backpack and handed Eno her binoculars. "Keep one eye out for Thomas. And the other one for yourself."

"Will do," Eno said, backing up.

"Police or not, you don't think you're getting away without a hug, do you?"

Before Eno could react, Elly put her arms around him. "I know you'll hate hearing this, but you've become like a brother to me."

"The truth is," Eno stammered, "you've become…like a sister to me."

"Ha. I know you don't mean that, but it's sweet of you to say."

Elly released Eno and Thomas could see the tears forming in her eyes, though she didn't lift a finger to stop them.

"Just so you know, I'm not going to wave goodbye because I'm not going to admit you're leaving. Given the beauty of time travel, you could be gone for a year and come back tomorrow morning, right Eno?"

"Technically true, Elly."

"So, you'll know where to find me. Now go save the world."

CHAPTER 31

As the cab pulled away from the hospital, Thomas looked up to the fourth floor, hoping to catch one last glimpse of Elly. But true to her word, she wasn't there.

In minutes, the Transamerica building loomed above them. What little traffic existed earlier was now gone, and the streets were completely empty.

"You can let us off in front of the park," Thomas told the cab driver, but when they pulled over, he looked out the window, puzzled. "What happened to the fountain?" he said.

The driver glanced at him in the rearview. "What do you mean?"

"We were here just an hour ago. It was on then."

"I don't know," he said. "They probably shut it off at midnight."

Thomas handed the driver the last of the money Elly had given him.

"This is too much, kid."

"That's all right," Thomas said. "Keep it."

"Paper's not a viable currency where we're going," Eno explained.

Thomas and Eno got out of the cab and started toward the park entrance. The Transamerica's rooftop beacon cast an eerie yellow glow over the transplanted redwoods. As they reached the entrance, Thomas abruptly put out his arm to stop Eno from taking another step.

"What's the matter?" Eno said.

"Where are the frogs?"

"What frogs?"

"The metal ones in the pond. You didn't notice them when we left?"

"Not really. What are you…?"

Thomas pulled Eno away. "Put your head down and keep walking."

"What are we doing?"

"Taking a detour around the park. We can't get through it right now."

"Why not?

"Because the Mastership's sitting in the middle. It's camouflaged to reflect its background, so it's taking up the space where the fountain and frogs should be."

They reached the corner and crossed the street to the next block. Thomas pulled Eno into the alley between buildings.

"Can I have the binocs?" Thomas said.

Eno reached into his backpack for the ones Elly gave him. "How are we going to get back in the building?"

"I'll use my magnetic pick. The one I made back on the Station. I just want to make sure there's no Redshirts near the entrance." Thomas scanned the area, then handed Eno the binocs. "I can't see any, but if they're here, they could be hiding anywhere."

"That's a comforting thought. Shall we run?"

"No, that might alert them. Just walk fast. If they show up, then we can run."

They emerged from the alley and walked briskly toward the building. They were halfway there when they heard footsteps behind them.

Eno looked at Thomas anxiously. "Time to run?"

"Wait until they show themselves."

Thomas and Eno were about ten feet from the entrance when they saw the reflection of Varik and the Moons in a ground floor window. They reached for their holstered laser guns.

"Run!" Thomas said.

As Varik and the Moons rounded the corner, Thomas swiped his pick against the handle and opened the door. He and Eno ducked inside seconds before the laser fire hit the building. Thomas locked the door from inside and ran toward the elevator bank when they heard the sizzle of a laser cutting through the door. Thomas pushed Eno past the elevators.

"Where are we going?"

"To the stairs."

"Why?"

"Because the Moons will never be able to keep up."

"What makes you think I can?"

"You'll be fine," Thomas said, throwing the stairway door open. "All that low-oxygen hiking in Colorado must've made your lungs stronger."

"We'll see about that," Eno said skeptically.

They ran up the first flight of stairs and were halfway to the second when they heard Varik and the Moons burst through the stairway door below. Thomas looked down through the handrail as Varik fired a shot, which barely missed his head. They continued running.

"I take it you remember," Eno panted, "that the observation deck is on—"

"The forty-eighth floor. As soon as we lose them, we'll hop in the elevator."

They raced up the third flight and turned toward the fourth. Varik and the Moons stopped at the second story landing and waited for Thomas and Eno to appear above. The moment they did, Varik and the Moons fired several shots, the lasers cutting through the railing. Thomas pulled it away and tossed it down the stairs. He could hear Varik and the Moons scrambling away as it crashed toward them.

Thomas kept going. Eno was panting heavily now.

"I can't make it much farther."

"Only two more floors. We'll get the elevator on six."

Eno nodded, too winded to speak. As Thomas got to the fifth floor, he looked down to see the Moons doubled over on the stairs, gasping for air. Varik grabbed Simon's laser gun and with a weapon in each hand, continued alone.

Eno got halfway to the sixth floor when he had to stop, out of breath. Thomas heard Varik gaining and pulled Eno the rest of the way to the landing. He shoved him through the door, then slammed it shut, planting his body against it.

"Get the elevator!" he yelled to Eno.

Eno staggered toward the two high-speed elevators that went to the observation deck. Thomas heard Varik running up the stairs, with the Moons thumping along behind, trying to catch up. When they arrived, they threw themselves against the door like battering rams, almost knocking Thomas over. But he held on until he heard the elevator's signature bing.

Thomas stood back and pulled the door open. The Moons fell inside, one over the other, Simon's gun skittering across the floor. Thomas grabbed it and ran for the elevator, where Eno was waiting. As Varik climbed over the Moons, Thomas jumped inside. In the hallway, Varik aimed both guns at the elevator. But the shots hit the door just as it closed.

Eno clutched his chest, trying to catch his breath. "That was close."

"It's not over. He'll use the other elevator."

The doors on their elevator opened on the forty-eighth floor, but as Eno started toward the observation deck, Thomas stopped outside the elevator.

"These doors…what are they made of?"

"Steel, most likely."

"What temperature does it melt?"

"Somewhere around…1,400 degrees. Why?"

"I'll fix them so you'll have time to program the globe. Go!"

Eno disappeared toward the cable car as Thomas pointed the laser gun he took from Simon at the elevator carrying Varik. He moved the high-powered beam down the seam that separated the door panels, melting the metal and fusing them together.

He finished just as the elevator arrived, and when Varik tried to open the doors, they whined in frustration. Thomas started for the cable car as Varik kicked at the elevator from the inside. Moments later, the banging stopped and Thomas realized that Varik would simply take the elevator back down and transfer to another. But it would buy them some precious time.

Thomas raced to the observation deck and poked his head inside the cable car to see Eno frantically programing the Time Globe. "How's it going?"

"Not good. The destination sphere is stuck."

"Can you fix it?"

"Yes, but it will take a minute or so."

"Do it. I'll try to hold off Varik."

Thomas surveyed the observation deck for a place to make a stand. But there was only one option on the wide open space. He looked up at the spire, a four-sided pyramid that covered the yellow warning beacon. It was a few hundred feet high and sheathed with aluminum panels, making it almost impossible to climb. But there was no better choice.

He tucked the laser guns under his belt, grabbed one of the panels and started up, planting one foot solidly on the slippery metal before moving the other. He was about ten feet up when he heard the door to the deck open and saw Varik emerge. He fired a shot that landed a few inches over Varik's head, forcing him to retreat back inside the door.

Thomas took the opportunity to maneuver around to the back of the spire, out of sight.

After a few moments, Varik threw the door open and ran onto the observation deck. He rolled toward the pyramid, directly under Thomas and got off several shots. He ducked back as the lasers ricocheted against the aluminum, flaring into the night sky.

Thomas quickly shifted to the other side of the pyramid so that Varik was forced to shoot in the opposite direction, away from the cable car.

But unable to see his target, Varik soon stopped shooting.

In the silence that followed, the deck door opened and the Moons started out, but Thomas got off a few quick shots, which sent them ducking back inside.

The glare of the beacon now flooded the deck, allowing Thomas to see Varik's silhouette as he flattened his back against the wall and slid to his feet.

For a moment, neither of them moved.

But without warning, Eno stepped onto the cable car platform. Unaware of Varik's presence, he shouted up at Thomas. "I've got it fixed!"

Varik jumped out from behind the wall and pointed his laser gun at Eno's head.

He shouted up at Thomas. "Drop the gun or your friend will need a replacement brain to go along with his eye!"

Thomas peeked down to see that Eno's situation was hopeless. He slid around to the front of the spire, and tossed the laser gun to the observation deck. It landed to the side of Varik, but far enough away so that he had to turn to retrieve it. The moment he did, a shadow crossed overhead and Varik swiveled to see Thomas in the air, diving toward him. He tried to react but was a moment too late as Thomas landed on top of him, taking them both to the ground. The lankier Varik used his height as leverage to roll Thomas on his back, but the quicker Thomas slid out and slammed Varik's arm against the concrete, forcing him to drop his weapon.

Thomas jumped to his feet and kicked the gun toward Eno, who picked it up. But as he did, Varik got up and launched a bony shoulder into Thomas's stomach, slamming him against the concrete wall that rimmed the observation deck. Thomas was momentarily stunned, long enough for Varik to grab him at the knees and flip him over the side of the building.

Eno let out an involuntary scream as Thomas disappeared from view.

Varik turned toward the stunned Eno and smiled triumphantly. Eno gripped the gun in his two hands, which were shaking. Varik moved toward the terrified Eno, who backed up toward the cable car.

Meanwhile, Thomas clutched the ledge a few feet below, dangling forty stories over the Mastership, his fingers burning against the rough surface.

Suddenly he got an idea. Up to now, Thomas had only used the Q-Rings to manipulate gravity against an aggressor. But with the adrenaline of the moment coursing through his body, he wondered if he could apply the same tactic to his own body. Since he'd given one of his Q-rings to Elly, he'd have to do it with one hand. Rapidly losing his grip on the ledge, it was worth a try.

Thomas swung his ring hand onto the ledge, then kicked his legs out to swing his body sideways. When they swung back, he dug the Q-Ring into the ledge and used every last ounce of energy to catapault himself up toward the ledge.

He was still in the air as a laser blast flared above him, accompanied by a scream. A body hit the deck a few feet from where Thomas landed, but in the darkness and confusion, it took a moment for him to realize that it wasn't Eno but Varik, lying on his back with his shoulder on fire.

Thomas ran to Eno, still in shock, and pulled the gun from his hand. He tossed it over the side of the building, then guided him into the cable car. As they got inside, the deck door blew open, revealing the Moons. They ran toward Varik, writhing in pain, and put out the flickering flames at his shoulder, a result of the point-blank shot.

A group of Redshirts finally arrived to help. Assuming Thomas was still on the spire, they dropped to their knees and began shooting at the pyramid.

"He's not there anymore, you idiots!" Varik shouted. "Don't let them get away!"

The Redshirts turned their aim on the cable car, but the mirrors reflected the laser fire back at them, forcing them to stop shooting and charge the car itself.

But now, the tornado of dark matter that preceded every time jump was whirling around the cable car with hurricane-like winds, blowing them across the deck.

The frustrated Varik finally got to his knees, only to be met with a blast of redshift, mixed with a swirl of yellow light from the tower beacon.

The mixture of the two transformed his face into a sickly orange.

CHAPTER 32

THOMAS WOKE WITH HIS hands still burning from the ledge on the Transamerica building. But a strange sight quickly distracted him from the pain. Despite the fact that time-flies were clustered on one side of the cabin, they were swaying back and forth to the opposite side.

"Eno?"

Eno opened his eyes. "What?"

"I think we've landed."

"So why are we still moving?"

Eno pulled himself up. "It feels like our first trip to San Francisco, on that ferry."

The cable car thumped over a solid object as Thomas tried to stand. He'd barely made it to his feet when he was jolted backward, and then to the other side of the cabin. Using the stabilizing straps, he made his way to the front of the cabin and pushed open the door. The horizon was barely visible under a thick blanket of mist. The only thing Thomas could make out was a river of greenish water carrying them forward. He leaned out to see that it seemed to emerge straight out of a jungle. The cable car was rocked by another object, and a huge tree trunk popped up in their wake.

"Can you see anything?" Eno shouted.

"We seem to be going down a river."

A spray of even thicker mist hit Thomas in the face, accompanied by a muted roar.

"What's that sound?" Eno said.

Thomas lifted himself up so he could see over the top of the cable car. His face fell. "That would be a...waterfall. We have to get off the car, now!"

"Into the river?"

"We have no choice! If we go over, it's all over."

The cable car was now rocking more violently as the platform door blew open and banged shut with every sidelong lurch. Thomas managed to sling their backpacks over his shoulders and pull Eno to his feet. They staggered onto the platform and were immediately engulfed in a mist so thick that the waterfall was no longer visible. The roar was still deafening, as if it was getting ready to devour them.

"The next time we swing toward the bank, jump, all right?"

Eno nodded, though he was holding the railing in a death grip.

"Here, give me your arm!"

Eno didn't move. Thomas reached over and gripped his wrist. As the cable car swung toward the bank, he yanked it from the railing and the momentum sent them off the platform and into an wave of green-white froth. Thomas spotted a downed tree stretching from the bank but still attached by its roots. With his free hand, he reached out and grabbed a branch, while the current continued to drag the cable car downriver.

Using the branch for leverage, Thomas slowly pulled himself and Eno toward the muddy bank, where they collapsed onto the soggy ground.

In the distance, they could see the cable car bouncing through the turbulent river, an eight-ton cork, as Muirin called it. It became so small so fast that it soon looked like one of the souvenir replicas in the car barn gift shop. They watched helplessly as it reached the lip of the waterfall, then drop off the face of the Earth.

"Well," Eno panted. "That's not good."

Thomas nodded. "It's worse than that."

"What do you mean?"

"The Time Globe's still in the cable car."

Eno flopped back in despair. It was one thing to lose the transport, but without the globe, they were stranded in whatever time and place they were in, possibly forever.

They hiked away from the river to the nearest patch of dry ground and took refuge under a canopy of trees at the edge of the jungle. The mist finally lifted, allowing a hot sun to emerge. Thomas put down their backpacks and checked to see if their meager possessions were damaged. While Eno's backpack contained nothing but his globe diagnostic kit, Thomas carried his keepsakes along with his own small library, his father's mountain climbing manual, and the books Elly had given him. He retrieved the precious volumes and laid them out to dry in the humid air.

That done, Thomas used the Tetrascope knife to carve out a large rectangle on the ground. He and Eno dragged several downed trees from the riverbank and framed out a crude shelter. By the time the sun was beginning its descent, they were able to sit inside and consume the crackers and bananas Thomas had brought from Iceland.

As soon as they'd eaten, Eno picked up the damp destination booklet that came with the Time Globe and pulled out a palm-sized digital device that accompanied it.

"What's that?" Thomas asked.

"It registers the coordinates of our time jumps. I can use it to determine where we are."

"How come you've never done that before?"

"It involves a time-consuming mathematical computation, so it's a last resort, mainly intended for landing in a hostile wasteland with no sign of civilization."

"So why didn't you use it when we were in Death Valley?"

"If you recall, there was a road, plus a sign, and then actual human beings. We've been here for a few hours, and so far, this place has none of the aforementioned."

"How long will it take you to figure it out?"

"With any luck, I'll can narrow it down to a two hundred mile radius before dark."

"While there's still some light left, I think I'll check out the neighborhood."

"Don't get lost."

"Don't worry, I'll leave a trail of breadcrumbs."

Eno looked up with a blank expression, unaware of Elly's use of the term.

"Never mind."

✦✦

THOMAS WALKED INTO THE jungle, which was so thick in every direction he was forced to use his Tetrascope laser to carve a narrow path. Along the way, there were small, strange looking creatures of every imaginable color, and he stopped a few times to watch snakes slither through the trees.

Several times, Thomas found himself distracted by the natural beauty that surrounded him. Instinctively, he thought about asking Elly a question, only to remind himself that she was no longer with him. He knew he'd have to break the habit of relying on her earthly expertise.

While the ground in the jungle was perfectly flat, the sheer overgrowth of every living thing made it impossible to see more than a few feet ahead. Thomas decided to climb the nearest tree and when he reached the top, could finally see over the jungle canopy, where the setting sun revealed a jungle that seemed to go on forever. In the distance was a magnificent mountain, where a trickle of silver water marked the source of the river. A few miles to the opposite side, he could see the waterfall they'd nearly gone over. It dropped a hundred feet or so, then became a river again, which ran for many miles before curving away from a small bronze colored lake. It was too far away to make out whether it held the cable car. But there was only one way to find out. Even worse, Thomas would now have to break the news to Eno.

✦✦

It was dusk when Thomas arrived back at their camp and Eno was using the destination booklet to swat away one of the many small insects gathered around his head.

"These bugs are a nightmare," Eno said.

"Unfortunately, we have a bigger problem."

"I know, we barely have enough food for breakfast tomorrow."

"I wouldn't worry about that. The jungle's filled with plants and insects. I've got Elly's foraging book, so we should be able to make do until we find the cable car."

"Assuming it hasn't sunk."

"Actually, the flotation material the Survivor kids added should keep it from sinking, so hopefully we'll be able to see it. And the river flows into a lake."

"That's good, right? We can just hike over in the morning and pick it up?"

"I wish it were that simple."

"Ah. So now we come to the bigger problem?"

"The lake is miles away, and the only way to get there is through the rainforest."

"I don't suppose there's a path of any sort?"

"Nothing but jungle, and a lot of small...creatures."

Eno considered that. "If there are small creatures, there are bound to be large ones."

"There's bound to be a lot of things we've never encountered. Wherever we are is stranger than any place we've been. It could almost be a different planet."

"How do you know it isn't?" Eno said, then shrugged. "Joking, of course, though it does have name to match it's unique nature."

"How do you know?"

Eno held up the destination booklet. "While you were gone, I computed the coordinates. We're on the continent of South America. The booklet is still damp, and some of the words are smudged. But as far as I can make out, it's called the Amazing."

Thomas let out a laugh.

"What?"

"I think you mean the Amazon."

"You know it?"

"I did my five-class report comparing medicines on Earth and Mars. The jungle is called a rainforest. It has lots of valuable plant extracts to make drugs that can cure illness. They're so unique that we still use them on Mars."

"Of course, I've used them in my own research. They're grown in a special terrafarm. But a lot of good they're going to do us here."

"Unless we get bitten by one of those larger creatures you were talking about."

"You think that's a possibility?"

"Actually, we're more likely to be swallowed hole. They have a famous creature here called the anaconda. It's a snake that can grow up to five hundred pounds and ingest something as large as that mountain goat we saw in Colorado."

"Now *you're* joking."

"I wish. They're members of the constrictor family, which means that they usually suffocate you to death before they eat you. If you're in the water, they drown you first."

Eno sighed deeply, as if this latest development had sucked out the last of his remaining resolve. "So, we've exchanged giant sharks for giant snakes. Why is everything on Earth so large and lethal?"

"Let me remind you that it's dangerous to even breathe on Mars. And you have to admit, the scenery here is pretty spectacular."

Eno looked around him. "All I see is a jungle. Everywhere."

✦✦

NIGHT CAME SUDDENLY AND completely, as if someone dropped a black blanket over the entire area. Thomas made a fire. In addition to the light, it also had the effect of driving away the bugs, which had become so plentiful that Eno was forced to cut out a piece of mesh from the lining of his backpack and wrap it around his head.

All around them, the jungle echoed with a cacophony of animal sounds, reducing the river's roar to a trickle. Eno, unsettled by Thomas's description of the anaconda, spent the evening building a smaller version of the Tesla coil they'd used against the megalodons in New York. Anything that ventured within ten yards of them would be warned off by a crackle of electricity.

When the fire began to wane, a deeper darkness enveloped their small camp. Eno, who was lying on his sleeping bag only a few feet from Thomas, was barely visible. As Thomas stoked the last of the fire, he caught a glimpse of Eno's eyes. He was surprised to see they were wide open.

"If it's any consolation," Eno said, "I miss her, too."

There was nothing Thomas could say to make either of them feel any better. They had to face a new reality. For the first time since landing on Earth, they'd need to get by on their own, without Elly's guidance, not to mention her intelligence, resourcefulness, and good humor. And from a purely selfish point of view, Thomas would have to live without someone very special to him. He remembered how Gabby had described her early relationship with Ignatius as "star-crossed." Perhaps that's what he and Elly were, two people kept apart by something beyond their control, not only geography, but time itself.

He forced himself to think of something else.

He wondered about the fate of the Survivor kids, and pictured them on the raft piloted by Thor and Muirin, with Ajax and Duck going about their daily business. He thought about Ignatius, recovering at Dr. Darwin's home, and imagined Josef learning to fish and Lina learning to cook. He thought about them eating one of Mrs. Teasely's elaborate dinners, which reminded him of the lake in Colorado, and the trout Elly's mother had cooked for lunch. He could see the look on Elly's face when she caught the fish.

And just like that, he found himself thinking about her again.

Thomas was suddenly distracted by a small red light blinking inside his backpack. It was the cell phone Elly had given him, signaling a message. He grabbed the phone and pressed the message button, and amazingly enough, her voice came alive.

"Hey, Thomas, it's me—Elly. Who else would it be, huh? I'm the only one that has your number. Or at least I hope! Anyway, you just left a few hours ago, and my father's sleeping peacefully, so I thought I'd check in before I went to bed. I was up on the hospital roof about twenty minutes after you left and looked over at the Transamerica building. I couldn't see you, but I did see some laser beams, so I hope you didn't run into any trouble on your jump. When I saw the redshift I knew everything must be okay, and… you were gone."

Elly paused, and Thomas hoped it wasn't the end of the message.

"Hey, Thomas, hold on a sec." Thomas could hear Elly's muffled voice talking to someone. "Hi, I'm back. The night nurse just told me I'm not supposed to be making phone calls this late, so I'll have to wrap it up. Anyway, I'll be sleeping in my father's room until he's well enough to go home, so I'll be here for a few days at least."

There was another long pause, but this time it was different, as if she was at a loss for words. That would be a first for Elly, Thomas thought.

"It doesn't feel right that we're not together, but I know that's the way it has to be for now, so I'm trying to get used to it." Elly's voice cracked, and then quickly recovered. "I don't know how I'm gonna get through the next few days without you guys. Note that I said *days*, because even if you're gone longer I'm trusting Eno can work his Time Globe magic and get you back here before I turn fifteen in a couple weeks. So that's officially my birthday wish. Anyway, I'll be waiting for you to blow out the candles. Remember that. Goodnight."

The message ended, and the red light went out, plunging Thomas back into darkness. Somehow, the sky seemed to have gotten even darker after hanging up, and he noticed that the first star of the night had made its appearance directly above him.

He tucked the phone into his backpack, but as he did, his hand grazed something smooth. It was the glass jar Elly had given him.

The jar of hope.

He carefully removed it. Almost like magic, the jar instantly caught the reflection of the star and pulled it into its glass interior. Thomas couldn't resist a smile. He knew that the little star was the spirit of Elly, and as long as he had it, he'd have her by his side. His secret weapon.

He closed his eyes and held it tightly.

www.ingramcontent.com/pod-product-compliance
Lightning Source LLC
LaVergne TN
LVHW041917160826
845644LV00007B/12/J
* 9 7 8 1 6 4 4 2 8 4 3 7 7 *